21/6/17

Books should be returned or renewed by the last
date above. Renew by phone **03000 41 31 31** or
online *www.kent.gov.uk/libs*

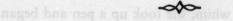

Shot in Southwold

SUZETTE A. HILL

Allison & Busby Limited
12 Fitzroy Mews
London W1T 6DW
allisonandbusby.com

First published in Great Britain by Allison & Busby in 2017.

A CIP catalogue record for this book is available from
the British Library.

First Edition

ISBN 978-0-7490-2131-3

Typeset in 10.5/15.5 pt Sabon by
Allison & Busby Ltd.

The paper used for this Allison & Busby publication
has been produced from trees that have been legally sourced
from well-managed and credibly certified forests.

Printed and bound by
CPI Group (UK) Ltd, Croydon, CR0 4YY

PROLOGUE

From his office window overlooking Parliament Square, Tom Carshalton MP surveyed the swirling traffic. He took a sip of tea, eyeing the few cyclists perilously weaving their way among the streams of vehicles, and thought of his young niece (or rather his half-niece by marriage) and her newly acquired bicycle.

Really, who on earth would choose to ride a bike in London these days? he mused. Only the vain and insane! But then of course, in his estimation Tippy was both. She always had to be different, which generally meant difficult. He took another sip, and continued to gaze at the mass of cars and lorries manoeuvring far below, and for a moment a smile twitched his lips. Perhaps the girl would get run over. A handy resolution! Ida would be upset, of course, but a trip to Paris and a new dress would soon settle that . . . For a few moments he allowed the convenient thought to flutter gently in his mind. But then, with a prick of shame, he banished it abruptly, put down his cup and took out a fountain pen. He picked up the telephone and dialled his secretary. 'I am ready to go over those accounts now, Miss Fielding,' he said briskly.

CHAPTER ONE

It was three o'clock in the afternoon, and Professor Cedric Dillworthy's mews house dozed sedately in the mellowing sun. Seated on the sofa, its occupant would also have liked to doze, but the crossword was being so beastly that scholarly pride denied such luxury until at least six clues were solved. The professor frowned, took another sip of tepid coffee, and was about to redouble his efforts when there was the sound of the doorbell. With a muted curse, he cast pencil and newspaper aside and went to the window to peer down into the little courtyard.

From that angle the bell ringer could just be discerned: slight, dapper and carrying a smart attaché case. It was his friend Felix Smythe, owner of the fashionable Sloane Street flower shop *Smythe's Bountiful Blooms* (with a royal warrant, no less). Cedric was puzzled. Why was Felix here at this hour? No arrangement had been made, and besides, couldn't he have telephoned – or was the Knightsbridge exchange out of order again? And what did the briefcase signify? Floral briefings from Clarence House? He smiled, thinking of his friend's devotion to the gracious patron. Well, if that was where he had been one could kiss goodbye to crossword clues, let alone a nap!

Easing the cat from the top of the stairs, Cedric went down and opened the door.

'Ah,' Felix said, 'glad I've found you; thought you might be napping or something.'

'I was,' Cedric lied, 'but I am fully awake *now*.' He stood back and ushered the visitor into the narrow hall and hence upstairs to the drawing room.

Felix surveyed the cooling coffee pot and the sofa's discarded crossword. 'But not asleep on your bed, I note. I should hate to think I had disturbed genuine slumber.'

'It was perfectly genuine until you rang the doorbell,' Cedric sniffed. 'Why are you here? It's Sunday. We never meet on Sundays.'

Felix gave a mild shrug. 'Indeed. But exceptions can be made and this is one such.'

'Evidently.'

'I thought you might be interested in my news. You see, I have had rather an intriguing proposition, and I wanted to discuss—'

'My dear chap, you don't mean that at long last old Blakely-Edwards has declared himself, do you? I knew he would one day!' Cedric leered, his disturbed peace no longer an issue.

'Oh, nothing so tiresome; much more diverting. The *proposition* is to do with me featuring in a film: I have been approached by the director. What do you think of that?' Felix slicked his hair and beamed.

Cedric, initially puzzled, said, 'Oh . . . you mean some sort of commercial venture to do with London flower shops? I don't have television, as you know, but I gather that nowadays there is a channel that displays advertisements. Is that what this is, a little item promoting porcelain *cache-pots* or royal florists? Will you be sharing the screen with a corgi?'

'Certainly not,' Felix replied, clearly nettled, 'this has nothing to do with advertising or commercial television! This is a *proper* film, a serious artefact for distribution in public cinemas and, who knows, possibly even in the United States.'

'Goodness! You mean like *Ben Hur*? Now that really was something. I had no idea that gladiators actually fought with—'

'Er, no, not quite on that scale – rather more intimate, more subtle. Apparently very British but essentially avant-garde; all to do with the current "New Wave" so I gather . . . although I have to admit I am not quite sure what that means. At least not entirely, but doubtless all will be revealed. The main thing is that he clearly feels I could contribute a certain *je ne sais quoi* and that my left profile is especially photogenic.'

'Who does?'

'What? Oh that boyfriend of Angela Fawcett's loud daughter: Bartholomew Hackle. He has been dabbling for ages, and now he actually has a sponsor who is prepared to back a full-length picture. Very enterprising, don't you think?'

Cedric said nothing, recalling that Bartholomew Hackle's enterprises were many and unremarkable. (Or possibly too remarkable: the stewards at Newbury were still smarting from his wild attempt to run his uncle's filly in the Hennessy – a disastrous undertaking resulting in five horses being brought down and two jockeys hospitalised.) Still, it seemed churlish to dampen his friend's excitement, and instead he enquired where the film was being shot.

There was a pause while Felix adjusted his cufflink and cleared his throat, and then said casually, 'Uhm, Southwold actually.'

Cedric stared in astonishment. '*Southwold*, in Suffolk?' But you said that nothing would induce you to go there again – not after that frightful flower festival drama we had to endure.[1] Why, only last week I heard you telling Rosy Gilchrist that even the very thought of the east coast was enough to give you a heart attack.'

'That was last week; circumstances do alter cases – or so our Latin master was always muttering. One cannot be too rigid in this life . . . Besides, Cynthia Paget's last party was so crashingly awful that one had to say something to enliven things.'

'Hmm. Not notably efficacious. In fact, rather the reverse, I seem to recall. But tell me more about this film; and when do you propose going up there?'

There was a further pause. And then Felix said winningly,

[1] See *A Southwold Mystery*

10

'Actually, Cedric, I rather thought that *we* might travel up at the end of next week . . . Oh, and by the way, I've brought you some chocolates, your favourite Charbonnel et Walker.' With a flourish he produced a large beribboned box from the snakeskin briefcase and laid it on the console.

Cedric regarded the package in silence, and then enquired sternly whether the assortment contained the rose or the violet creams.

'Both!' Felix declared triumphantly. '*And* the vanilla ganache!'

'Most kind,' Cedric murmured. 'Remarkably so.'

In the purlieus of London's Sloane Street, blackmail was also being applied . . . or at any rate its way was being paved. Lady Fawcett's drawing room was considerably larger than the professor's, and in this domain it was the guest who was the target not the incumbent.

They were discussing her daughter's marriage prospects. 'You see,' she said earnestly to Rosy Gilchrist, 'although Bartholomew seems perfectly pleasant, one cannot be *sure*. Fundamentally decent, of course – I knew his father – but just a trifle headstrong, though I daresay age will remedy that. And his manners are impeccable, not like that terrible Desmond she produced last year. He was a disaster – almost as bad as the extraordinary Frenchman she had in tow when we returned from Suffolk that time. Do you remember? Well, at least that's all over, thank goodness!' Lady Fawcett closed her eyes in painful recollection. Opening them, she added, 'After all, the dear girl is nearly twenty-five; it is high time she was settled. Wouldn't you agree?'

At thirty-six and unmarried, Rosy wasn't entirely sure what she was expected to say. 'Er, well, I suppose—' she began tentatively.

The supposition was unfinished for in the next instant the older woman had said hastily, 'Well of course it's different for you, Rosy dear. I mean you have that important post at the British Museum and your fiancé was killed in the war – a real hero – but Amy has no such excuse. She really must pull herself together.'

Rosy smiled. 'Are you feeling broody for grandchildren?'

'Not in the least. One generation is quite enough. No, as it happens I am thinking of Amy's future; marriage would be so *stabilising* . . . Besides, I am becoming just a teeny bit tired of Mr Bates; he's so shifty. I found him eating jam in the pantry the other day.'

Rosy was startled. 'Mr Bates? Who's he?'

'Oh, didn't I tell you? A replacement for Mr Bones; he died and we've buried him under the pear tree. Amy was inconsolable so I bought her this whippet. Not as cuddly as the pug but less lazy, and actually he is quite lucrative. It certainly means I don't have to increase Amy's allowance.' She laughed.

'Really? In what way lucrative?' Rosy was puzzled.

Lady Fawcett lowered her voice. 'He has *stud* potential, if you see what I mean. She takes him on little missions and charges the most outrageous fees . . . And that is why I need your help.'

Had she not been eating a slice of cake, Rosy's jaw might have dropped. What on earth was the woman talking about? How could the whippet's amatory missions have anything to do with her?

'Er, I don't quite follow . . .' she began.

'Well it's Bartholomew, you see. He is about to make a film, or "movie" as he calls it. It's his first proper go and he is most eager for Amy and me to visit and lend support – you know the sort of thing: dispensing sandwiches and being generally helpful on the set.'

An image of Lady Fawcett being helpful on a film set did not come readily to Rosy's mind; but she nodded, still unclear of her link with the whippet or indeed the latter's connection with the cinema. She was to learn.

'Anyway, the problem is that Amy tells me she cannot possibly oblige as it cuts across Mr Bates's busy schedule in Shropshire, and she suggests that I go alone . . . Frankly, I'm not too keen on that as I don't know Bartholomew all that well, and anyway such ventures are much more fun with a chum. Thus I was about to bow out gracefully, when it suddenly occurred to me that it would be an excellent chance to get to know the young man better, while at the same time making a *crafty* assessment of his suitability for Amy. Indeed, with the dear girl absent one might get a better perspective.' She laughed gaily. 'Don't you think that's a neat wheeze? Pretty canny, as my Gregory used to say!'

Politely Rosy agreed that it was very neat, and enquired the film's location.

'Well that's just it,' her hostess exclaimed merrily, 'Southwold. It is being shot in Southwold. Would you believe it?'

Coincidences being more frequent than popularly supposed, Rosy did believe it. She was surprised, nevertheless; but even more so by Lady Fawcett's evident elation. After all, with two murders and a suicide, their visit to the little place a couple of years previously had not been what you might call a feast of gaiety. The town, of course, was delightful, but the circumstances had been less than enlivening.

'But don't you think that could be a bit worrying?' she asked. 'I mean, you might feel haunted by certain memories – your friend Delia, for example, buried in St Edmund's churchyard . . .'

'Oh no,' the other replied blithely, 'few things haunt me – except perhaps that frightful Frenchman of Amy's in his beret! In fact, returning to Southwold in happier circumstances will probably be a good thing; lay the ghosts, as it were. And as for dear Delia, well naturally I shall pay her my respects, and I am sure she will welcome me at her graveside . . . Uhm, remind me, it was the *third* yew they put her under, wasn't it?'

Rosy assured her that it was, and then asked if she might not feel at a bit of a loose end on her own: 'Obviously during the day there will be Bartholomew and his film crew, but the evenings could be a little dull; and without Amy to do the driving won't it be a bit tricky getting about?' And then feeling that sounded too negative, she added hastily, 'although naturally there are bound to be local buses.'

Lady Fawcett looked faintly puzzled (a not infrequent expression) and said vaguely, 'I don't think I am mad about local buses . . .' She took a sip of tea, while the mild eyes abstractedly roamed the room before once more alighting on the young woman opposite. She flashed a dazzling smile and proffered more cake. 'And that brings me to *you*, Rosy dear.'

Oh yes – it would, wouldn't it, Rosy thought grimly. I asked for that; walked straight in!

But before she could muster any sort of response, with practised agility Lady Fawcett had outlined her proposal. This was to the effect that Rosy should come as her guest to Southwold. ('No worries, my dear, it is totally all my treat! They say the bedrooms at The Swan are so restful, and don't you remember those superb dinners we had at The Crown last time?') She urged that when not 'hobnobbing' with those 'doubtless delightful film people', she and Rosy could explore the Suffolk countryside, immersing themselves in local history and toying with cream teas at Aldeburgh or Snape. It would be, she assured the lucky chauffeuse, a veritable feast for mind and palate. Rosy sighed . . . Hmm, perhaps.

In fact, Rosy was warily fond of Angela Fawcett and could certainly think of far worse people to spend time with in Suffolk. And in spite of its grisly events, her earlier trip with the older woman had been largely congenial . . . Yes, she had to admit that the prospect was quite appealing – especially as apparently expenses would be minimal! But what about the film business? Did she really want to be roped in to serve sandwiches and be factotum to a novice camera crew and a bunch of amateur actors? Instinctively she thought not . . . Yet from the back of her mind she heard her mother's voice of long ago: 'Oh, go on, Rosy, don't be such an old stick-in-the-mud. You'll love it, really.'

And echoing the past, her companion's voice exclaimed: 'You know, I think we might love it – a treat for both of us!' And then more pressingly: 'I really do need a second opinion of Bartholomew, and an ally in these matters is such a comfort. Gregory would undoubtedly have had a view. But alas, the dear man is no longer here. So you *will* come, won't you?'

Rosy nodded. 'I would love to,' she said.

CHAPTER TWO

Once home and mission completed, Felix busied himself with making preparations for Southwold. During their previous sojourn when attending its flower festival, they had stayed at The Sandworth in Aldeburgh, glad to be distanced from the hurly-burly of jousting gardeners and crowded marquees. Indeed, the quieter town had been a refuge not simply from the drama of the festival but also from the melodrama of murder . . . or nearly so, at any rate.

This time, however, there would be no murder, and the public melee of the festival would be replaced by the private melee of a film set . . . a film in which he, Felix, was to play a modest role. Thus, to be at the heart of things in Southwold itself was essential – which is why he had already made arrangements to rent a most charming cottage on the edge of the town. This was pleasantly secluded, and yet the film 'studio' (a large, unkempt villa on the East Cliff, procured from a Hackle cousin) could be reached in only a few minutes' walk. It had been an excellent choice and he knew that Cedric would approve.

Recalling the afternoon's visit he smiled at how compliant his friend had been. Not at first, of course, he rarely was. (The professor had a tendency to object to things on principle.) But it had taken only a little cajoling to persuade him that such a trip would be mutually beneficial: gratifying for Felix, and for Cedric a welcome rest after the chore of indexing *Cappadocian Capers*, his new geological memoir. Personally, Felix rather questioned this title, unable to envisage Cedric capering anywhere, let alone amidst the rocky heights of Cappadocia. But the author had defended his choice by declaring that the note of levity had 'layman's appeal' and that fingers would thus reach more readily into wallets. After being shown the cover proofs of a dauntingly harsh and arid landscape, Felix rather doubted this. His quizzical reaction had not been well received, and saying no more he had privately dwelt on capering amidst the seductive charms of Biarritz.

Currently, however, it was not the charms of Biarritz that occupied him but those of Southwold. The sartorial question was paramount.

It was all very well for Cedric, Felix reflected, for his friend's garb rarely varied: the statutory dark suit and cream shirt (with just an occasional blue alternative to lend a touch of frivolity). Even on the beach Cedric's bathing trunks were uniformly black. But for those of a more creative ilk, such as himself, a wider repertoire was required.

18

Thus Felix pondered his meticulously arranged wardrobe. A selection of the usual items would be needed: an assortment of stylish shirts, slightly raffish ties, a couple of natty jackets (plus the new smoking one) and a tailored suit or two for evening; and to fit any occasion, a range of footwear, from casual moccasins to highly polished Oxfords. Yes, naturally he would take all the main stuff. Two suitcases should suffice, though a third might be safer . . .

Well, those were the broad generalities. But what specifically should be worn in a film studio? The last thing he wanted was to commit the faux pas of being overdressed. Still, he was damned if he was going to sport Hawaiian shorts and 'sloppy Joe' jumpers as seen in those movie magazines idly scanned at the barber's. Or, indeed, blue jeans as favoured by the followers of the late American star James Dean. Felix had never worn jeans in his life and he certainly wasn't going to start now! He frowned, thinking of his own heroes: James Mason, George Sanders and David Niven. What did *they* wear when not in costume and lounging about in casual mufti? Something comfortable, no doubt, but essentially English and with just the merest nod in the direction of elegance . . . Ah yes, of course, beige slacks and a silk neck scarf. Ideal! He would go to Jermyn Street the very next day.

With that happy prospect he was about to pour himself a glass of sherry; but before he did so another thought struck him. What about headgear? Being 'on location' many of the scenes would be shot in the open air; and thus when not personally on call surely some sort of casual hat might be appropriate – *not,* of course, one of those Hemingway forage caps (Felix shuddered) no, a jaunty panama was the thing. His present one was beginning to look a trifle worn, a bit bendy in fact; high time for a replacement. Yes, indeed, after Jermyn Street a short stroll to Lock's was clearly indicated.

The sherry was consumed with much satisfaction.

Meanwhile Cedric, having fewer sartorial choices, was less concerned with the number of suitcases he should take than whether the cottage had an efficient heating system. Admittedly at that time of year one was not expecting icy blasts. But even in London the unseasonal cold day was not unknown; and that east coast wind blew in straight from the Urals! A scarf and gloves might be a wise precaution. He made a mental note to put some in the car.

Of course, assuming the place *was* decently heated and not dripping with damp, it could indeed be very agreeable. Felix's report had been glowing – which was just as well, for when his friend had revealed its name, *Cot O'Bedlam*, he had very nearly refused to go. However, apparently the amenities were entirely in order and offered everything to ensure a reasonable stay: large sitting room, two bedrooms and bathrooms, a hyper-modern kitchen, a conservatory with terrace, plus a small *sheltered* garden (most reassuring).

Yes, the prospect was not unpleasant; and after all, as Felix had insisted, it would be a way of relaxing after the tedious index business. What a chore that had been! Still, all finished now and he could take his ease and indulge in a little light reading. He must decide what to take to

Southwold: a couple of Forsters and some Waugh perhaps, Saki naturally (his vade mecum), splendid Sydney Smith – and oh yes, the chance to reacquaint himself with the stories of WSM, a volume presented by the author himself when they had last visited his villa at Cap Ferrat. He was tempted to take a Simenon – but given the events of their previous visit to Southwold, crime, however cerebral, seemed not quite the thing. It wouldn't do to strew further hostages in Fortune's way!

Immersed in thoughts of his reading schedule, Cedric had momentarily overlooked the main point of their prospective visit: the film and Felix's part in it. Thus selection made, and sipping a cup of lapsang, he sat on the sofa and contemplated.

What on earth was it all about? Felix had been appallingly vague, and apart from stressing that it was 'terribly experimental' didn't even seem to know the title. But then with Barthlomew Hackle in charge any title probably changed from day to day. The young man's mind was not of the most constant . . . And why had he chosen Felix for a role? (Luckily not a large one, the strain would have been intolerable!) The dear chap certainly exhibited thespian sensitivity; but as to having actual talent in that direction, Cedric rather doubted – unless of course you counted melodrama a skill. Perhaps it was indeed the photogenic profile, as Felix had coyly hinted. Certainly his profile was very clear, but it was *sharp* surely rather than 'chiselled' or 'sculptured'; and those thin cheekbones and short spiky hair did not exactly bring to mind Clark Gable. For a moment Cedric harboured an image of Felix with the latter's moustache . . . Impossible, he would look like a spiv. He smiled. Personally he found his friend's face rather endearing; but the profile, clear though it was, was not exactly of the Novello mode . . . unless perhaps shot in a dim light with brilliantine and black hair dye.

Cedric's reverie was interrupted by the telephone. It was Angela Fawcett.

'My dear,' she announced, 'I am so sorry, but I am afraid I shall have to forgo your birthday lunch next week – overcome by events, as one might say. Rather exciting, really, and I've had to reschedule *everything*. You see, I shall be going to Southwold to see a film being shot. It's the Hackle boy – you know, Amy's current beau – he has a backer at last and is all poised to try his directional skills on the Suffolk coast. Great swathes of swirling clouds and freezing sea, I suppose. Anyway, he is full of enthusiasm and has very sweetly suggested that I go as a sort of encouraging observer . . . and, well, to be generally useful, I gather. Amy can't go, so therefore I've asked—'

Interrupting the breathless spiel, Cedric replied casually that yes, he had heard about the film and that, as it happened, Felix would be playing a major role in it.

There was a gasp followed by a long pause. 'Felix? But why? . . . And did you say a *major* role? How strange – I shouldn't have thought that . . .'

Cedric smiled, and admitted that, actually, as far as he knew the part was very small; and that as to the reason he had no idea, but presumably the Hackle boy knew what he was doing (something which he firmly doubted). He added politely that Amy must be thrilled at the prospect.

'Oh, indeed she is – but as I said, she won't be there. Or certainly not to begin with. It's the new whippet, you see: he is going to make her a lot of money in Shropshire.'

'Really? Going to be the star turn in some dog show and win rosettes, is he?'

'Ye-es. That is one way of putting it, I suppose... Anyway, luckily I shan't be alone as dear Rosy is coming with me. I clinched the deal this afternoon. It's all arranged!'

Lady Fawcett's triumph was not especially shared by Cedric. He had nothing against Rosy Gilchrist; but to learn that she was to be with them as in the earlier visit with all its dire vicissitudes, gave him an uneasy flash of déjà vu. 'How nice,' he said smoothly, 'just like old times . . . So where will you be staying?'

'At The Swan. I have fixed everything. And then my Amy will join us after' – she cleared her throat – 'after Mr Bates has, er, dealt with things . . .'

'Will that take long?' Cedric enquired.

Lady Fawcett indicated that she was not cognisant with such matters, but was sure that Amy would arrive as speedily as possible. 'She's awfully fond of young Hackle, you know. Actually I think this might be the *one*!'

'And does he think so?'

'That's what I aim to find out,' she replied firmly. 'Now, mind you keep on the qui vive and let me have your opinion as to his suitability. I trust your judgement, Cedric.'

With such faith ringing in his ears, she rang off.

Cedric lit a cigarette and reflected. Really, was he expected to act as some sort of voyeur or Fifth Columnist in the Fawcett affairs? It was a bit much.

However, irritation was soon dispersed, for the prospect of the forthcoming trip began to take a hold on his imagination. His memories of being stationed in the little town during the war were still sharp, and held a pleasurable nostalgia that the grim events of the previous visit had failed to eclipse. This time, without the menace of murder to cast a shadow, he could indulge those memories freely and retrace some of the old haunts . . . Yes, with his books and the cabaret of dear Felix's film performance to keep him amused, it could indeed prove a most civilised holiday.

He lifted the telephone and dialled his friend's number. 'Dear boy,' he began . . .

CHAPTER THREE

This time the drive up to Southwold proved smoother than before, Rosy being more familiar with the route, and Lady Fawcett being less prone to gesticulate wildly at grazing ruminants while wrenching the chauffeur's eye from the road to admire the passing scenery. Evidently the novelty of uncharctered territory beyond the metropolis had waned somewhat, and thus the journey was without hazard.

However, after Blythburgh, and approaching the large girls' school in the vicinity of Reydon, Rosy felt a nervous jolt as memory of the earlier experience became disturbingly real. They had just driven past the narrow turn to the house from which so much of the drama had emanated; and while the house itself had been peaceful, the events surrounding it had been considerably less so . . . She glanced at her companion. But Lady Fawcett's thoughts were clearly elsewhere: not of the past but the imminent future, for she had taken out her compact and was busily powdering her nose in readiness for The Swan.

Installed in her bedroom, Rosy unpacked, chose something suitable for the evening, and then spent five minutes at the open window gazing down at the high street.

A little later they were to meet Bartholomew Hackle whom Angela had invited for a drink in the hotel lounge. Rosy had never met the young man, but knew him by reputation and Amy's garbled reports. From all accounts he was an amiable chap, cheerful and kindly but given to wild enthusiasms not always productive. Well, it was to be hoped that the film project worked – and perhaps, more importantly, that his current interest in Lady Fawcett's daughter proved one of his more viable ventures! Rosy was quite fond of the younger girl (despite the latter's noise and unremitting mirth) and, like her mother, felt it would be nice to see her 'settled'. Much as an exuberant spaniel, Amy Fawcett needed a firm hand and loving playfellow. Would Bartholomew fit the bill? It remained to be seen.

With such thoughts in mind Rosy idly scanned the street below, alert for any changes from their last visit. But all was much as she remembered: charm without contrivance and a general air of quiet busyness. In Market Place the stalls beneath the Victorian lamp post were slowly packing up, women gossiped, dogs scuttled, the sun shone . . . and the wind blew. Rosy surveyed the string of hectically flapping bunting on the shopfront opposite. Oh yes, some things never altered!

Before turning back to the room she glanced to her right, and halfway down the street saw a couple of men engaged in animated conversation – or at least, one of them was certainly animated: a tall youth astride a bicycle and waving his arms with graphic gusto as if making some vital point. His companion was also distinctive, less by his gestures than by his hat: a smart panama worn at a distinctly jaunty angle. The promenade at Cannes sported many such hats, but here in Southwold it seemed just a trifle too chic. Rosy gazed – and then gasped. Oh lord, it was Felix!

Ah, of course – she had momentarily forgotten. According to Angela, the two friends had rented a cottage somewhere in the town to facilitate Felix's involvement in this much-vaunted film of Bartholomew's. Thus one could expect the pair to be ubiquitous . . . But who was the cyclist? Perhaps one of the film crew; yes, bound to be. She couldn't imagine Felix chatting to a complete stranger, let alone one attached to a ramshackle bicycle. Oh well, presumably all would be revealed the next day 'on set'. She smiled, and decided to take a quick bath before joining Angela and her guest for the preprandial drink.

Rosy was right in her recognition of Felix. He and Cedric had arrived at *Cot O'Bedlam* the previous day, and apart from its excruciating name, were well pleased with their temporary home. As Felix had hoped, it offered all the listed amenities, and Cedric was impressed with the spacious sitting room, large collection of books, small conservatory and its surprisingly comfortable veranda. 'Film or no film,' he had observed, 'this couldn't be a better place for a well-earned rest.' Felix had agreed but muttered something about the film being paramount.

To celebrate matters they had dined at The Crown that night. But the following day Felix was eager to sample the pristine kitchen, and that afternoon had wandered into the high street in search of wine and ingredients for '*une casserole du poisson à la* Southwold'. Mission accomplished, and immersed in plans for his special concoction, he had stepped off the kerb unaware of the bicycle bearing down upon him.

'Christ!' exclaimed Bartholomew Hackle, 'that was a near one. You almost had me in the gutter!'

'Could have rung your bell,' Felix retorted testily, and adjusted his panama.

They glowered at each other; and then as recognition dawned, simultaneously uttered 'Ah!'

Mutual apologies were exchanged and hands shaken. Felix, still clueless about the projected film and eager to hear more of his own role, took the opportunity to invite the young man back to the cottage for a cup of tea to 'discuss logistics'.

Bartholomew deemed this a good idea as he could then outline the shooting schedule and tell Felix about the other members of the cast. 'You'll love them,' he enthused, 'an absolutely first-rate bunch!' Felix wondered about that, but nodded compliantly.

Thus with the movie director trundling the bicycle, its basket and panniers freighted with undisclosed ballast, they walked back to the cottage. Here Bartholomew leant the bike against the side of the porch and started to unload its cargo.

Felix was mildly surprised. 'What's in there?' he enquired. 'Film stuff?'

'You could say so,' was the cheerful reply. 'Vital provisions for the set – Adnams' Special. The cameramen won't work without their tipple, and the grips get shirty if we don't have the right brew.' He paused and grinned: 'Come to that, so does the director. But I daren't leave it on the bike, you've no idea how sneaky people can be . . . at least, they are in London; maybe it's different here. Still, one doesn't want to risk it.' He heaved the bags into the porch, while Felix went inside to alert Cedric.

Settled on the sofa with a cup of tea and munching a garibaldi biscuit, Bartholomew surveyed the room and nodded his appreciation. 'Hmm, this is a bit of all right, isn't it,' he observed. 'Very cosy. Much better than that barracks of a place we've got on the East Cliff! Far more civilised.'

'But I thought that belonged to your cousin; surely it's quite habitable?' Cedric enquired. 'I should have thought that at that size it must accommodate you all very comfortably.'

'Oh it *accommodates* us all right,' the young man replied, 'but I don't think comfort figures very strongly. It's bleak, barren and draughty, and with some very dodgy plumbing. Shouldn't wonder if there aren't rats too; the girls won't like that. Still, one isn't there for sybaritic gaiety, we have a job to do: to make *The Languid Labyrinth* a howling success and to pot bags of money.' He gave his biscuit a decisive bite, scattering crumbs over Cedric's neatly folded jacket on the cushion next to him.

Felix craned forward. 'Oh, is that its title? I had meant to ask you . . . Er, what does it mean exactly?'

'Oh no meaning is exact,' Bartholomew replied airily, 'and even in its generality there is always the subjective factor, wouldn't you agree?'

Felix replied uncertainly that he did agree but that surely the word 'labyrinth' was likely to hold some special significance.

'You bet it does,' Bartholomew exclaimed, 'it's what you might call an "existential conundrum", a conundrum that evolves variously and whose resolution is determined by the skill of the exponent. It's all to do with inner nuance and the play of shadows.'

'I see,' said Felix blankly.

'But why "languid"?' Cedric enquired. 'I mean, if I got lost in a labyrinth I doubt if I should be in a state of languor . . . after all, one might encounter the Minotaur.' He gave a dry laugh.

The other regarded him solemnly. 'I say, that's quite a good idea; I hadn't thought of it like that. We could use the motif of the Minotaur as an underlying metaphor for the helplessness of man's condition in the face of nihilism and grief. It could be given a—'

'Fascinating,' Cedric interrupted hastily. 'Now, do give us a rundown on your team – quite a mixed group, I imagine. Any established stars among them?'

Bartholomew grinned, his earnestness gone. 'Not unless you count the dog, Pixie. She belongs to Fred, the chief cameraman, and he won't go anywhere without her.'

'Oh yes? Nice little thing is she?'

The other grinned again. 'You could say that . . . but presumably you mean the humans.'

Cedric nodded.

'Well, my great coup is Alicia Gorringe. She was rather well thought of at RADA and won a prize in her final year. Currently she is "resting", as these actresses put it, but she has had some filming experience and is very photogenic. Except that she's brunette and not blonde; she's a sort of Monica Vitti type.' He paused, and then added thoughtfully, 'Hips a bit wider perhaps – verging on the voluptuous, you might say. Walking away from the camera she'll look jolly good, and I know Fred will do her justice. Actually,' he added, taking another garibaldi, 'I'm a bit worried that there could be a whiff of tension between her and Tippy Tildred, you know what the girls are like!'

Cedric was vague on the subject, but asked who Tippy Tildred was.

'One of Hector Klein's casualties. They had a spectacular bust-up a couple of months ago; and as she was at a loose end, and to stop her banging on about Hector's beastliness, I asked if she would like to join the cast.' He frowned. 'It seemed a good idea at the time and I've given her quite a significant part. With luck it will work; she's certainly got plenty of zest.'

'Is she amusing?' Cedric asked.

Bartholomew reflected. 'She thinks she is.'

'Ah – tedious you mean.'

'I wouldn't say *that* exactly.'

'But verging?' Felix suggested.

The young man shrugged and smiled. 'Verging or not,

the point is she's got the looks plus all the confidence to prance about in front of a camera. With a bit of polish she could be most useful. If our leading man, Robert Kestrel, does his stuff the scenes between them might be rather good.'

Cedric cleared his throat. 'And what is his stuff exactly?' he enquired with interest.

'He smoulders.'

'He does what?'

'Smoulders – it's his forte. He likes being dark and brooding.'

'You mean like Mr Rochester?' Felix asked brightly.

'More like Marlon Brando, I should say. He met him once in New York. I gather Brando shook his hand, mumbled for twenty seconds, lit a cigarette and then went silent. Ever since then Kestrel has gone around declaring the chap is his mentor.'

'So apart from smouldering, what's his normal job?' Felix asked.

'He's an insurance clerk in Surbiton.'

As a lavish provider of blooms for the Queen Mother, and in any case being far more concerned with his own part, Felix was unimpressed. He was about to quiz Bartholomew about this part, when the latter looked at his watch, gave a gasp of horror and said that he had to dash as he had been summoned for a drink with Lady Fawcett at The Swan.

'You never know,' he chortled, 'she may become my future mother-in-law. Mustn't keep the lady waiting, and I've got to take this stuff back to the studio first.' He stood up and started to gather his impedimenta from the porch.

'But what about my—' began Felix.

'Oh, it's frightfully subtle,' the other said hastily over his shoulder. 'But don't worry, all will be revealed tomorrow!' So saying, he threw himself on to his saddle and pedalled precariously towards the high street.

Felix was none too pleased at such scant information; and after the visitor had gone grumbled crossly to his friend. However, he was mollified by Cedric's assurances that the Southwold bouillabaisse was bound to be a performance of the most exquisite artistry. It was too.

CHAPTER FOUR

Refreshed after her bath, and relishing the prospect of a drink, Rosy went downstairs to investigate the bar. She was rather earlier than arranged, and at that hour and with only two other people present, the room was pleasantly quiet. She ordered a dry sherry and wondered if she should do the same for Angela, but decided against it. Other than a penchant for champagne, Rosy knew little of her companion's preferences, and it was frustrating to be faced with a drink not of one's own choice. Thus, taking her sherry, she settled in a comfortable chair at the side of the bar and awaited events.

She contemplated the arrival of Bartholomew Hackle and hoped she would like him, though by all accounts he sounded pleasant enough. Angela had said he was bound to be late as she had never known a Hackle that wasn't. Well, if so, it hardly mattered: they weren't going anywhere and the surroundings were very agreeable.

She looked around at the softly lit room and at the couple sitting near the door. They were a striking pair: the young woman's dark auburn hair was long and wavy, and she wore a close-fitting dress that flattered a fulsome figure. The man was handsome in a rugged, sultry sort of way . . . nice if you liked the style. Rosy did not especially. They were smoking, and talking earnestly in low voices; but the girl broke off to put on her wrap, and then with eyes scanning the room, stood up abruptly. 'Oh, do let's move,' Rosy heard her say, 'that doorway is hellishly draughty. I shall get a stiff neck, and that won't suit His Nibs at all!' She laughed and led the way to another table near to Rosy's.

'So what's your agent like?' her companion asked as he put down the drinks.

She shrugged. 'Could do better. Willing enough I suppose, but not exactly a go-getter. That's why I've had to take this current bit of nonsense – a useful stopgap while I look for a brighter spark.'

'I'm sure you won't have to look far – not someone with your talent, sweetie. They'll be falling over themselves to have you on their books, and doubtless an MGM scout is prowling Wardour Street even as we speak. Just be patient, Cleopatra!' The man laughed and blew her a smoke ring. 'Oh, and talking of sparks, guess who is joining our merry throng. It's—'

She cut him short. 'I know exactly who you are going to say: it's that bloody Tildred brat. Bartho must be mad; she's such a frightful little show-off and can't act for toffee –

though with that absurd cropped hair she obviously thinks she is Jean Seberg. I tell you, she minces about like some cretinous fairy!'

'Hmm, but as cretinous fairies go, rather cute wouldn't you say?'

'Oh yes: cute as a pain in the arse,' the girl agreed coldly.

At that moment Lady Fawcett appeared in the doorway, garnished in pearls and swathed in Je Reviens.

'Ah, Rosy dear, I've just caught that nice waiter in the hall and ordered a bottle of Moët for the three of us. A little treat to prompt good fortune! I've told him we'll have it in the lounge.'

Rosy followed the wafting scent, pleased at the prospect of champagne but slightly regretful not to hear more of her neighbours' views. If the two were who she guessed them to be, perhaps more might be learnt the following day!

As they entered the lounge they almost collided with a tall young man in a suit, looking slightly dishevelled. 'I do apologise,' he exclaimed breathlessly, 'in a bit of a hurry . . . Ah, it's you, Lady Fawcett! So sorry, I thought I was going to be fearfully late.' He beamed engagingly.

'Yes, I did wonder,' Angela replied, 'but your arrival is most timely: we're just about to split a bottle.' She smiled and began to make introductions, but was diverted by the waiter bearing an ice bucket and enquiring where they would be sitting. She drifted towards a corner alcove.

Hackle hovered. 'You must be Rosy Gilchrist,' he said. 'Amy thinks you are splendid – she is always going on about you.'

'Oh dear, how boring for you,' Rosy laughed. 'But I can return the compliment: you are the great movie mogul, Mr Bartholomew Hackle.' Even as she said it, she realised he had been the boy on the bicycle talking to Felix.

He laughed. 'Exactly. But named not after the martyred and flayed saint, but that rather precocious child star, the angelic Freddie Bartholomew . . . Actually, I was christened Herbert after my grandfather, but once Ma had been entranced by the boy's smile in *David Copperfield* she insisted otherwise. Probably as well: I don't think I could have coped with Herb Hackle – Bartholomew's bad enough.'

'Oh, but it's a very distinguished name – though possibly a bit of a mouthful?'

'Only if one has a mincing mouth,' the other replied, and then doubled up in a spasm of mirth. Rosy was vaguely reminded of the absent Amy. Once recovered, he explained that actually his close friends called him Bartho and that she was welcome to do so. Rosy smiled, and with suitably pursed lips said she would consider it an honour.

By this time they had joined their hostess, who, with the wine poured, was clearly poised for refreshment. 'We must toast the film,' she said gaily. 'Is there a title?'

'It's called *The Languid Labyrinth*,' the mogul informed her solemnly.

Lady Fawcett blinked slightly. 'How nice,' she said, and raised her glass.

The hour passed quickly and agreeably. Some of the talk was taken up with Amy in Shropshire and the exploits of

Mr Bates, who, according to Lady Fawcett, was reported to be in good spirits (as well he might, Rosy thought); but inevitably it was the film that was the main topic.

'So apart from its intriguing title,' Lady Fawcett enquired, 'what actually goes on?'

Bartho took a deep breath, and accepting his second glass began to explain. 'It is *deeply* metaphysical with a burgeoning complexity, and ostensibly deals with the Battle of Sole Bay of the seventeenth century (which is why the Southwold location is so vital) and with ravaged Europe of the indeterminate future. There is a sort of subtle interchange between the two periods and places, which entails a lot of cutting back and forth, and—'

'Why ostensible?' Rosy asked.

'What?'

'You said "ostensible". What's the significance?'

'Ah well, that's an aspect of the labyrinth. You see nothing is quite what it seems and at any moment one could take a turn into the past or into the future. And then sometimes the protagonists arrive at a T-junction, which marks the moment of existential crisis, and when they must make the Kierkegaardian leap and decide whether to plunge back into the Sole Bay fiasco with all its snares and tensions, or forward to the Somme . . . uhm, though it could even be the last war and Tobruk, we haven't quite decided yet. Anyway, the point is that some of the combatants are left quivering on the cusp . . . which is where Felix comes in.'

'Goodness,' exclaimed Rosy, 'whatever happens to him?'

'Ultimately he fades into the unknown, but his essential

role is cuspian and he moves hesitantly between past and future, a sort of spectral Janus figure: a pensive observer linking the personal carnage of Sole Bay with the vortex of the Somme.'

'Or Tobruk,' murmured Lady Fawcett.

'Does Felix know this yet?' Rosy asked.

'No, but he will tomorrow. Everyone's gathering in the morning for a preliminary briefing at HQ, Cousin Walter's barn of a place on the East Cliff. And then if it all goes to schedule we'll shoot the first couple of scenes in the afternoon. You'll enjoy those: there's a torrid love scene set in the drawing room of Admiral Daventry just before the battle. I've put that in at the beginning to grip the audience before moving on to the deeper stuff.'

Lady Fawcett cleared her throat. 'How wise,' she murmured.

'This love scene,' Rosy said, 'does it feature a good-looking girl with long legs and auburn hair?'

'Yes, that sounds like our Alicia all right – why, do you know her?'

Rosy explained that she had seen such a one in the bar earlier on. 'There was a man with her, broad shoulders and heavy brows.'

'Oh, bound to be Kestrel,' Bartho replied. 'He's quite a stalwart in his way; not a pro like Alicia (well she's a sort of pro, got her Equity card) but he's a keen amateur and is rather strong on doing silent masterful stuff. They've acted together before, some charity thing at the Guildhall last year. They were pretty good, actually, so with luck they'll deliver the goods.' He paused, and then added, 'Did you say you had seen them here?'

Rosy nodded.

'Ah, then they're probably staying; that would explain why there's been no sign of them at the studio. Most of the others have dossed down in the bedrooms. It's a big house, but I don't blame them for preferring this place – rather more creature comforts.' He grinned, and then looking at his watch, exclaimed, 'Crikey, time for the kitchen! Our gaffer is arriving tonight, the chief cameraman, and he's bound to want a big fry-up plus chips. I must get back and start on the potatoes; he loves them, and so does Pixie. She can't get enough of them.'

With fond farewells, and urging them to attend the shooting of the next day's opening scene, Bartholomew Hackle took his leave; and from the lounge window they glimpsed him crouched over handlebars, pedalling furiously in the direction of the seafront.

'It's very nice that he has culinary interests, don't you think?' observed Lady Fawcett once he was out of sight. 'I mean, that will be so good for Amy *should* things become serious – her cooking is hopeless.' She paused, and then added, 'And, uhm . . . who is Pixie?'

Rosy said that she had no idea, but whoever the lady was she clearly had a good appetite.

The other agreed and lapsed into silence, but after a moment said ruminatively: 'You know, I don't think my Gregory would have been terribly keen on this film. The last one we saw together was *The Lady Vanishes*. Now that was awfully good, and we both enjoyed it so! But I can't help feeling that this one is just a trifle *complicated* – at least, I am sure dear Gregory would have thought so. Strange really; despite all those years in the diplomatic service, he much preferred things to be obvious and straightforward, could never abide muddle . . .' She gave a wistful sigh.

'Yes, it does sound a bit oblique,' Rosy agreed, 'but I think it's something to do with the "New Wave" genre, which is currently so fashionable in France and Italy. It's beginning to get a following here too – so I suppose one might say Bartholomew is in the vanguard.'

Lady Fawcett intimated that on the whole she might prefer the 'Old Wave' but that doubtless all would become clear once the cameras had 'started to roll', and that meanwhile there was a simpler matter in prospect: supper. Handing Rosy one of the menus, she said, 'I don't normally eat steak – too much for me – but I suspect tomorrow may be a gruelling day, mentally at any rate. A good dose of protein might be advisable; I shall opt for the tournedos. What about you, Rosy dear?'

Over dinner they continued to discuss the film and speculated on Felix's role. 'It does sound a little nebulous,' Lady Fawcett remarked, 'I hope it won't strain his sensibilities; I think he was expecting something more defined.'

'I don't know about his sensibilities,' Rosy grinned, 'but if it's too ill-defined it will certainly strain his ego. And I doubt whether the idea of his fading into the unknown, as Bartho implied, will be entirely to his taste.'

The other wagged a finger in mock rebuke. 'Ah, but while he lasts I am sure his performance will be masterly. A cameo part – isn't that what they call it? He'll dine out on it for months.' She smiled benignly.

Sipping coffee in the lounge, Rosy described the conversation she had overheard in the bar. 'Bartholomew may be glad to have those two heading the cast,' she said, 'but I had the impression that the Alicia lady was none too pleased about one of the other members: she referred to her as "that Tildred brat", and seemed very put out that she would be here.'

'Oh well, I suppose such petty rivalries are to be expected – after all, they are thespians! I remember when Gregory's department in our Paris embassy put on the Christmas pantomime, there was a tremendous kerfuffle among the—' Lady Fawcett broke off and frowned. 'Did you say the name was Tildred?'

Rosy nodded. 'Yes, but I didn't catch the first name. Why, does it ring a bell?'

'Possibly. The term "brat" suggests youth or adolescence. I wonder if it's the same Tildred girl who used to be a kind of appendage to the Carshaltons . . . you know, Tom Carshalton, that rather earnest MP in Kensington; he's her uncle or his wife is the aunt, something like that. Anyway, she used to stay with them occasionally when she was a schoolgirl . . . rather a feeble little thing in those days – whiney and always seemed to have a cold.'

Rosy remarked that in that case she had better watch out for the winds on the East Cliff. 'If she's feeble she might catch a chill and get the sniffles – not something to impress the cameramen.'

'Ah, but I don't think she is feeble now, not if it's

the one I am thinking of; rather the reverse, really. She was at the Astleys' dance last month. One gathered she had just been sacked from some drama or ballet school, not that it seemed to bother her. A bit showy and pushy, I thought – not quite *comme il faut*, if you take my meaning.' She paused, and then added, 'If it is her, I just hope she doesn't distract Bartholomew.'

'Is she likely to?'

'*Very* likely,' was the grim reply.

CHAPTER FIVE

The next day, despite the success of the bouillabaisse, Felix seemed twitchy; and Cedric guessed he was worried about the studio induction scheduled for that morning. He assured his friend that once Bartholomew had divulged more of the plot and explained Felix's part in it things would go swimmingly – adding that Felix's stylish attire and amiable manner were bound to impress everybody. 'Absolutely no need to feel nervous,' he had said. 'And you'll see, once the shooting starts you'll act 'em off the set!'

Felix had thanked him for his kind words, but stressed that he wasn't the least bit nervous, merely in a mood of heightened anticipation – such as doubtless beset even his gracious patron on the rare occasions when she was faced with the unknown.

Cedric was about to say, 'You mean when one of the corgis has bolted?' but thought better of it.

As it happened, such concern proved unnecessary, initially at least. Bartholomew telephoned, full of apologies, to say that owing to a contretemps with his car, Fred, the vital cameraman, had been forced to delay his previous night's arrival, and instead would be appearing that morning at Darsham Railway Station. As Bartholomew would have to motor over to collect him, the briefing was postponed until later that afternoon.

So with a sunny day in prospect, they decided to take the opportunity to saunter around the town, imbibing the sea air and bracing draughts of Adnams' ale. With wartime memories still upon him, Cedric was eager to show Felix some of his old haunts – something which, due to the pressing events of their previous visit, he had been unable to do. 'We might also go down and have a look at those smart beach huts,' he suggested. 'They have become quite a feature. Although of course when I was here in forty-two, that part of the promenade was covered in tank traps and barbed wire entanglements. It's less encumbered now and distinctly more decorative!'

'Good idea,' Felix agreed, 'and I might see if I can buy some decent flowers. Nice as the cottage is, I do rather object to those plastic petunias festooned all over the hallway. There's a decent greengrocer in the high street that may have a few . . . Oh, and talking of beach huts, didn't Hackle say that he owned one or that he had borrowed it from somebody?'

'Yes. From his cousin Walter up in Scotland, the one who is a landowner and knows Vincent Ramsgate.'

'Who's he?'

'The travel writer and broadcaster; the one that's always on the wireless prosing on about some place nobody's ever been to – or wants to. I mean, does one really relish the idea of eating desiccated yak on the Russian Steppes in a howling blizzard? It's not my idea of fun! Much more interesting if he talked about the drinking dens of Dresden or the brothels of Berlin. Wouldn't you agree?'

'Oh yes,' Felix replied, 'far more civilised.'

They spent a pleasurable two hours dawdling in the high street, admiring St Edmund's, pottering on the promenade and revisiting the Sailors' Reading Room, before (in serious need of refreshment) gravitating towards East Green's Sole Bay Inn.

As they passed the brewery, two men came towards them; one was middle-aged and stoutish, the other dark-haired and younger. As they drew level the latter seemed to look at Felix quizzically; and out of the corner of his eye Cedric saw him say something to his companion. The other nodded.

'Huh,' Cedric muttered, 'anyone would think he knew you.'

'He does,' said Felix tightly.

Cedric was startled. 'Really? Whatever do you mean?'

'Didn't you recognise them?'

'Certainly not.'

Felix sighed. 'They were those two police officers who

were so officious the last time we were here – the ones who kept pestering me about Delia Dovedale. Frightful they were – rotten so-and-sos!'

'Ah, of course, when you were a key witness. Yes, they were a bit nosy . . . still, only doing their duty I suppose. And it's nice to think that one of them is sufficiently alert to remember your face so clearly; most reassuring in these troubled times, I consider. After all, one has to be so careful, there being such odd types about. One should be grateful for such vigilance,' he added primly.

Felix, about to seethe at his friend's indifference, caught Cedric's wink just in time. 'And I consider it is your turn to stand the drinks,' he said.

Plain, scrubbed and restful, the little pub's interior was much as Cedric remembered it from the war; and putting down the two halves of best local bitter, he settled happily at the small table that Felix had chosen by the window. The window let in considerably more light than it had in Cedric's time; for in those days the thick blackout curtains, despite being drawn back in the day, had always given the place a somewhat shrouded effect. For a brief moment he felt an odd wave of nostalgia . . .

'Posteriors up!' Felix announced, lifting his glass. 'And let's hope we don't see those wretched police people again!'

Cedric raised his own glass and smiled. 'Oh, I expect the younger one is quite a film fan. Once he hears of Hackle's project I daresay he'll be only too ready to do a spot of essential surveillance – probably ask you to wangle him a spectator's place on the set.'

Felix tossed his head. 'Just let him try!' he snorted.

Sipping their beer, they relapsed into a companionable silence.

However, the silence was not to last. From outside there was the sudden blast of a klaxon, followed by the squeal of brakes and a loud slamming of car doors. The next moment the door to the pub was flung open and three people stood on the threshold: two youths of about twenty and a girl. The youths were big, the girl small: petite, slender and with blonde cropped hair. She wore shorts, and without his glasses Cedric at first took her for a boy. However, the shrill voice and expansive gestures suggested otherwise.

'Oh, isn't this quaint!' Tippy Tildred exclaimed. 'And *so* authentic – a real old fishermen's cubbyhole!' She gazed around, her eyes taking in the wooden floors, plain walls and the two 'old fishermen' sitting po-faced by the window.

One of the youths laughed. 'Oh yes? And what do you know of fishermen's cubbyholes? Damn all, I should say.'

The girl pouted and flounced her hip. 'I do read, you know. And a few of us have imaginations – not like some people I could mention. Now, how about some drinkies? I'm parched!' She turned to the other boy: 'Darling Charlie, I'll have a double rum and Coke. Phew! I'm going to need that for this afternoon's wake. I shan't understand a word Bartholomew is saying – but at least he's found me a marvellous costume. I can't wait to put it on; I'll look *fantastico*! It's scarlet and full-skirted, with laces at the back and sequins and black pom-poms down the front.' She gave a little pirouette.

'Christ,' said Charlie.

Felix silently echoed the observation. He was about to nudge Cedric's foot to signal their departure, but at that moment, to his horror, the girl had pranced up to their table.

'Oh, that is the snazziest panama.' she cooed, pointing to Felix's hat lying on the chair next to him. 'My uncle wears that kind; they are *so* smart!'

Coming from anyone else, the endorsement might have pleased Felix; but as it was, he was furious. 'What a coincidence,' he remarked stiffly.

However, worse was to follow. Without warning, the girl stretched out her hand, picked up the hat and put it on her head, tilting it rakishly over one eye. And before Felix could protest, she had rushed to the small mirror over the bar, crying, 'I say, look at me! Talk about Burlington Bertie!' This was followed by gales of laughter and more pirouettes. Felix sat frozen.

Hastily, Cedric stood up and held out his hand. 'Actually, I am afraid we must be off. If you don't mind, Miss . . . ?'

'Oh, my name's Tippy, Tippy Tildred,' she beamed, returning the hat. 'I'm up here to do some filming, and so are Charlie and Frank. They're the grips, and fearfully important.' She turned to her companions: 'Aren't you, darlings?'

Charlie and Frank looked a trifle uncertain.

With hat retrieved and fixed smile, Cedric steered Felix out of the pub and on to the sanctuary of the pavement. 'I suggest,' he said quietly,' that we go and inspect the beach huts and see if we can spot Hackle's. It's blue, I think.'

* * *

Back at *Cot O'Bedlam* Felix announced that he had a slight headache and would lie down before setting off for the studio. 'On the whole,' he said, 'I think that for this preliminary session it would be better if I were to go alone. There's bound to be masses of introductions and instructions and it is essential that I immerse myself thoroughly in the general style of things without distraction. Once I am properly au fait with matters it would be most agreeable to have you with me to lend support and applause.' He smiled graciously.

'Most wise,' said Cedric (rather pleased at the prospect of a lazy afternoon with a good book), 'and then, when you get back, you can tell me *all* about it . . . Uhm, will you be taking your panama? It could be a little breezy up there, you may have to hold—'

'No,' Felix sniffed, 'it might be wrested from me.'

As envisaged, Cedric spent a most reposeful afternoon reading, toying with the crossword, composing a postcard and then indulging in the merest soupçon of some chocolates and a snooze. When he awoke it was nearly six o'clock, and the click of the front door latch signalled his friend's return.

'Busy schedule?' he enquired. 'What was the studio like – all lights and cameras and continuity girls?

'Oh yes, plenty of that . . . well, lights and cameras. I didn't see much of the last, unless you count some crone called Mabel who sat on a packing case chain-smoking and muttering that all the sequences were up the spout.' Felix paused, and added, 'She may just have had a point . . . Anyway we didn't stay long in the studio itself,

51

because after Hackle had outlined the agenda and assured us that the film was about to make cinematic history, he insisted on giving us a protracted tour of Gun Hill and the adjacent area. Some of the scenes are set there, and he felt it would help us to "absorb the spirit of the place".'

'Really? Given your earlier experience in that location, I should think you've absorbed quite enough of its spirit. Not one of life's more reassuring events, I seem to remember!'[2]

'Exactly,' Felix replied with a shudder, 'and the less said the better; we don't want *that* business raked up again . . . Still, I must toughen the sinews, or whatever one does, as apparently some of the part I am playing involves a couple of shots of me loitering amidst the artillery on the wind-torn cliff.'

Cedric looked doubtful. 'Sounds a mite chilly, I should say . . . But if you don't mind my asking, what exactly is your part?' he enquired curiously.

'It hasn't been totally defined yet but it's obviously rather subtle.'

'Oh yes? In what way subtle – what do you have to do?'

Felix hesitated, and then explained that so far it involved his leaning against the barrel of the third cannon on Gun Hill and gazing out to sea with right shoulder down and left profile up. 'At an angle,' he added.

'Hmm, sounds a bit uncomfortable. Do you have to say anything?'

'I am required to whisper: "the seagull, the seagull".'

'Well, that won't tax the memory. And why the whispering – are you supposed to have laryngitis?'

[2] See *A Southwold Mystery*

Felix scowled. 'Of course not. Apparently it's part of the character's mysterious aura.'

'I see . . . And will you be wearing any clothes?'

'Clothes? What are you talking about? Of *course* I shall be wearing bloody clothes! You don't think I am going to be poncing around as some nudist, do you!' Felix glared.

'Calm down, dear boy,' Cedric said soothingly, 'I was merely wondering whether you would be in costume – an ornithologist's smock, for example.'

There was silence as Felix seethed. And then glancing at the clock, he said tightly, 'I propose taking my martini on the veranda. Doubtless you have something better to do.'

Ten minutes later, bearing his own drink and a dish of olives, Cedric joined him. 'Do you know,' he said genially, 'there's an awfully good grocer's in the high street that actually stocks these, and even sells Camembert. It's a sort of delicatessen; most enterprising. I don't recall it being there the last time we came, do you?' Other than stretching out an indifferent hand for an olive, Felix made no response.

His friend tried another tack: 'I say, do you think that Tippy Tildred girl is entirely all there?'

'Absolutely not! Totally barking – and nasty with it,' Felix exploded happily. 'And do you know what . . .'

The rest of the evening passed most amicably.

CHAPTER SIX

The following day, with the vital Fred now arrived and the cast tenuously acquainted with their roles, shooting began in earnest.

When Rosy and Lady Fawcett arrived at 'Cousin Walter's' rambling mansion they found themselves plunged into a confusion of lights, cameras, amplifiers, piles of packing cases, trailing wires and an abundance of discarded coffee cups. There was also much noise and toing and froing.

In the midst of it all, or rather ensconced in a corner, sat Cedric reading a book. Passive and oblivious, he could have been Eliot's still point in a turning world. Felix was nowhere to be seen – presumably in some nether room practising being gnomic and Janus-like.

The two spectators seated themselves on a couple of canvas chairs conveniently placed near the action area;

but moved hastily when told by an electrician that these were the special preserve of the 'big shots, Him and Him'. He stuck his thumb in the direction of Bartho and Sam. The scriptwriter was looking somewhat peeved, and Rosy wondered if he had had to fight his corner over some aspect of the text.

From a door behind them Alicia appeared and sat down in the chair next to Rosy. With aggressively tousled hair, highly rouged cheeks and clad in the tumbling folds of an eighteenth-century negligee, she was clearly in seduction mode. She carried a cup of coffee, and rather incongruously was smoking a cigarette.

'I'm worn out already,' she grumbled, 'and we haven't even started the bloody thing! God knows where Robert has got to, he was still gobbling eggs and bacon when I left the hotel. No sense of timing, that man!' She took another drag of her cigarette, and gesturing to the chaise longue in the centre of the set, snorted derisively. 'Well, that's on its last legs all right. I daresay it belongs to Bartho's cousin, one of the relics of the place. If that's what we are supposed to do our love scene on I shan't answer for the consequences – broken frame and bruised backsides!'

'I knew the feeling once,' Lady Fawcett sighed nostalgically.

Alicia's momentary interest was diverted by the entrance of Robert at the far end of the room, looking mildly dashing in ruffled shirt and knee breeches. 'About time too,' she said, 'but I just hope he isn't soaked in that awful Old Mice, I can't stand it.'

'Soaked in what?' Rosy asked startled.

'Oh, you know: that dreary aftershave, Old Spice. It's so unsubtle.'

'Ah, you mean the one with a picture of a galleon on the bottle. Yes, I agree it's not the most delicate. But perhaps with that ship motif he may think it fits the Sole Bay theme,' Rosy laughed.

'You could just be right,' the other replied gloomily.

Their conversation was interrupted by a microphoned bellow from Bartho demanding silence and action.

'Ah, at last,' Alicia muttered, 'so here I come, lover boy.' She stubbed out her cigarette on the floor next to Rosy's foot, and gathering the billowing negligee, glided forth to do battle with her smouldering buccaneer.

On the whole the scene had not gone badly. And evidently 'Old Mice' had failed to feature, as the leading lady had seemed obligingly compliant. It was fortunate, too, that the scorned chaise longue had stayed the course – and indeed coped valiantly with the lunges and languors being enacted on its faded brocade. Yes, as amatory hurly-burly goes, the little scene had been moderately convincing.

It had been rapidly replaced by a large photographed backdrop of the retreat from Tobruk, with one of the cast (a budding Paul Scofield) intoning poignant lines about the ravages of war. Picture and poetry had been moving; but as Lady Fawcett observed to Rosy, it had been difficult to see its link with the preceding dalliance in a Suffolk drawing room three centuries past.

'I expect it's all part of the *labyrinth*,' Rosy had whispered. 'What you might call a juxtaposition of the gay and the gross, pulsating life and dreadful death. A sort of transcendent pastiche.'

'How frightful,' her companion murmured.

At eleven o'clock there was a pause for rest and recuperation, and people dispersed to the garden or to make fresh coffee. In an area adjacent to the studio, and which originally must have been a study or morning room, there was a sideboard with a tea urn, a selection of raddled rock cakes and assorted cans of fizzy drinks. Rosy and Lady Fawcett studied these dubiously and decided that they could wait until lunchtime for proper refreshment.

'Well, it's all very fascinating,' Lady Fawcett remarked to Rosy, 'but I am not *quite* sure that I'm any the wiser. And when I asked Sam to explain a little, he looked rather fierce and said that the concept of summary was alien to him, and that I would need to see the finished product to grasp its spiritual essence. And then when I said that—'

But her words were never finished, for Felix had suddenly appeared on the threshold looking white and scandalised. 'Oh my God,' he cried, 'I have just encountered a bear – it's huge and black and dreadful! It came towards me. I've only just escaped with my life! Quick, we must defend ourselves.' He grabbed a nearby chair and rammed its back under the door handle.

Stunned, the others gazed at him fascinated, and then at each other. 'Has he been taking dope?' Tippy giggled.

Cedric gripped him by the arm and whispered firmly, 'This is absurd, Felix. Just because the last time we were here you were ambushed by a coypu, doesn't mean to say there should now be a whole zoo after you. Do be sensible, dear boy – it was probably a trick of the light.'

'Some damn light!' the other squeaked, casting fearful glances towards the door.

At that moment another voice was heard coming from the garden. Its tone was light and coaxing: 'Pixie, Pixie,' it crooned, 'come along now, don't be a silly girlie-whirlie. See what daddy's got for *yoo-hoo* . . .'

The crooning stopped, and Fred put his head in at the open window. 'Here,' he said in normal basso voice, 'has anyone seen that bloody dog of mine? She's been playing silly beggars all morning, crafty old cow.'

There was a momentary silence; and then Alicia said, 'Actually, Fred, I think she may be on the other side of that door. One rather gathers she has been chatting up Mr Smythe.' She approached the door, dislodged the chair, and threw it open.

There, sprawled on the floor like a shaggy coal heap or beached whale (or bear), lay what Rosy assumed to be the errant Pixie. The creature was indeed huge – the biggest Newfoundland she had ever seen. And as Felix had said, she was very black; a colour that accentuated the bright pink of the tongue peeping from the slumbering jowl.

Instantly, Tippy Tildred emitted peals of derisive laughter: 'Oh, Felix, fancy mistaking that stupid old hearthrug for a dangerous bear, you are a silly ass!'

It was difficult to say which of the two, Fred or Felix, was the more stung by her reaction: Fred for her calling his beloved pet a stupid old hearthrug (and whose coat he assiduously groomed every day); or Felix for being dubbed an ass by a girl less than half his age.

Both men glowered. But it was the latter who spoke: 'I may be an ass, Miss Tildred, but at least I am a *polite* one.' With the merest shrug, he deftly lit a cigarette, and with left profile well displayed, gazed indifferently at the clouds wafting beyond the window. Cedric regarded him with some pride, while Tippy looked sullen, and the dog woke up and yawned.

In the studio that afternoon there had been a minor shindig. Bartho, true to his inconstancy, had changed the shooting schedule. Aesthetically a reasonable adjustment; socially less so. It had entailed swapping the sequence of scenes from one featuring Robert and two supporting characters, to one involving Tippy. The switch was generally deemed sensible, but there was one dissonant voice: Tippy's. She had planned to be elsewhere, and was none too pleased to learn that her presence was required on set.

'Sorry, Tippy,' Bartho breezed, 'it can't be helped. Lie back and think of England – or better still, stand up and think of all that money and fame so nearly in your grasp.'

Tippy pouted. 'Oh hell,' she whined, 'that's messed everything up. I had organised a lift to Darsham to catch the Ipswich train. There's a wonderful new boutique there. It's fearfully hip and wildly expensive. This is the last day of its sale and there'll be some fantastic bargains – but now I'll never get another chance. It's too bad!'

She looked defiant and then winsomely tearful; and Cedric, not without sympathy, was prompted to say, 'Ah well, that's life, I'm afraid: a medley of fun and fury. There will be many other such blows to endure – but like the rest of us, doubtless you'll cope valiantly.' He flashed a kindly smile.

It was not returned. And instead, she said coldly: 'It may be *your* life, Professor, but I do not intend it to be mine.' With a toss of her head, she flounced to the sideboard and poured a Coca-Cola.

There was an awkward pause, during which Lady Fawcett raised an eyebrow, Cedric cleared his throat and Felix hated her.

Later, over coffee in the lounge of The Swan, the four of them agreed that on the whole Tippy Tildred was not an asset to proceedings, Felix going so far as to suggest that she should have been drowned at birth.

Shelving the topic, they were about to get up and go their separate ways, when Bartholomew appeared in the doorway. He scanned the room, and seeing them, approached quickly. 'Ah,' he said, 'glad I've caught you. We've had an invitation – or at least I have – and I've wangled it so that you can come too. I hope that's all right because, frankly, I don't really want to go on my own, I hardly know the chap.' He grinned at them hopefully.

'What chap and where?' Rosy asked.

'Vincent Ramsgate, the travel writer. He knows Cousin Walter, and Walter happened to mention that he had lent me his place for the filming. Ramsgate lives not far from here – Reydon, I think, or near it – and he's just telephoned to ask if I would like to go over for a party that he is throwing to toast his latest travel book; I gather it has won some prize or other. Most of the other guests will be locals and I shan't know a soul. So I thanked him for his kind thought, and then

61

mumbled something about being spoken for that evening as it was Angela's birthday, and a few of us were going down to the Harbour Inn to celebrate, and thus regretfully—'

'Do you mean *my* birthday?' Lady Fawcett exclaimed. 'But that's not till November!'

'Well, now you've got two, like the queen,' Bartholomew chuckled. 'But, anyway, the excuse didn't work, because he was most insistent that I should bring you all with me; said his friends would be fascinated to meet members of a real-life film company, especially one as renowned as the mighty Hackle Enterprises and we would enhance their evening.' He laughed again, and added, 'Actually, he sounded perfectly genuine, quite keen in fact, so I said we would go. I hope that's all right?'

'But except for Felix, *we're* not members of your company or its cast,' Rosy said doubtfully, looking at Cedric and Angela. 'I mean, we're just here to cheer things along.'

'And you do it so beautifully,' the young man laughed. 'Yes, of course you are included. After all, it is you who are the vital birthday celebrants all poised for the revels of the Harbour Inn. Ramsgate owes you a party!'

'Oh really, Bartho,' Lady Fawcett exclaimed in feigned annoyance, 'you are no better than Amy: both weavers of rampant invention. Suppose Mr Ramsgate gives me a present?'

'In that case, dear Angela,' Cedric observed, 'you will doubtless accept it with your usual grace and charm. As it happens,' he continued, 'I should be intrigued to see Reydon again. The last time I was there was during the war when it was virtually off limits to all but the military, and covered in guns galore. I imagine its peacetime aspect is rather more appealing. I seem to remember a rather striking medieval church and some bluebell woods, though it's too late in the season for—'

'Well, I am all for going,' Felix interrupted. 'With luck he will be serving champagne – although I trust one will not be required to buy the book. Currently, *Cappadocian Capers* is as much as I can handle!' He winked at Cedric.

Rosy also evinced an interest, and enquired if anyone else was included.

Bartholomew nodded and said he had asked Robert and Alicia. 'They will doubtless strike the expected note of glamour for the locals. Oh yes, and I'll ask Tippy too: it might soothe ruffled feathers, and I am sure they will appreciate our sprightly starlet.'

'Sprightly? A posturing gnome!' Felix was about to mutter. But his mind had already whisked to his new smoking jacket: a matter of greater concern than Tippy Tildred. So far it had not had an airing, and this would be an ideal opportunity. He wondered which tie would look best.

Thus the outing was arranged. And the following evening they set off in two cars for Reydon and Ramsgate's residence.

This turned out to be a large, aggressively modern house seemingly inspired by the New Brutalism, aspects of art deco and the whims of the local builder. It was on the far outskirts of the town and thickly surrounded by trees – a feature which, Cedric opined, was no bad thing. ('I certainly don't recall this being here before,' he observed tartly, 'but it's amazing how quickly new buildings are thrown up these days: they appear from nowhere like disagreeable mushrooms in the night.')

As they continued up the long drive they saw on the left an expansive lawn populated by a group of sculptures in a strangely eclectic style: a decapitated ostrich, a mermaid with her tail wrapped round her neck, and a cuboid shape of no discernible significance.

'I say,' said Felix nervously, 'do you think there are any more inside?'

But the interior, far from being brutal or eclectic, was in fact surprisingly bland: universally pale grey, spacious, sparsely furnished, and with randomly chosen flowers badly arranged (a detail Felix was quick to notice). In contrast, its owner cut quite a dash. He greeted them effusively, wearing a pair of vivid plaid trews, mustard velvet slippers and, rather bizarrely, a jaunty skullcap (or sort of hybrid fez). Mercifully, his jacket was dark. All the same, Rosy couldn't help thinking she was being ushered forward by some flunky from a pantomime. Clutching a large cigar, he welcomed them in the richly gravelly tones familiar from his radio talks.

CHAPTER SEVEN

With practised ease they were manoeuvred among the other guests, plied with Felix's hoped-for champagne, and quickly assimilated into the throng of kindly and inquisitive locals.

Rosy was approached by an elderly gentleman who seemed convinced she was Lana Turner. He produced a biro, and, in the absence of an autograph album, wondered if she would be so kind as to sign the back of his hand. Explaining she was a mere appendage to the film group, she pointed him in the direction of Tippy Tildred, encased from neck to toe in black satin, and looking – as Alicia had once remarked – like a thin eyebrow pencil with yellow top. 'Now, she's a real star,' Rosy laughed, and glancing at the proffered wrist, added, 'she'll sign anything.'

'Wow!' the old boy exclaimed, and without further utterance, trundled off towards the obliging Tippy.

'That was neatly done,' a low voice said from behind, 'very slick, if you don't mind my saying.'

Rosy turned quickly, flustered to have been overheard making such a comment. 'Oh dear,' she exclaimed, 'that was a bit clumsy! I really didn't mean—'

'Oh, don't apologise,' a tall man with grey cropped hair said, 'I enjoyed the cabaret – in fact it's not over yet.' He nodded to where Tippy stood frowning. The girl was clearly piqued to have been entrapped by one quite so ancient. The biro was still being flourished. 'You watch,' the man said quietly, 'he'll roll up his trouser leg next.'

They both laughed, and he introduced himself as Mickey Standish, an old friend of their host. 'Well, more than a friend, really. For my sins I am also his financial advisor: tax and investments and so on. Vincent is hopeless with money, always has been. At school he would blow his pocket money the day he got it, and then wonder why there were no reserves. I put him straight then and I'm still at it.' He took a sip from his glass; not alcohol, Rosy noticed, but apparently water.

Rosy sipped her own drink and regarded her companion. She rather liked what she saw. Height and hair were complemented by a casual but well-cut suit, and which – unlike the taste of his old friend – was of sober hue. She asked if he lived locally.

'Oh no,' he replied, 'London mainly, that is when I'm not abroad on business. But I come up here from time to time to sort out Vincent's affairs and to do a spot of fishing. And when he has any London broadcasts he usually stays at my flat. Rather a good arrangement, really: he enjoys the occasional glitz of the metropolis and I bask in the peace of Suffolk. This is a beautiful strip of the coast.'

Rosy agreed, and was about to ask politely whereabouts abroad his business took him, when he enquired of her own job: 'So since you are not of the movie glitterati, what is it that *you* do to keep the wolf from the door – or are you a lady of leisure?' He smiled, glancing around at a number who obviously were.

She told him a little of her work at the British Museum: compiling catalogues and arranging some of its exhibitions; and of the more arduous task of organising her boss, the wayward Dr Stanley. 'That's the tricky part,' she laughed.

'Yes, I can believe you; I've come across him once or twice. Mad as a hatter and brilliant. If you can manage him you must have redoubtable powers. My compliments.' He gave a wry smile. And then he looked slightly puzzled and stared at her searchingly. 'I know it sounds odd, but I am pretty sure I've seen your photograph somewhere, but can't think when.'

Rosy was taken aback. 'I can't think when either – and it wasn't in the *Tatler* that's for certain!' She laughed.

'No,' he said thoughtfully, 'not that, but some other rag possibly . . . Ah yes, *The Times* about four years ago. Yes that's it: in connection with the Marcia Beasley case. Weren't you the niece?'

The question was not what Rosy wanted to hear, not at all! At the time of the case she had tried her level best to keep out of the limelight. Her aunt's bizarre death and the mystery surrounding it had been a source of acute embarrassment, both initially and even more so later when most of the facts had been revealed (not, mercifully, to the public but to the inner circle of MI5). She had been sworn to secrecy (hardly a penance) but had been living beneath its shadow ever since. The last thing she wanted was for this man, or anyone else, to start raking up a matter she chose to ignore. Frankly, with the lady in question safely dead and buried, she had no desire to talk about Aunt Marcia and her dubious lifestyle.

'Er, yes,' she replied uncomfortably, 'I was the niece. But it all seems rather a long time ago now.' She laughed again, but this time in a tone she knew must sound false.

Would he leave off? No, of course not! 'As it happens,' he continued, 'I knew her briefly. Quite a girl in her way, but always a bit of a dark horse.' He paused, and then added, 'Very dark. In fact, the whole thing was rather a funny old business, wasn't it? One always thought there was far more there than appeared on the surface . . . but then, I suppose that's true of most things – or people.' He smiled; but it was a smile not so much friendly as sharply quizzical.

Rosy shrugged, and mumbled something evasive about having been scarcely involved and knowing little about the case. Ostensibly this was the truth, but in reality she had been involved up to her neck. The whole thing had been godawful!

Luckily, at that point the topic was interrupted by the arrival of Felix who, having modestly told a group of respectful ladies that in addition to being part of the film company he was *also* one of the Queen Mother's most frequent suppliers of flowers, had escaped to draw breath and to review his repertoire. However, so riveting had been the narrative that one from his audience still adhered.

She plucked at his sleeve. 'A final question, Mr Smythe,' she pleaded. 'Tell me, which is Her Majesty's most favourite flower? Do divulge!'

Felix gazed pensively into the distance, and then with a wistful smile replied: 'Oh, undoubtedly, it is the gracious delphinium . . .' He paused, and then murmured, 'which of course echoes those peerless blue eyes.'

Just for an instant Rosy saw why Bartholomew had chosen him for a part in that outlandish film! She glanced round to catch her companion's eye, and saw his tall back disappearing among the crowd of guests.

She turned back to Felix. 'The last time you were asked that question,' she said accusingly, 'you said it was a pink peony to match the delicate bloom of her cheeks.'

'Yes, well all truth is relative,' he said, scanning the room for some more smoked caviar.

A little later Rosy saw Alicia Gorringe and Robert Kestrel over by the window. They stood close together, the one looking sullen, the other characteristically smouldering. Their attention was clearly fixed on Tippy, who (by now having extricated herself from the clutches of the autograph hunter) was being gamine and winsome among a group of chortling young men. Alicia's thunderous gaze was diverted by a sudden blast from the gramophone, and seeing Rosy she waved and beckoned her over.

Moving in their direction, she passed Cedric in close conversation with Ramsgate. The two writers formed an incongruous pair: the professor's cloistered look contrasting sharply with Ramsgate's flamboyance and assertive gestures. The academic had the earnest air of one conducting a graduate seminar, while the travel pundit chatted freely and volubly, the gravelly voice punctuated with staccato barks of mirth. Cedric was smiling politely – but inwardly wondering why on earth the man was wearing that ridiculous headgear.

'You know, that child is such a cow,' Alicia muttered as soon as Rosy had joined them, 'vain and stupid, *and* calculating!'

Rosy was startled by her tone: quietly venomous. 'You sound a bit fed up,' she said lightly. 'What's she done now?'

'Bought a red bikini,' Kestrel announced.

Rosy stared at him open-mouthed. Was the man mad? Did the pair harbour a joint hatred of socialism? Or give secret support to Prudes Anonymous?

'Er, so what?' she stammered, 'I've got a yellow one with pink—'

'She has bought a red bikini *because*,' Alicia interrupted with gritted teeth, 'that fool Bartho has altered the beach scene. Instead of having *me* languishing by the breakwater to seduce the unsuspecting sea captain as he plods his weary way across the dunes, Bartho and that idiot scriptwriter have decided to use *her* instead . . . I ask you, scrapped the professional and substituted that cheap little stick insect! The stupid bikini is a present to herself for being so favoured: a sort of self-conferred trophy.' As if to stress the grossness of the insult, she tugged angrily at her ample bodice; and in so doing bumped against Kestrel's glass. Its contents splashed liberally down her cleavage.

'Christ, that's all I need!' she hissed.

'Oh dear,' Rosy exclaimed, dabbing ineffectually at the other's dress, 'I hope that's not too chilly. Shall I get you another glass?'

'Several would be helpful – and oh, while you're at it you could spike that bloody girl's drink. It might keep her quiet.'

Rosy couldn't help grinning, while Alicia glared at Robert Kestrel; and indeed at anyone else who happened to catch her eye.

Elsewhere in the room things were proceeding more equably. Lady Fawcett had just encountered Mickey Standish, and they were engaged in an amiable exchange of pleasantries – something that emboldened the former to enquire if Vincent Ramsgate was always in the habit of wearing a hat indoors.

'No, fortunately,' Standish replied. 'Only if he is hosting a party or celebrating a new book – which, I suppose, is about fifty per cent of the time. A friend of his, Ida Carshalton, gave it to him a few years ago as a joke, since then it's become a sort of fetish.' He shrugged. 'Absurd, really, but I suppose we all have our little quirks.'

'Oh, indeed,' Angela agreed earnestly. 'I remember my dear late husband used to—' She broke off in surprise. 'Oh, you don't mean Ida Carshalton, the MP's wife, do you? We used to know them moderately well at some point – but you know how it is, one loses touch so easily, especially in London. Mind you, he is always most assiduous in dispatching his emissaries to come canvassing on my doorstep when the need arises. These politicians, they never miss a trick do they!'

Standish agreed that they didn't, adding wryly that perhaps it was just as well as it fed the public's taste for lurid gossip. 'And after all, without that, think how dull the newspapers would be.'

'Yes, perhaps you are right,' she mused, 'one hadn't thought of it like that. But, oh dear, in that case just think what the readers of the *Manchester Guardian* must be missing!' She chuckled, and rather to her own surprise, accepted his proffered cigarette.

He asked about the film and her connection with its young director. She began to explain about Amy, and the girl's absence on account of Mr Bates's Shropshire mission, but then stopped. Vincent Ramsgate was approaching (cap slightly askew).

'Ah, Lady Fawcett,' he cried, 'I've been looking for you. The birthday girl, I gather! How noble of you to forsake the hotspots of Southwold for my meagre gathering. You deserve a prize for fortitude: in short, a little birthday token . . . I shall present you, dear lady, with the veritable limes of paradise!' He executed a theatrical bow.

Lady Fawcett was flummoxed. Really! It was bad enough being faced with the bogus birthday, but what on earth were these limes the man was babbling about?

Her confusion must have shown, for Standish said patiently, 'He means he is going to give you his new book, *The Limes of Paradise*.'

'Indeed, I am,' the author beamed unctuously, 'and here it is: my latest collection of travel essays all signed and sealed.' He thrust the volume into her hand and made another bow.

'*How* kind,' the startled recipient replied – and wondered how much longer his fez would stay the course.

After he had gone, Standish said, 'So today is your birthday?'

'Oh most certainly,' Lady Fawcett lied, 'it's the same date every year.'

As Felix and Cedric hovered in the entrance hall, waiting for the others to say goodnight to their host, the latter remarked that on the whole it had been a moderately congenial evening. 'One has known far worse, wouldn't you agree? But I just hope that young Bartholomew is sufficiently steady to get us back to Southwold without incident, he looks a trifle flushed.'

'Most of them do,' replied Felix, 'even Rosy Gilchrist. I noticed her in a huddle with Robert and Alicia. Alicia looked tigerish and was obviously effing and blinding about something.'

'Sozzled?'

'More sodden, I should say.'

Cedric laughed. 'Well, Tippy Tildred was certainly having fun. Extraordinary, really: I happened to be standing minding my own business inspecting that Bechstein, when all of a sudden she rushed up to me spluttering that she had taken a shine to Mickey Standish and didn't I think he was an absolute dish!'

'Oh, indeed? And without wishing to be inquisitive, what did you say, exactly?'

'There wasn't time to compose an answer, dear boy. She had run off.'

'Hmm. If you ask my opinion, Tippy Tildred takes a shine to most people providing they are male and with money,' Felix observed dryly. 'But she won't get far with that fellow. I should say he's immune to frippery, wouldn't you?'

Cedric glanced behind him to the drawing room where the tall figure of Standish could be seen by the French window, passive and alone. In his hand was a glass of colourless liquid, which some might have assumed to be vodka, but which Cedric suspected was water. 'You could be right,' he said.

Revelry over, Bartho drove back to the centre of Southwold with commendable caution.

Rosy pressed her face against the car window, and absorbed by the moonlight, the sleeping fields and spectral trees, was content to let the others conduct the autopsy. But when there was a lull in the conversation, she said brightly: 'I say, do you think I look like Lana Turner?'

There was a silence. And then Lady Fawcett murmured, 'Uhm . . . well not entirely, I shouldn't think – though, of course, *some* might see a resemblance. Er, what do you think, Felix?'

'Obviously two sheets to the wind,' was the answer.

CHAPTER EIGHT

Felix had cooked a superb supper. And Cedric, in mellow mood after the shrimp ravioli and Alsatian Riesling, suggested they took an evening stroll to complete the evening's pleasure. Felix agreed but said he had had enough of the sea for one day, having been required by Bartholomew to hover endlessly around a breakwater while Robert Kestrel strutted and declaimed. The scene had not been notably successful and would doubtless have to be reshot the following day.

'Let's go the other way,' he said, 'down to those marshes by Buss Creek.'

Cedric was slightly surprised but said nothing, recalling that the last time Felix had been near marshland the dear boy had suffered an unfortunate experience . . . But it was an excellent idea as he could then show his friend where he had been strafed by a Messerschmidt in '43 and the exact spot by

Might's Bridge where he had taken cover. Thus turning left they sauntered on down towards Buss Creek where Cedric, to the murmured appreciation of Felix, spent a happy ten minutes recreating his ordeal and discovering the abandoned pillbox that had also served as shelter during the ordeal.

Drama exhausted, they retraced their footsteps up towards the town. For once Cedric was talking volubly, clearly still reliving those fraught moments: 'And then it turned round, dipped its wings and—'

Felix gripped his arm. 'Ssh,' he whispered. 'Watch out!'

'What?'

'Move over, it's that bloody girl!' He pulled Cedric into the shadow of the hedge by the library.

A chattering trio passed them, two youths and a girl: Tippy Tildred. Her companions appeared to be the two young men from the film crew who had been with her in the Sole Bay. Their arms were linked, their feet unsteady and from their mouths issued a mangled version of Paul Anka's 'Put your Head on My Shoulder' interspersed with stifled guffaws.

'Well, she's certainly having fun,' Cedric observed, 'probably won't remember a thing in the morning. Just as well she didn't see us – might have wanted to try on another of your garments!' He gave a sly laugh.

'Doubtless,' Felix said disdainfully. 'So vulgar!' Clutching Cedric's sleeve he continued to hover in the lee of the library, glaring at the trio's retreating backs as they entered and stumbled across North Green.

Cedric cleared his throat. 'Uhm – do you think it's safe for us to move on now? I am sure Tippy is far too preoccupied to notice us and it's getting a little chilly.' Pointedly, he turned up his jacket collar against the mild air.

'Hold on a bit,' Felix breathed, 'with luck they'll turn off up Victoria Road and we can walk on unmolested.'

Then, just as Felix declared it safe to detach themselves from the hedge, they saw the figure of a man cross the road from the King's Head on the corner, and begin to walk slowly in the same direction as Tippy and her cavaliers. He seemed in no hurry. And when the group stopped, and amid gales of giggles the girl struck a pose and did a little jig in the middle of the green, he remained in the shadows as if watching the performance from the wings.

The three moved on; as did the man, keeping several yards behind.

'Looks as if she's got a hidden admirer,' Cedric said.

'Huh! I can't think why. Nobody but a—' He broke off as Cedric nudged him.

'Oh, look,' the latter whispered, 'it's Robert Kestrel. What's he doing slouching around Southwold at this hour?'

'Doubtless looking for where he was strafed by a Messerschmidt,' Felix tittered. It was a foolish riposte for it nearly cost him his bedtime Calvados and cocoa.

For a few moments they watched Kestrel as he sloped on behind Tippy and her escorts rollicking up Victoria Road. He kept his distance and was clearly in no hurry to catch up – stopping whenever they did, and melting into the shadows like some hack private eye.

'But he is staying at The Swan, surely the quicker route would be the high street,' Cedric said.

Felix sniffed. 'Clearly enjoying the night air and that excruciating scent the girl wears. I can think of more congenial pursuits.'

They turned, and crossing the road made their way back to the discreet fragrance of *Cot O'Bedlam*.

Meanwhile, in the lounge of The Swan, Lady Fawcett pored over her crossword, the gnomic clues an invaluable antidote to insomnia. If she could just manage to complete that top corner she would call it a day and retire to bed, brain happily exhausted.

Inspiration flashed, and smiling in triumph she started to complete one of the longer clues. With a flourish she pencilled in the final letter – at which point she was aware of a presence in front of her. She looked up and saw it was Alicia, equipped with a large brandy and a scowl.

'You haven't seen Robert, have you?' she asked. 'We were supposed to meet for a nightcap at least twenty minutes ago and there's not a sign of him. It's too bad!'

The other hesitated, reviewing the events of her evening. 'Er – yes, as a matter of fact, about an hour ago. He said he was going to have a stroll along the seafront to rehearse his lines and hone his part.'

The young woman raised an eyebrow. 'Hone his part? Well, that might be an idea; it could help him no end.' Angela thought she detected a gleam of mirth, but couldn't be sure.

She invited Alicia to sit down. 'I am sure he'll turn up at any moment,' she said. 'Men are like that, no idea of time. The times I had to wait for my Gregory! And then they suddenly turn up . . . I won't say like bad pennies: a bit like gold dust, actually.'

The other swirled her brandy and took a sip. 'Hmm. I don't know about gold dust where Robert is concerned, more like silver foil, I should say.'

At that point, and as predicted, the errant companion did indeed appear; and seeing the two of them on the sofa, walked briskly over. 'I am *so* sorry, sweetie,' he said, addressing Alicia, 'I had gone for a walk along the promenade and got so immersed going over that scene where I have to sit on the breakwater and gaze at the wraith of Felix Smythe, that before I realised it I was right down by the putting green and the pier!' He beamed at Lady Fawcett: 'That's the trouble with us thespians, we get so absorbed by our roles that everything else just *fades* into the ether!'

'Well, I don't know if I can manage the ether, but I am going to fade into my bedroom,' she replied. 'I have been awake far too long for one day.' Lady Fawcett rose, and tucking the crossword under one arm, waved them a kindly goodnight with the other.

At the door she caught the sound of Robert's voice earnestly regaling Alicia with his nocturnal impressions of the canons on South Green and the outline of Southwold's pier. ('*So* striking and romantic in the moonlight!' he enthused.) She suspected it was a topic not entirely to the other's interest. She was also uncertain about the quality of the moon: it hadn't been much in evidence when she had last looked out. In fact, the evening had been decidedly dull and misty. But then, with a name like Kestrel perhaps he had hawk-like eyes.

CHAPTER NINE

The following morning was tough – for Felix at least. There had been a small dispute between Bartholomew and Fred regarding the rushes of his 'seagull' scene, the director deciding that dawn, not dusk, would give the better effect. Thus a reshooting had been scheduled for first light – a time not entirely congenial to Felix. However, in a mood of noble martyrdom he joined the rest of the team on the clifftop, and draping himself across one of the guns thrust his profile towards the camera, and intoned the familiar spiel.

'Cut!' yelled Bartho.

Oh hell, had he messed up? Out of the corner of his eye he glimpsed Tippy with a big smirk on her face. Bitch! He was about to reset his features for another take, when to his surprise Bartho said: 'That's absolutely fine, just the job. Now you can go back to bed.' He looked quite pleased.

Felix, now also pleased, gave a jaunty bow and turned to leave – but not before Tippy had scampered up and said, 'Oh my, you looked *just* like Laurence Olivier, although you are just a *teeny* bit shorter.' She sniggered. 'What a pity you've got such a tiny role, and you are trying *so* hard! Perhaps if you're nice to me I can pull a string or two to get His Nibs to expand it a bit.' She gave a patronising smile.

Unsmiling, Felix wandered back across the turf knowing exactly why murders were committed.

At the cottage, boosted by breakfast and Cedric's emollient words, he felt better. Nevertheless, when Rosy rang to ask if they would be lunching in Walberswick to watch some more location work by the estuary, Felix declined.

'I gather Miss Tildred has a scene there this afternoon,' he replied, 'and having already encountered the lady once today I do not need to repeat the experience. Besides,' he added rather grandly, 'Cedric and I have a prior engagement, which we really cannot miss.'

The former looked slightly surprised. 'Have we?' he asked, after Felix had replaced the receiver.

'Surely you remember,' his friend beamed, 'an exploration of Orford Castle followed by a leisurely lunch of delicious oysters, Chablis and grilled sardines at Mrs Pinney's seafood place. What could be nicer? Beats filming any day!'

'You could be right,' Cedric replied. 'And the sun's coming out; you might wear your panama.'

Alas, Felix could not wear his panama as he had lost it (a blow which had nearly stymied the whole Orford project).

* * *

But meanwhile, sitting next to Rosy in The Bell at Walberswick, Tippy Tildred made it clear to her neighbour how much she was looking forward to sporting her new scarlet bikini. She had bought it at Denny's in Market Place just the other day, she confided, and couldn't wait to show it off. 'You see,' she exclaimed, 'I have this little anklet from Selfridges, and the red beads will match the bikini exactly!' She stretched out a neatly shaped calf adorned by a ring of chichi nonsense.

'Very pretty,' said Rosy politely, 'but will you have time to wear it? And besides, the bikini sounds more typical of Le Touquet than Southwold. From what I've seen, most of the bathing costumes here are woollen one-pieces. You might create a disturbance!' She laughed.

'Exactly what I intend,' the girl said airily, 'this place needs shaking up!'

She turned her attention to one of the grips sitting opposite. 'I say, Charlie, you'll take me swimming, won't you? What with your muscles and my wiggle we'll turn every head on the beach!'

Charlie looked shifty and took refuge in his pint and cheese sandwich. The girl persisted. '*Won't* you, Charlie?' she cried.

The young man seemed embarrassed. 'Er, well I would, I suppose,' he mumbled, 'if I could swim; but I can't really, never got the hang of it somehow. But I'll wade about a bit if you like,' he offered vaguely.

Tippy tossed her head scornfully. 'Oh, don't bother. I'm certainly not going around with a mere *paddler*!' Rosy had the impression the youth was rather relieved to hear this.

Yet despite her irritation, she felt slightly sorry for the girl: a silly little show-off; but underneath the flounce and bounce, perhaps lonely. She had known one or two like that in the ATS: insecure youngsters putting on the style. Thus, as a kindly gesture, she complimented the girl on her performance the previous day. It hadn't really been much good, but propriety dictates the occasional lie.

'Oh, but it could have been *much* better if Bartho hadn't been so boring,' Tippy lamented. 'I mean, every time I really wanted to express myself he accused me of overacting. Honestly, it made me feel so confined, so *thwarted*. Terribly frustrating!' She pulled a face.

'I am sure it will turn out beautifully,' Rosy said encouragingly. 'And that scene shot with just you and Robert was most convincing. There was such a good contrast: you looking all fragile and gamine, and he so tough and imposing.'

Rather to Rosy's surprise this remark elicited a fit of giggles. 'Imposing? I wouldn't call him that, exactly. Far from it!' There were more giggles. 'In fact,' she continued, 'Robert Kestrel is the least *imposing* person I know.' Rosy must have looked curious, for by way of explanation the other said in a loud stage whisper, 'He has *difficulties*, if you see what I mean.'

Rosy thought that she probably did see, but had no intention of pursuing the matter with the sniggering Tippy. She was about to turn the conversation but was forestalled.

'Frankly,' the girl said with confiding relish, 'he made an enormous pass at me the other day: wined and dined and all the usual old preliminaries, and then, if you please, the idiot couldn't cope. Simply could not cope. *Pas du tout!* It would have been pathetic if it hadn't been so humiliating – for me, I mean.' She lowered her voice, and added, 'He's got a wife in Surbiton, and I was so angry that I told him I would spill the beans – *all* of them, I may say. He didn't like that, I can tell you. Not one little bit, he didn't!' She gave a malevolent grin.

'Oh, but you wouldn't do that, surely?' Rosy murmured, rather shocked. 'It would hardly be wise.'

'Perhaps not wise,' the girl said, 'but definitely fun, don't you think?'

Luckily, Rosy did not have to answer that question, for at that moment her sleeve was tugged by Fred on her left. 'Do you think,' he asked earnestly, 'that I should have Pixie's toenails clipped before she gets married? You see it might make her more responsive, sort of more comfortable. What do you think?'

'Oh, most certainly,' Rosy said firmly, 'a good pedicure is essential at such times.'

'Hmm, that's what I was thinking,' the solicitous owner replied thoughtfully. 'And I suppose a spot of worming wouldn't be a bad thing?'

Rosy nodded vigorously, glad to be rid of Robert Kestrel's problems. Somehow the Newfoundland's intimacies seemed the more manageable.

A little later, as they were about to leave the pub, Rosy noticed Robert alone at the bar draped over the last drops of his pint. It might have been her imagination, but she couldn't help thinking he looked decidedly down in the mouth. Was he brooding on how to handle his next appearance before the cameras . . . or his wife's fury in Surbiton should Tippy's threat be delivered? Judging from the Brando scowl it could have been either.

Other than the drama of Felix's lost hat and the occasional joust between director and scriptwriter, the next few days proceeded fairly well. True to form, Tippy had been a universal irritant (and Robert discernibly tense in her presence), but by and large there had been no overt hostilities. The grips and technicians had applauded the local beer and sandwiches; and, apart from Felix, Pixie had enamoured herself to everyone.

Admittedly, Lady Fawcett, after making a close study of her aspiring son-in-law, did observe to Rosy that she wasn't really sure whether the young man was fearfully intelligent or abysmally simple. But it was a remark made without malice, and Rosy felt that on the whole the Bartholomew prospects were good. It also occurred to her that Angela's perplexity regarding the young man's intellectual ability might equally apply to her daughter Amy . . . in which case the two might be ideally suited.

By the end of the week half of the essential scenes had been covered and the results approved by director and scriptwriter alike. As a consequence the movie mogul was clearly pleased, and as a respite (for himself at any rate) he suggested to Rosy that she and perhaps Cedric and Felix might enjoy a twilight stroll along the beach before joining the others for a nightcap in the Red Lion. The weather was good and the idea appealing, and she readily agreed.

They set off west, across South Green, down on to the

shore and then onwards to the tussocky dunes. It was the most delightful evening: no wind, a pale dulcet sea, and mellow rays casting shadows from the declining sun. Except for Cedric (shod in black plimsolls), all went barefoot, enjoying the lost sensation of wet sand between unfettered toes.

'The last time I did this,' chuckled Bartholomew, 'I was a kid in Cannes. I was playing boules with the French boys while Daddy chatted up the new nanny on the Croisette and Mummy guzzled champagne with de Gaulle's private secretary in The Majestic.'

Felix wasn't having that. 'The last time I did this was years before you were born – at Southend, eating whelks and waving my toy flag at the troops returning from Passchendaele. *My* mother was walking out with a sergeant major who gave her port and lemon on a breakwater.' He turned to Cedric. 'Where were you? Scrabbling for fossils by the Dead Sea, I suppose.'

Cedric looked vague. 'Er, can't remember, dear boy . . .' He looked down anxiously at his feet. 'You know, I'm sure these things are letting in the wet. Perhaps I should have worn socks after all, but they did say they were waterproof and—'

'What's that?' Rosy said suddenly, pointing towards the hillocks of sand. 'That pale thing – it's not your hat is it, Felix?'

They looked to where she gestured, and Felix screwed up his eyes. 'Highly unlikely; it would hardly be here. I told you, I must have left it in one of the hotels; the boy at The Crown said he would make a good search for it.'

'Well, it looks like some sort of headgear to me. Come on.'

They followed Rosy as she led the way from the beach towards the small ridge of rock and shingle. Here they encountered a mass of desiccated seaweed topped by a basking sand crab. Next to the crab, its rim caught in a crevice of the rock, fluttered a cream panama hat.

For a few seconds they gazed, fascinated by the curious melange. 'Rather rum,' mused Bartho, 'it's like a motif from a Dali painting: animal, vegetable and Felix's hat!' He stepped forward to pick it up. The crab scuttled off at alarming speed, and he laughed.

'Shut up! Shut up!' Rosy suddenly cried, her eyes fixed on an image beyond the hat's banality. 'Look over there!' She had wrenched at Cedric's arm, and was violently gesturing to the left where the sand dipped into a basin of sparse gorse. They turned to where she pointed, and their eyes were confronted by the sprawled languid limbs of what, earlier in the day, might have been a sunbather . . . but which, illuminated by the rising moon, was quite clearly the lifeless body of a woman.

CHAPTER TEN

Clustered around the body, they stared mesmerised at the figure's cropped blonde hair and distinctive scarlet bikini, and knew it could be none other than the girl: Tippy Tildred. She was on her front with arms splayed out and right leg drawn up; the other, its ankle encircled by the cheap beads, was stretched at full length. Tilted to the left, her head showed the tight curls behind her ear and temple. They were spattered in blood – blood from the small crater in her back.

Mechanically, knowing he would find nothing, Cedric knelt down to feel her pulse. As he did so, he glimpsed the eyes – wide and staring. For an instant it was as if he was back in the war, seeking the stilled pulse of Bertie Simmonds sprawled in Stradbroke Road, strafed by a Stuka returning to base in Normandy . . . But this was not wartime, there were no enemy planes circling above, and the victim was a young girl in a red bikini.

He stood up. 'She has been shot,' he announced. 'We had better get the police.' He looked at Bartholomew. 'I suggest you go; you can probably sprint more quickly than us.'

The other nodded, and was about to set off when Felix said listlessly, 'If you don't mind, I'll take my hat.' He held out his hand.

'Actually,' Rosy murmured, 'perhaps we ought to show it to the police when they come. I mean, being so near the body it might be of relevance – they'll probably say it's part of the crime scene or something.'

'Exactly,' Felix said quickly, 'which is precisely why I have no intention of mentioning it – and I like to think that no one else will either.' He glared at them in anxious defiance, and then almost under his breath muttered, 'It's a bit much!'

'Are you sure it's your hat?' Rosy asked him ten minutes later as they waited for the police to arrive.

'Quite sure,' replied Felix glumly. 'The size tag is right and it has Lock's label.' He sighed. 'It was damned expensive too, and now just look at it – all dirty and crumpled. Besides, I couldn't possibly wear it after this ghastliness. I should have nightmares of that wretched girl every time I put it on. It's too bad!' He shifted his position on the piece of driftwood he and Rosy were sitting on, and stared morosely in the direction of the town. 'It's high time the police were here, isn't it? Bartholomew has been gone for ages and it's getting cold. Just look at my toes, they've gone all white.'

Rosy glanced down at her companion's feet, now safely encased in his sandals. 'Shock, I daresay,' she said without much sympathy. She looked over to where Cedric was standing guard over the body of Tippy Tildred. Who on earth would want to do that to the girl? To shoot her down in cold blood: defenceless and virtually naked. From the look of things the bullet had presumably come from behind. If so, what had she been doing? Running away or standing admiring the sea? And what about Felix's errant hat – had that been part of the drama? Or was its presence a mere chance, blown to the spot from some other place? The latter presumably. Nevertheless, she felt slightly uneasy about his refusal to have its presence declared. After all, it *could* have a bearing, she supposed. But she understood his reluctance: the events of their previous visit to Southwold had not endeared the constabulary to Felix – nor, she rather suspected, they to him. The routine questioning had been a somewhat taut encounter, and Felix was not one to ignore old wounds – or indeed old scratches. She gave a wry smile. But it quickly vanished as her mind leapt from the past to the present and the thought of the poor girl's dreadful end. She shivered; and like Felix, wished that the police would hurry up.

A few yards away Cedric gazed down at Tippy's diminutive corpse, his attention caught by the small hands with their brightly varnished nails. For some reason that detail seemed to accentuate the pathos, the vicious reality . . . Poor kid. He had not liked the girl, not at all.

But doubtless she would have improved with maturity, and now she would never have the chance. Somebody had wrested that from her, denied her that potential. But who, for God's sake? A silly simpering little piece, that's what she had been; so why on earth go to such cruel and unnecessary lengths? . . . And what about Felix's panama – why should that be there? Chance or reason? He shrugged inwardly, feeling sorry for his friend: either way it was not something likely to enhance the poor chap's equilibrium! He sighed and then looked up angrily, and to his relief saw a police car approaching.

The first vehicle was closely followed by a second. Uniformed and non-uniformed figures emerged.

Questions were asked, addresses and initial statements taken, brisk notes made. Two officers were detailed to go over to inspect the victim while another used a walkie-talkie to summon reinforcements – presumably medics and pathologists. There seemed to be a man in charge whom Cedric vaguely recognised as being one of the pair he and Felix had encountered on their way to the Sole Bay. If so, they had also met a couple of years ago in similar circumstances, but he couldn't be sure and frankly wasn't bothered. All he wanted was to get away, back to the sanctuary of the cottage. Glancing at Felix he guessed that he felt the same. His friend's thin features were very pale, and the hand grasping the panama distinctly shaky. Bartho, who had returned with the police, looked more composed; probably because his brief time at the station and talk with the officers had calmed what nerves he may have had. Rosy, he saw, looked strained but also composed.

At last they were told they could leave but to be

available the next day for further questions; and Bartho was reminded that his whole film crew should also be ready for interrogation. 'Since Miss Tildred was one of your group we shall naturally need to interview all those with whom she was associated,' he was told. 'Ensure that everyone is present at ten-thirty tomorrow. Too many for the station – be at your relative's place, on the set or wherever it is you do your stuff.'

Bartho nodded meekly and was heard to mutter, 'Right-o, Officer.'

The four of them walked back slowly towards the town centre, at first saying nothing but by tacit agreement taking the longer route, away from the dunes and up Ferry Road. Perhaps instinctively they were avoiding the area of the tragedy, or perhaps walking in the evening air was a means of delaying more intensive reflections in private rooms.

Felix was the first to speak. 'Of course she *was* frightful,' he said, 'still it does seem a bit extreme. I wonder whether—'

His speculation, whatever it might have been, was cut short by Bartholomew. 'On the whole,' he said musingly, 'she wasn't really a very good actress. Alicia is streets ahead. But Tippy had tremendous brio, if you see what I mean. It's going to be awfully difficult to replace her . . . Perhaps I can get Sam to rewrite the part.' He looked up at the stars, lost in thought.

'Er, do you mean to say that you are going to go on with the filming?' Rosy asked curiously.

'Well, yes,' he replied, sounding somewhat surprised. 'I

mean, it's all very shocking but I cannot see that by not continuing we are helping one jot. Can you?'

Rosy wasn't sure what to answer but couldn't help feeling a little uneasy. Somehow it didn't seem quite right, but she was hard-pressed to explain why.

'Ah,' the young man said, 'you mean we should cancel the thing as a mark of respect. Rather an expensive mark, if you don't mind my saying, and frankly not one that would be particularly noticed. Let us do something positive, i.e. push on and make the film. Death is bloody awful but it shouldn't be allowed to mess things up. Who wants to limp home having achieved nothing? I don't. It would be pointless.' He spoke with a severity alien to his usual good humour.

Rosy was about to point out that Tippy's fate wasn't just any death but outlandish murder; however, she was stopped by Cedric. 'How refreshing,' he remarked, 'to hear such utilitarian sentiments, especially at a time like this when commonplace pieties are the order of the day. I applaud your clarity of thought, Mr Hackle!'

'Er, Bartho,' the other muttered, clearly unsure whether Cedric was being genuine or beastly – as neither was Rosy. But then she was often not sure which way to take Cedric's pronouncements.

The topic was interrupted by Felix declaring that he was feeling sick, and that he knew for a fact that at least two of the policemen had been eyeing him suspiciously. 'And what's more,' he protested, 'how on earth they expect one to be on parade at the crack of dawn after this horror, I cannot imagine. I shan't sleep a single wink.

Typical of the law, they have no finer feelings!' By this time the crumpled panama had been crushed irrevocably.

Bidding the others goodnight, Rosy entered the warmth and enfolding civility of The Swan. What a relief! Given the gruesome discovery barely a mile away, the hotel's staid normality was both reassuring and oddly unreal. She was about to go to her room, but looked into the lounge on the off chance that Angela might still be up. To her surprise she was – sitting in a corner with the *Telegraph* and pencil in hand, evidently doing battle with the crossword.

Seeing Rosy, she hailed her. 'Ah, so you're back, safe from the ravages of crabs and starfish I see! So how was your walk, my dear? I'll order more coffee, you look a bit cold.' She paused, and added, 'Indeed, if you don't mind my saying, blue actually.' She regarded Rosy quizzically.

'Er, well, ye-es,' Rosy agreed, 'I do feel a bit chilly. Shock, I suppose.' And then before the coffee had been brought, and before she could stop herself, she gave a whispered account of the recent events.

'*Murdered?*' Lady Fawcett's voice rang out, 'But that's absurd, she was far too young!'

Rosy winced and looked around nervously. But fortunately there was only one other guest in sight – an old man seemingly fast asleep and, unless he was a government spy, unlikely to have registered anything.

Desperate for coffee, Rosy assured her companion that she would deliver the full details upstairs in the privacy of one of their bedrooms.

'Very sensible,' the other whispered, and then as an afterthought, observed: 'One has to admit that the silly girl was an awful pain in the neck, but one hardly expected this!'

As a summation of the whole affair, Rosy felt it was fair comment.

CHAPTER ELEVEN

'You know, I am not *entirely* surprised,' Lady Fawcett confided to Rosy over breakfast the next morning.

'Really? You certainly sounded surprised last night,' Rosy replied, 'as well you might. It was a ghastly shock to us all!'

'Yes, but since then I have been giving it some thought and—'

'Oddly enough it has been on my mind too,' Rosy said dryly, 'kept me awake, in fact. But I can't say it has lessened the shock. I mean, it just seems so brutal, so arbitrary.' She shuddered inwardly, recalling the awful scene.

'Brutal, yes, but not necessarily arbitrary. In my experience few things are truly arbitrary; most actions are governed by reason – however peculiar or oblique.'

'Perhaps. But in this case it could simply have been a

random attack by some warped creature harbouring a dislike of red bikinis. One does hear of such things.'

'Oh, one *hears*, but I suspect that in this case the reality is more logical. The poor girl wasn't too bright. Ironically, it is often the witless who do the most damage, or have the capacity for damage. Tippy Tildred was a provocative irritant and I think she paid for it in a terrible way. To the murderer she was either dangerous or intolerable. *We* didn't take her seriously – a tiresome flibbertigibbet – but somebody did, and acted accordingly.' Lady Fawcett took a decisive bite of her toast and hailed the waiter to bring some more jam.

As Angela munched her toast and spoke with firm assurance on the matter, Cedric was making an early perambulation of the high street. Felix (contrary to his forecasted insomnia) had enjoyed an uninterrupted slumber throughout the night – and indeed at eight o'clock that morning was still blissfully detached from the rigours of the day.

But the professor had found sleep almost impossible. Though retiring late after the night's horror, he had managed no more than two hours. And thus by dawn, and weary of such boredom, it had seemed sensible to do something constructive: arise, make tea and seek out the daily paper from the newsagent. With luck, such early exercise might induce an afternoon's shut-eye.

Leaving the cottage he paused to gaze at the wide marshes stretching far over to Walberswick, and where, shrouded in the early mist, he could just discern the outline of its church tower. Despite the lightest breeze wafting the grasses, the morning air held a bated silence, and for a couple of minutes Cedric stood contemplating the tranquil scene of sky, marsh and distant spire. Gradually he began to feel an ease denied him in the night. And relaxing his gaze, he turned and strolled up the lane and into the high street.

At that hour Southwold may have been busier than the Walberswick marshes, but even so it held the pretence of sleep with few people about and traffic sparse. This suited Cedric, who, with newspaper under his arm, took the opportunity to dawdle at shop windows unimpeded by pram or wayward dog. He had intended to cross the road to inspect the range of titles in the little bookshop (and perchance see an early copy of his own *Cappadocian Capers* displayed – the shop was select enough). But his attention was caught by a larger building on the same side, a few yards further down.

Thus he paused to contemplate the modestly elegant Montague House. With an eighteenth-century facade, its name was presumably a reference to Sir Edward Montagu, victor of the Sole Bay engagement . . . but now of course its principal association lay with that remarkable maverick, George Orwell. His parents had bought it in the thirties, and while claiming to have been uncomfortable in Southwold, the writer had produced some of his best work there.

Cedric smiled, fondly imagining the man pounding away at the typewriter late into the night – and through clouds of tobacco smoke producing such pungent brilliance. His death a few years earlier had been a sadness, and for a moment Cedric dwelt ruefully on the cliché of the good dying young – or at least in Orwell's case, the masterly. Yes, he reflected, the end had come cruelly soon . . .

With a jolt, his mind jumped back to the present as he thought of another cruelty: the fate of the Tildred girl. He doubted whether she had been particularly good (and certainly not masterly), but it was still an unnecessary severance. And what on earth had it all been for? Why should such a silly little baggage inspire that degree of malice – or that *risk*! He sighed. Presumably, the authorities were wrestling with exactly the same question. And at least this time he and Felix had not been witnesses to the killing itself . . . *merely* among its shocked discoverers. With luck the police would not prolong their interviews: one had come to Southwold for a rest not a catechism!

He frowned, recollecting the scene. Oddly enough, the aspect that lodged most vividly in his mind was not the victim in her red swimsuit, but Felix's panama. Its presence there, so far removed from the town centre and their usual haunts, had been peculiar. True, Southwold was a windy spot; but if Felix had dropped the thing in the vicinity of their cottage or near one of the hotels, could it really have been blown quite so far? He had an absurd image of the thing merrily bowling its way along the high street, past the Red Lion, traversing South Green, fluttering merrily among the cannons, and then blowing on to the promenade, until finally coming to rest on the dunes and the tussock of grass next to the girl's body. Quite a marathon. And quite a puzzle.

Yes, he brooded, Felix was probably right in not wanting its presence noted. It was amazing how such trivial enigmas could lead to endless trouble. There had been enough of that on their previous visit!

With a final glance at the house opposite, and savouring the illusion of having glimpsed a cigarette's glow at an upper window, he turned and walked briskly back to the cottage to rally the slumberer.

Rallied and shaved, Felix indicated that he was moderately ready to undergo more questioning by the police and to be on parade at the allotted ten-thirty. 'I can't see why we should be further detained,' he grumbled, 'they only do it to annoy! I told them everything I knew last night.'

'Hmm. Not exactly *everything*,' Cedric reminded him.

'Everything of any consequence,' was the quick reply.

As they were about to leave, Cedric noticed a book lying on the sofa table. He hadn't noticed it before and it certainly wasn't one of his own. 'What's this?' he asked, moving to pick it up. 'Something you've been reading?'

'What? Oh, that. No, it's that one to do with limes or something – the one written by the Ramsgate fellow. I meant to tell you – he called the other day when you were out slurping coffee with Angela in The Crown, and insisted you should have a copy. Apparently he had meant to give it to you the other night when we were there, but was diverted by playing the lavish host all over the place. He said you had expressed a particular interest. Had you?'

Cedric shrugged. 'Not specially, though the cover's pretty.'

He set it aside, and the two of them left to do battle with the law on the East Cliff.

CHAPTER TWELVE

Early the following morning, with the previous night's alarm behind them and its initial protocol discharged, Chief Inspector Nathan and Detective Sergeant Jennings had returned to where the body had been found. The day held an aura of serenity and kindly optimism – the tide was out, the sky was blue, children were already building industrious sandcastles and dogs scampered gaily. In short, it was a typical seaside scene with Southwold looking its best.

Nathan sighed, lit his pipe and contemplated the distant waves. 'Ten to one it was her young man,' he announced. 'She was probably leading him a dance and he couldn't stand the pace, so he shot her.'

Jennings considered this. 'Er, how do you know she had a young man?' he ventured.

'They all do,' was the firm answer.

'Hmm . . . So what was her young man doing with a revolver? I mean, I never had one when I was that age.' (At nearly thirty, and newly promoted from DC to DS, Jennings was beginning to feel the weight of his years.)

'Ah, well, you wouldn't, would you? – I mean you being a pillar of the establishment and all that. Not your style at all I shouldn't think, not at all.' The chief inspector continued to study the waves while Jennings frowned, unsure whether he was being complimented or mocked. That was the trouble with his boss: some of his observations were what you might call *opaque*. Jennings liked that word and had used it twice in the last couple of days. He had first encountered it in an Agatha Christie and had docketed it away for future use.

Turning his gaze from the sea, Nathan scanned the immediate ground knowing that such scrutiny was pretty pointless: the forensics had already examined the area and apparently found nothing. An initialled cigarette lighter would have been handy or a dropped wallet, but such convenient gifts were rarely granted. In fact, he wasn't really sure why he had bothered to return to the place at all: probably to indulge old Eager-Beaver over there. He glanced to where Jennings was standing, deep in thought.

What was it the boy had said? Something about it being important to immerse oneself in the 'essential ambience' of a crime site, to try to get the 'subtle feel of the place' – a sensation that would, allegedly, enhance the intuitive process. As an aid to detection, the chief inspector did not hold with intuition, favouring the solidity of facts and tangible clues to get him the right answers. But in any case, dry sand, shingle and windswept tussocks . . . what sort of 'feeling' was he to get here? None, unless you counted earache from the coastal wind. He sighed bleakly. Those detective novels the lad was so keen on had a lot to answer for. His arthritic knee had started to throb; and signalling to Jennings that they were leaving, he turned to walk back to the car. He had only gone a few steps, when he tripped and fell to his knees.

'Ruddy hell!' he cursed, getting up and brushing the sand from his trouser legs. He saw there was something sticking up from a mound of dried seaweed: a piece of dark leather or rubber, slightly crescent-shaped.

'What's that, then?' he grumbled to Jennings, who had joined him and picked it up. 'Some sort of kids' boomerang, I suppose!'

'Oh no, sir,' the other replied, turning it over in his hand, 'that's an orthotic.'

'A *what*?'

'An orthotic – you know, those support things for people with flat feet or bunions. They go inside your shoe. My old granny's got one.' He paused, and then added excitedly, 'You never know, perhaps it belonged to the murderer!'

'Ah, I see,' Nathan mused, 'so you think it was your old granny who did her in, do you? Fired the gun and then sat down to rub her bunion, and in the heat of the moment forgot to put the thing back in her shoe . . . Very likely, I should say, Detective Sergeant.'

Jennings pursed his lips. Hilarious, he thought grimly.

'Mind you,' the other conceded more seriously, 'it could have belonged to the victim herself. We shouldn't discount that, I suppose.' He gave Jennings an encouraging nod.

'Oh, I think we can, sir,' the young man replied quickly. 'You may not have noticed that this orthotic is obviously a man's, or at least someone with big feet. Tippy Tildred was small, no taller than five foot, I should guess. It would be unusual for someone so short to wear that size shoe – wouldn't you say? Though perhaps not beyond the bounds of possibility . . .' He fixed the chief inspector with a look of bland enquiry.

Nathan scowled and gave an indifferent shrug, and Jennings felt so much better. He took the item back to the car with him and placed it safely under the dashboard.

That evening the chief inspector sat at his desk and ruminated. It had been a hell of a day: officious comments from the super about the Blyford burglary case, the typist scarpered off home with a migraine just when there was a load of reports to do, his front tyre blown – and to cap it all, Jennings incessantly bleating about that sodding orthotic. He would be glad when retirement came. 'Nice to go out on a tide of glory,' some smug colleague had once declared. Huh! Currently he would be glad to go out on a tide of sleep and Blue Label bass. However, with neither in the offing, he lit his pipe and thought more about the corpse on the sand dunes.

Unless luck had guided his hand, the killer would seem to have known what he was doing as it had taken only one shot. And since the pathologist had found nothing in the flesh the thing must have passed straight through her: through the intercostals, smack into the heart and out the other side. Relatively speaking there had been little mess, which suggested the missile may have been jacketed. Still, there was no means of knowing as there was no sign of the bullet. Combing the immediate terrain, the forensics had found nothing. He had directed them to do it again, but still there was no trace . . . It would seem there were two possibilities: either the murderer had located the spent bullet and carefully pocketed it *or* the deed had not been done there at all, but somewhere else and the body randomly dumped.

Nathan brooded, considering the first scenario. Feasible, but was it likely? It would have been a lucky fluke if the assailant had immediately seen the bullet lying amidst the tangle of scrub and gorse; and to make a deliberate search he would have had to get down on hands and knees and grope about in the semi-dark. With secrecy paramount, would he have risked doing that with the body strewn at his feet, and the chance of some invasive dog-walker appearing at any minute? It seemed doubtful.

Nathan relit his expired pipe, and to bolster thought, groped for the plastic mug and half-bottle of Scotch in the desk drawer. Then, spiritually fortified and with pipe aglow, he dwelt on the second possibility: relocation.

If the body had been shifted from A to B it was unlikely to have been from just one part of the immediate area to another. After all, would it have mattered if she had been found on the shore, say, or further along on some similar strip of dune? Hardly. And what about the absence of other clothes or a beach towel? You would expect someone wandering around in a bathing costume to have some bits and pieces nearby. And yet none had been found – unless, of course, the killer had diligently gathered them up . . . Nathan chewed the stem of his pipe. Yes, he reflected, much more likely that she had been shot in a different spot altogether – somewhere away from the dunes; somewhere like a private garden perhaps, a friend's house or a swimming pool, even. The sort of place where bathing gear might have been casually worn but from which the task of dumping the body would have entailed transport.

Transport? Then how about recent tyre marks? Ferry Road was the obvious place to look, but it had rained in the night and thus traces were unlikely. Still, he would get Jennings to look into that aspect; he could make enquiries about any unusual vehicular activity seen in the vicinity at that time of evening. Might keep his mind off the orthotic theme!

Nathan's thoughts turned to wider issues: motive. Well, as he had told Jennings, it was bound to have been a crime of passion – some youth spurned by a pretty girl too big for her sexual boots, and driven to a frenzy by jealousy or mockery. It happened all the time . . . though it had to be admitted that the firearm element was a rarity: Jennings had been right there. Not many youngsters had those – knives occasionally, but not guns. Besides, it suggested an element of premeditation, not some heat-of-the-moment attack, and she had certainly not been 'interfered with' as the *News of the World* still quaintly put it. He cast his mind back to his own youth and thought of ruddy Hilda Birtwhistle: a right little madam she had been. Enough to send anyone berserk! Yes, he would readily have strangled her if he'd had the nerve! A pity he hadn't, really. Still, he thought maliciously, the minx was already a grandmother now with grizzled hair, slack jowls and running to fat. An altogether more satisfactory conclusion. He toasted the thought with another tot of Scotch; and then locking the office and with a wave to the duty sergeant, set off for the home-stretch down Pier Avenue and to a good supper.

Like his superior, Detective Sergeant Jennings was also reviewing the evolutions of the day. But in his case this was being done in a spirit of slightly greater optimism than that of his chief. Discrepancy in age and temperament lent an eagerness denied to his jaded colleague, and the recent promotion conferred a zeal waning in the latter.

For the third time that day he took out the leather insole Nathan had tripped on, and wondered what Christie's Hercule Poirot would have made of it. Amazing what one could learn from that lady's pen. Such insights! He thought proudly of the collection of her novels adorning the shelf on his bedroom wall, and mentally gave thanks to the aunt who had presented him with his first volume (*The Murder of Roger Ackroyd*) at the age of thirteen. 'Here,' she had said, 'this'll keep you quiet, if we're lucky.' And it did. It had also inspired him to join the police and become a detective.

In fact, in terms of personality, Jennings was not entirely enamoured of the Belgian sleuth – a bit of an old ponce, really. But he admired the 'little grey cells' bit and his attention to apparent trivia. Thus pondering the piece of leather in front of him, Jennings wondered if it had the significance the great detective would undoubtedly have accorded it. Or was it merely the bit of dross that Nathan had implied? Probably . . . but you *never knew*! It might just have a bearing. He returned it to his desk drawer and noted it on the list of other queries he had assiduously compiled that day.

These related to the interrogation of the film bunch, the victim's associates. He had been put in charge of that, and liked to think he had conducted the procedure with just the right blend of authority and affable ease. In fact, he had said as much to Nathan. 'It's the human touch, sir,' he had explained, 'it sort of relaxes them, you know.' The response had not been encouraging: 'Ah, the human touch is it, Jennings? That'll be the day,' the inspector had snorted, and returned to his sandwiches. For some reason he seemed to be grinning.

Really, Jennings thought stiffly, a little appreciation wouldn't go amiss. That was the trouble with the chief inspector, a sound copper all right but with few finer feelings. Not what you would call a man of sensibility: whereas he himself was trying to achieve a fine blend of tact and . . .

He returned his mind to the morning's interviews with the movie people. A peculiar lot, really. And what that film was about was anyone's guess! In a matey way he had enquired of a cameraman, who had shrugged and said how on earth was he supposed to know – he only shot the bloody thing.

And what an odd coincidence having to deal with that professor and his sidekick the Felix chap again. He hadn't liked them the first time around[3] (a bit too superior for his

[3] See *A Southwold Mystery*

liking), and this time they had seemed evasive – well not so much evasive as tight-lipped. Although they hadn't said anything derogatory, he had the impression they hadn't much liked the girl. But then from what he could make out, few of those questioned had. In fact, the only one who had said anything complimentary about the victim had been that busty femme fatale woman, Alicia somebody. She had said the girl had been 'an absolute sweetie and *so* cute!' But now he came to think of it, the tone had held so much gush that she was probably lying through her teeth.

Far less fulsome had been the big fellow with the thick eyebrows and cultivated vowels, who declared he barely knew the girl and that it was all very sad but, alas, such things did happen. For one who had apparently shared a couple of romantic scenes with her, so bland a dismissal seemed curious. Jennings took his pen and carefully underlined the name, Robert Kestrel, and wrote the word OPAQUE next to it.

He continued to consult his list and paused at one of the key witnesses, Bartholomew Hackle. Evidently, he was the big noise of the outfit, the director or whatever: nice enough in a cheery way and probably more intelligent than he appeared; but not easy to gauge. However, he had obviously been impatient to get on with the job. The chap's main concern had seemed less for the victim than for the disruption her death had caused to his production schedule. So if the girl was so vital to his plans, presumably he could be ruled out as a suspect. (But then, inevitably, Jennings recalled Agatha Christie; and knowing that presumption was not to be trusted, inserted a tentative question mark.)

His eye came back to the name of Felix Smythe, and he frowned. Shifty, that's what, and hoity-toity with it! In fact, Smythe's attitude had been much the same as when questioned about that other murder only two years previously. Still, the chap looked too nervous to be a serial killer – and besides, they had already nailed the culprit for that one. But he would lay ten-to-one that he had been hiding something. When asked if anything had been seen or found near the corpse, he had flinched like a startled rabbit and muttered, 'No, not really.' Then when urged to be more explicit he had tensed up and said curtly, 'Nothing that I recall.' It hadn't sounded terribly convincing, but then of course he might just be thick. In Jennings' estimation there was a lot of thickness about.

And with that satisfying judgement the detective sergeant, like Nathan, decided to call it a day and cycle homeward to his flat in Walberswick and the benison of fried sausages – plus a happy perusal of *Murder in the Vicarage*.

CHAPTER THIRTEEN

It really had been a dreadful shock – appalling, actually, when one came to think of it. Not that one cared to think of it too much, or at least certainly not the details – bizarre to say the least! Of course, the child always had been one for drama, but nobody had expected this kind of thing! What on earth had been going on?

Ida Carshalton fumbled in her bag for a cigarette, and lit it with the crystal table lighter. For a few seconds she contemplated the flickering flame, and then with a snap extinguished it. Briefly her eyes looked pensive . . . Tippy's end had been just like that: one moment vivid and sprightly (too damn sprightly), and the next moment, amid sand and seaweed, snuffed out. Extraordinary.

And yes, all very sad and distressing, of course, but nevertheless *inconvenient*. It would mean cancelling their appearance at the party conference – or at least she would have to cancel hers. Tommy would attend and do the usual backslapping and string-pulling, but ideally she ought to be with him. It was what the public liked to see: the devoted husband and wife radiating marital bliss and public duty. Besides, Tommy operated so much better with her at his side to nudge things along. Much better. On his own that essential spark was inclined to subside into a reliable glow – which was all very well, but in political life it was the sparks that mattered, which ensured the real triumphs.

She frowned and lit another cigarette, but this time the expiring flame awoke no rueful reflection. For by now Ida's thoughts were preoccupied with the tiresome (and distasteful) task of identifying the body. When the Suffolk police had contacted her about that, she had been startled. Except for a cairn terrier she had once owned, she had never seen a dead body before, and the prospect was uninviting to say the least. As the process was only a formality she had suggested that Hackle (or was it Cackle?) and his cronies might meet that requirement – after all, they must have known the girl well enough. But she had been told rather curtly that it was customary for a family member or relative to take the responsibility, and that in any case she would presumably wish to collect the victim's belongings (Ida didn't particularly).

The officer had asked about the girl's parents, and she had explained that there had been a divorce years ago, and that the mother – naturally devastated by the news – was living in South Africa and was too distraught to make the journey. (Actually her stepsister was not in the least distraught, merely reluctant to desert the claims of Cape Town's high life for so morbid an experience. 'One must be practical, Ida,' she had urged, 'you are so much better placed than I am. After all, you only have to whizz up there from London, not from halfway across the world like me. Currently all I can do is to *mourn* and *brood* . . .')

Recalling this reaction, Ida was reminded of the victim herself. Yes, she reflected, like mother like daughter: utterly self-engrossed! Indeed, it was the girl's cocksure egotism – not to say predatory greed – that had been a source of some continuing disquiet in the Carshalton household. At first, after the divorce, they had been sorry for the girl – in those days diffident and waif-like – and in a spirit of kindly duty had rather taken her under their wing. However, in the course of adolescence the waif's diffidence had waned, and her self-esteem waxed – annoyingly so. There had been complaints from the school, tantrums, truancies, manipulative wheedling, exploitative dramas. In short, the girl had started to become distinctly tedious, or as Tommy had observed, a vexing pain in the arse. And then just when they were wondering how to rid themselves of their tiresome protégée without appearing unduly harsh, there had been that *ghastly* incident.

Ida's eyes closed in painful recollection. It really had been most unfortunate. So embarrassing, and not to say costly. Wretched girl! Yet even as she mentally flinched, a smile twitched her lips. It had to be admitted, the thing did have its funny side. Oh yes. Quite absurd really! She grinned, and then immediately scowled. But oh God, they had been paying for it all right. Tacitly, indulgently, *bitterly* they had been paying . . . But now, well now the weight was lifted and one could sleep easy. She stretched languorously as if enacting the prospect; and then with a sigh glanced at the clock on the mantelpiece: four o'clock, teatime. In his Westminster office Tommy would be sipping his usual cup of strong Darjeeling and nibbling a chocolate wafer. She would keep him company.

Thus, rising from the sofa Ida smoothed her dress, and with a twinge of guilt at the early hour, poured a large gin and tentatively raised the glass. To whom was she drinking? To the memory of the poor dead girl? Or to the girl's reluctant custodians and the easing of their burden? The answer could well have been both. She herself was not entirely certain; but the sensation was pleasant.

By half past four and libation finished, she was briskly consulting railway timetables for the journey to Suffolk, and preparing to telephone their old friend Vincent Ramsgate.

Apart from a natural reluctance, the prospect of travelling up to Southwold for such a task now seemed less irksome than before. All the same, she would prefer that the inspection business itself could be done with a companion at hand; and with a bit of luck Vincent might offer to put her up for a couple of days. Naturally one could always stay in some local hotel, but given the circumstances, a friendly private house would be preferable. Besides, she hadn't seen him for well over a year (though they had heard his voice regularly enough on the wireless). Yes, it would be good to chat over old times – a cheery diversion from the grisly task.

Grisly? She paused fractionally, wondering what to expect. With luck, nothing too beastly! After all, didn't they sort of adjust the features to make them more palatable, less dead-looking? She certainly hoped so. Should she wear black or would that appear too heavy? Perhaps a pallid grey would be better . . . My corpse-viewing garb, she thought grimly.

Braced by the gin and with brighter thoughts, she picked up the telephone, dialled Ramsgate's number and achieved her purpose.

Meanwhile, munching the predicted chocolate wafer and staring out over the traffic, Tommy Carshalton also felt braced.

It really was amazing how well things could turn out. The press had been more than generous in their recent political coverage, his speech for the forthcoming conference was honed to a tee, (the ghostwriter predicting a triumph), the opposition had been complimentary about yesterday's questions in the House (though of course that was sometimes a poisoned chalice!), Ida had looked superb hobnobbing with Princess Margaret at the Festival Hall, his majority at the recent by-election had vastly increased . . . and to cap it all, the child was dead. What you might call a most satisfactory week!

His gaze fell on the intrepid cyclists pedalling feverishly through the rush-hour traffic. Well, he mused, at least now there would be one less of their number to affright London's bus and cab drivers. And with that in mind, he selected another wafer and smiled.

He returned to his desk; but before resuming work, glanced up at the photograph of the prime minister looking po-faced from the wall. Tommy winked at the photograph. 'Your days are numbered, matey,' he murmured.

CHAPTER FOURTEEN

Film-making, like time and tide, wait for no man – or in Tippy's sad case, no woman. And thus, after the initial consternation (and as Bartho had resolved), *The Languid Labyrinth* continued to evolve.

Director and scriptwriter spent a long and slightly alcoholic Monday night making the required adjustments to storyline, character and casting. The result, Bartho assured everybody, was twice as good as the original and bound to secure its success.

Alicia, reinstated as the wayward seductress, and with the role substantially enlarged, went about being purringly nice to everyone. Felix, fearing that his own role might have been subsumed by the changes, was gratified to be told that it was an essential element. Sam had even written him a further line, to wit: *Look yonder where the halcyon flies . . . but our time, brothers, alas must fade.* (With the seagull image in mind, Felix wondered if Sam had a thing about birds, but didn't like to ask.) Robert Kestrel, despite Alicia's allusion to his 'awful state', seemed similarly satisfied, being now required to play not only the Dutch sea captain but also a blighted member of the French aristocracy bankrupted by the loss of his vessel. Both parts gave ample scope for more Brandoesque brooding.

The first shootings of the revamped screenplay had gone well. Disturbingly well, Lady Fawcett thought wryly. It was as if the girl's death was a universal bonus.

To take her mind off the gruesome business, she had made a point of attending the new rehearsal, and it struck her immediately that the dire event had somehow focused the mind of actors and technicians alike. There was, she sensed, a spirit of resolution in the air, a latent force that imbued the performances with a verve and pathos not previously noted. Alicia's sultry syllables suddenly convinced; and even Felix's line about the halcyon seemed mildly effective and carried a sort of puzzling poignancy. Robert too, despite the overtight breeches, really did begin to emerge as a menacing presence . . . How strange, how sad that so terrible a thing should have such an enlivening effect. Tippy's loss was Bartho's gain – what an appalling irony!

She looked over to where the latter was standing, talking earnestly with Fred and gesturing at one of the cameras. Was it an illusion, or did the boy seem to be showing a fresh authority, a new poise? Far from being weakened by the event, he seemed to have become curiously strengthened, awakened. Perhaps he saw it as a sort of personal challenge, a hurdle to be defied and overcome.

There flashed before Lady Fawcett's eyes the hurdles on Newbury racecourse and Bartholomew's spectacular defeat, unseating himself and five others. Hmm. That little challenge had hit the dust all right! Still, he had been younger then, virtually a schoolboy; and perhaps this time things would be different. She certainly hoped so. His good-natured bonhomie had grown on her; and as hinted to Rosy, she could think of far worse candidates for a son-in-law . . . But then good nature wasn't everything; many idiots were thus endowed. A little success never came amiss. If the two could be combined, dear Amy's future might be bright.

And in thinking of Amy, her mind wandered to Mr Bates and his antics. She hadn't liked to telephone the ghastly news for fear of interrupting things. But surely the mission might be finished by now? Yes, she would contact the girl that very afternoon and tactfully suggest she leave Shropshire forthwith. Her fiancé-elect had need of her! (And in a way, so did her mother.)

Fortunately it turned out that Mr Bates had behaved impeccably, and Amy (especially when she heard the '*fascinating*' news) was only too eager to forsake Shropshire for Southwold. She would arrive two days' hence, she announced. And how lovely if Bartho or Rosy could meet her at Darsham Station – the latter was such a brick and she hadn't seen her for *ages*!

'I tell you what,' Bartholomew said to Rosy and Felix, 'we'll give her a special welcome. We'll put on a little "hello" party with some fizz and Adnams' best brew. Nothing big, simply the five of us: you two, and Cedric if he'll come. I know just the place.'

Rosy laughed. 'Where – some louche dive, I suppose?'

'Oh no, Southwold is far too respectable for louche dives – though admittedly the place I'm thinking of *is* a bit intimate. After this beastliness we deserve some gaiety, and I don't suppose Amy will want to be faced with doom and gloom the moment she arrives. It'll give her a sort of breathing space.'

They looked at him enquiringly. 'Where?' Rosy asked.

'A beach hut.'

'In a *beach hut*!' Felix echoed indignantly.

Rosy laughed. 'Honestly, Felix, you sound just like Lady Bracknell. It must be all this acting, it's getting into the system!' She turned to Bartho. 'What do you mean? What beach hut?'

'The one to which I have the key,' he replied smugly. 'Cousin Walter sent it to me before we left, and said I was welcome to use the place – though it was essential that it was kept clean and tidy as he occasionally lent it to friends for weekends. He said he didn't think it was being used this month, but in any case it would certainly be free during the week, Monday to Thursday. Since Amy arrives tomorrow, we could hold our little celebration Thursday evening. I'll tell the others I am taking my beloved girl out for a special treat.' He grinned.

Felix sniffed. 'I am not sure that I associate treats with beach huts, even those of the Southwold calibre; but then people's tastes do differ, of course . . .'

'Oh, come on, Felix, it could be rather fun,' Rosy said coaxingly. 'We could open the doors and picnic on the veranda in the moonlight to the sound of the waves. It would be terribly romantic – and who knows, Cedric might be persuaded to serenade us with his violin.'

Felix looked askance. 'Oh, don't tell me, he's not brought that with him, has he?' he cried. 'He must have sneaked it into the car when I wasn't looking. I thought he seemed a bit shifty. All that fuss about his books, and all the time he was secreting that confounded instrument. It's too bad!'

'Do I take it you don't approve of the instrument?' Bartho asked.

'Not the way he plays it,' the other replied darkly.

However, plied with emollient praise re his recent performance, Felix became more enthusiastic and said he would have a word with Cedric. 'As it happens, I am due to meet him in the Lord Nelson shortly, I'll mention it then.'

'We might as well join you,' Bartho said. 'I like the Nelly and I deserve a rest. It's been a tough morning dealing with Alicia's whims; and stubbing my toe on Pixie's great hide hasn't helped. She is what might be termed a stumbling block, but if Fred doesn't bring her to the studio she gets grumpy and his camera work goes to pieces.'

When they arrived at the pub they found Cedric already seated in a corner immersed in the newspaper. 'I see that Carshalton chap is in the limelight again,' he observed. 'He's got some bee in his bonnet about illicit arms trading and is determined to have it stopped. It's his latest crusade.'

'That'll be the day,' Bartho said, 'it's too useful and too lucrative. Still, I suppose it gets him a good press.'

'Does it say anything about Tippy?' Rosy asked.

'What? Oh, I see – you mean about his being some sort of relation. Yes, there are a couple of lines at the bottom saying her mysterious death in Southwold has been a great blow to the family, and being relatives he and his wife trust justice will be done.'

'Well, amen to that,' said Bartho briskly. 'Now, meanwhile . . .' and he started to apprise Cedric of the beach hut proposal.

'Charming,' the professor agreed, 'and I could bring my fiddle.' He beamed at them, while the corners of Felix's mouth went down.

Having imbibed and recuperated sufficiently, Bartho suggested that since he still had a little time before being back on set, it would be sensible if they reconnoitred the hut: 'After all, it might be awash with crabs and spiders. Amy can't stand either; she goes ballistic!'

Thus they strolled down to the seafront and its long row of colourful shelters. There was some initial confusion as Bartho had the numbers confused, but eventually the hut was located: blue with a green door and looking very smart. It even flew a small flag, though of what provenance no one was sure. He unlocked the door, and the sun flooded into the small space making the electric light almost redundant.

What they saw was very pleasing: scrubbed wooden floor, gaily striped mat, pale cream walls with plenty of hooks for towels, a large mirror (presumably just in case you needed to check the shade of your tan or the set of your swimming cap), a wicker table and a couple of stools. Rosy had rather thought there might have been deckchairs for its tiny veranda, but there clearly weren't. 'Oh well,' she said, 'we can always bring cushions from the studio. We can strew them on the floor and loll about like Romans.'

Cedric wasn't sure if he wanted to loll about like a Roman, but said nothing. However, the place was entirely salubrious and might indeed lend itself to an intimate twilight soirée. And being the oldest of the group he could doubtless appropriate one of the two stools . . . and yes, he most certainly *would* bring his violin. If Paganini could play in the moonlight so could he!

Rosy, too, was impressed. 'It's awfully spruce. You must be careful with the red wine, Felix. Don't get too wild! Still, I daresay there's a regular cleaner – especially if Bartho's cousin lets it out from time to time.'

'In that case,' the other replied, 'the char has missed something over there.' He stepped forward to one of the corners and bent down. In the palm of his hand were two items: a coin and a piece of plastic. The latter could have been the cap of a lipstick, and it bore faint smudges of scarlet wax.

Bartho laughed. 'Ah, obviously one of the other tenants has been entertaining some moll here, and in her raptures she dropped her handbag.'

'In that case, she was a French moll,' Felix said. He held out the coin. 'You see, it's a franc piece. There's some geezer's head on it.'

Cedric peered. 'That geezer is Prince Rainier. It's a

Monégasque franc, if I'm not mistaken.' He looked up at Felix. 'Oh, and that reminds me, we simply must go back to Monaco soon – perhaps after my book comes out. We had such a good time there, and I could take my fiddle. You know how you love it.' He gave a sly grin, and despite himself, Felix grinned back.

'What's that?' Rosy asked suddenly, pointing at the mirror.

'Your fair features,' quipped Bartho.

'*No*, idiot, that splotch just to its right. It looks like a hole, actually, as if some picture had been there or a different mirror, and the nail has been wrenched out. What a shame when everything else is so fresh.'

Cedric walked over to where she pointed, and examined the wooden wall.

'No,' he said thoughtfully, 'there has been no nail here – but there has been something else.' He paused, frowning. 'In fact, I should say . . . well, a bullet. You see?' He tilted the mirror slightly so that its frame cast no shadow and revealed the extent of the 'wound'. It was a round hole of about an inch in diameter, its edges sharply splintered and charred.

They regarded it in silence. And then Bartho exclaimed, 'But that's absurd. Who would be using that wall for target practice? I mean, I know Cousin Walter can be a bit nutty, but he's not as nutty as that. Besides, he is on holiday in Australia. You must be mistaken.'

Cedric shook his head. 'No chance of that; I've seen enough of these in the war. And I suspect Rosy might have encountered the occasional one too; she was in the ATS.' He glanced at her enquiringly. 'You must have seen quite a bit of firearm practice down in Dover, I imagine.'

'Yes,' she said slowly, 'but those were rifles, not pistols.'

'Exactly. And this has been done with a pistol: a Colt, quite likely.'

They gazed at one another in puzzlement.

'What about the bullet?' Felix asked. 'Is it still stuck in it?'

Cedric shook his head. 'No. It looks as if it's been gouged out, probably by a penknife. Whoever fired the thing either has a clean and tidy mind or didn't want it found and identified.'

The silence was broken by Rosy. 'Oh my God,' she breathed. 'Oh my *God*.' Her eyes were fixed on the wicker table where Felix had placed the coin and piece of plastic.

They were startled. 'What's that supposed to mean?' Bartho asked. 'Had a vision, have you?'

She shook her head impatiently. 'Don't you see? It's obvious: a single bullet hole, a lipstick top, the Monaco franc . . . This is where Tippy was shot. Not on the dunes, but *here*, in this hut. Just where we are standing!'

Bartho and Felix looked bewildered. But Cedric said grimly: 'It's the franc piece, isn't it? That's what you are thinking of.'

Rosy nodded silently.

'Well, I've no idea what you are talking about,' Felix sighed impatiently. 'The subtleties escape me – not unlike Bartho's film!'

The latter ignored his words, and addressing Rosy, said: 'Ah, I see . . . you are thinking of that time when she was banging on about Monte Carlo, saying she had stayed there recently with the Carshaltons, and what a marvellous time they had spent at the Monaco Grand Prix and in the casino. I can tell you, *that* didn't go down too well with Alicia. She complained later that masses of people visited Monaco and Monte Carlo but only Tippy would swank about it.'

'So when was she there?' asked Felix.

'From what I gather about three weeks ago; just before she came up here,' Cedric told him. 'Recently enough to still have the odd foreign coin in her purse, or to be saving it as a keepsake, perhaps: French francs are two a penny, but not the Monaco ones.'

'But the girl was found on the dunes,' Bartho protested. '*We* found her, for God's sake!'

'Corpses can be moved,' Rosy murmured. 'It wouldn't be the first time.'

'Seems a bit tenuous to me,' Felix said. 'There's no proof that those bits belonged to her. Besides, how would she have got in here? I take it that Bartho didn't give her the key?' He glanced enquiringly at the other.

Bartho shook his head. 'No, it's been with me all the time.'

'All the same,' Cedric said thoughtfully, 'it looks as if she might have been here somehow. One knows coincidences often occur, but in this case there seems a curious number: the girl was killed by a single bullet a few days ago; the bullet hole in that wall is fresh – perhaps no more than a week old; two items have been found, which could very well have belonged to her – though as Felix has pointed out – that is hardly conclusive. Nevertheless, it is . . .'

Rosy, who had been scrutinising the lipstick cap, interrupted him: 'You can just make out the letters REV – Revlon. It's the brand; it's the one she used. I heard her and Alicia chatting about make-up one evening.'

'There you are,' Cedric said, 'a further coincidence; though I don't know what the police will make of it all. Probably dismiss it as empty speculation. But if nothing else, at least the bullet hole may intrigue them.'

Bartho stared at Cedric, and then said evenly: 'The police will not dismiss it as speculation because the police are not going to be told. It would be far too dangerous.'

Cedric was slightly taken aback. 'Dangerous? In what way?'

Bartho sighed. 'I may not be an expert in these things, but from what one reads in the newspapers the police usually evince an interest in the owner of the premises in which a murder has occurred. For some silly reason they assume there could be a connection.' He paused, and then added, 'This place belongs to my cousin, and having been given the key and the permission to use it, I am its custodian or proxy owner. One or both of us could come under suspicion. Personally, I don't fancy being reported as "helping police with their enquiries". As you know, it's a charming euphemism for "probably guilty as hell". And apart from the embarrassment, I have a film to make. I haven't time to joust with the law or its representatives.'

'But surely—' Rosy began.

'Look,' Bartho continued, 'why do you think Felix was keen to take his hat back? It was hardly because of sentiment. He knew damn well that if it was left by the corpse he could be incriminated and subject to all manner of tedious probings. That's right, isn't it, Felix?'

The latter nodded. 'It most certainly is,' he said. 'I have no intention of being compromised by a panama hat!'

'Exactly. And the same goes for me. Frankly, the more we are distanced from this whole thing the better. There could be a perfectly simple explanation, which has nothing to do with the wretched girl. Why should we offer the police a plate of vague suspicions when they've got their own bloodhounds to deal with things? It's called muddying the waters.'

'Quite right,' chimed Felix. 'And after all, one does have one's reputation to consider – the mud of those waters can stick.' He turned to the other two: 'Besides, it is pure chance that we came in here at all. If Bartholomew hadn't suggested this as a venue for a beach party we shouldn't know a *thing* about it . . . and just as well, in my opinion. Ignorance, like silence, can be golden.' He regarded them anxiously, and Rosy knew he was thinking of his royal patron.

'Good. That's settled, then,' the custodian of the key declared briskly. He held out his hand to Cedric who had been about to slip the coin and lipstick cap into his pocket. 'I think I had better take those, if you don't mind.' He glanced at his watch and added, 'High time I was back at my post. Fred is going to try out some new camera angles on Robert and Alicia. I can't keep them waiting. I'll leave it to you to think of another place for Amy's reception . . . Oh, and by the way, for God's sake don't mention this to her when she comes – or to her mother: the whole of Southwold might hear of it!' He ushered

130

them out. And turning the key firmly in the lock, strode off in the direction of the studio.

'He's in a bit of a tizz,' observed Cedric.

'Are you surprised?' Rosy asked. 'He's got a point. The hut belongs to his cousin. I suppose he is thinking of the headlines: *Woman murdered in Hackle's Hut: Scottish Landowner Denies Everything*. You must admit it wouldn't look too good.'

Felix tittered. 'Perhaps he did it.'

'Who, Bartho?'

'No, the cousin. Slipped down to Southwold for a few days' paddle, went for a kip in his hut, found some giggling girl he didn't like the look of and took a potshot with the trusty service revolver he always carries in his sporran. Then, deed done, he drove her to the dunes, left her there and buggered back to Scotland . . . What do you think of that?'

Cedric regarded his friend with some irritation. 'Very little. Firstly, the cousin is currently in Australia. And secondly, not content with honing your acting talent, I see you are now practising your scriptwriting skills. Personally, dear boy, I think you should stick to your real forte – arranging flowers. Chelsea has need of you.'

Felix sighed. 'It's my nerves, you know.'

CHAPTER FIFTEEN

Mindful of Bartho's warning to say nothing to Angela about the bullet hole in his cousin's hut, Rosy had dutifully kept quiet.

Nevertheless, she felt uneasy about this, not sure whether it was entirely fair to conceal the matter from one whose daughter was so closely involved with the young man. If their conclusions were correct – that it was in Walter Hackle's hut, not on the beach, that the girl had been murdered – then surely Angela (and Amy) had the right to know . . . But then, she debated, with 'clues' being so often misleading or misread, their conclusions might *not* be correct. In which case she could fully see Bartho's point in not wishing to spread undue alarm.

Were the matter reported to the police there would be an awful brouhaha and the ramifications for the Hackles embarrassing to say the least: Walter Hackle would be recalled from his sojourn in Australia, enquiries would be made of all those to whom he had ever lent the beach hut (and thus perhaps in possession of a key), Bartholomew himself would be endlessly grilled, and doubtless – as he had clearly feared – the whole film project either seriously delayed or more than likely cancelled. And after all that fuss, supposing their discovery had no substance – nothing to do with the murder at all. Would such upheaval have been worth it?

No, she decided, it wouldn't. Wasn't it enough that the four of them should be faced with the matter, without roping in others and unleashing a whole spate of speculation and possibly slander? In his insistence on ignorance being golden, in this case Felix had surely been right. Thus, as far as she could she dismissed it from her mind – which admittedly wasn't very far.

Like Rosy, Cedric too had been dismayed by the beach hut discovery and later that afternoon, leaving Felix immersed in the pages of *House & Garden*, he had strolled down to the boating lake to mull things over and take stock. As he ambled around its perimeter, surveying the placid waters and assailed by the squeals of laughter from youthful paddlers and punters, the whole affair seemed not only remote but absurd – or at least this latest aspect of it did.

He reviewed his initial suspicions, and dismissed them as being foolishly premature. In a way Bartholomew was absolutely right: the only real link – if any – with Tippy's murder was the evidence of a solitary shot having been fired in his cousin's property. And while the splintering of the wood appeared recent, there was little to suggest exactly how recent – three days ago, a fortnight, a month even? And yes, the girl had been found shot, but there was no real reason to suppose that the killing had been done in the beach hut. After all, people did own guns quite innocently (many left over from the war) and occasionally these were fired, either deliberately or inadvertently. Perhaps a borrower of the hut had been cleaning their gun, fooling around, showing off to a friend, drunk in charge of et cetera . . . Stupid accidents happened all the time.

But what about the coin and lipstick top? It was pretty tenuous, wasn't it, to assume they had belonged to the girl? Rosy Gilchrist had been quick to spot the name (or half-name) of Revlon. But then surely that was a popular brand with women, almost as popular as Max Factor (or so he vaguely recalled his ex-wife once declaring). There would be masses of women both in Southwold and beyond who favoured that type.

And the Monégasque coin? Well, yes, that was a bit more unusual, admittedly. But Tippy Tildred was hardly the only person to visit the principality. After all, what about himself and Felix? They had been there only a year ago. And besides, following the Rainier–Kelly marriage the place had become fashionable again and was often featured in the films or in travel articles. It was not inconceivable that someone other than Tippy should have had a Monaco coin in their pocket or purse.

Cedric brooded. Taken individually the three things pointed to nothing . . . but together? Well, possibly a *cumulative* significance . . . but then, equally they could be a random set of fragile coincidences.

A set of coincidences worth mentioning to the police? Cedric frowned, and gazed ruminatively at a gently eddying dinghy. And then, glancing towards the town and its lighthouse, he was once more put in mind of wartime Southwold and the dead fire-watcher he had once seen sprawled pathetically in Stradbroke Road, victim of a casual air raid. Like the girl, he too had been struck down – suddenly, fatally, cruelly. And just like thousands of others, nothing had brought him back however much the circumstances had been discussed and analysed . . . Yes, Cedric told himself firmly, the deed was done: the girl dead. Nothing could alter that. Preventing a crime was one thing, but rushing around afterwards in pursuit of culprits was like shutting the proverbial stable door: worthy but too late. It was an exercise for the authorities, not for the bumbling laity.

Having reached that convenient conclusion and about to retrace his footsteps, he was waylaid by a small boy of about seven, wielding an enormous ice-cream cornet. The child stood four-square facing him, feet apart and thrusting the thing towards him. 'Here, Mister,' it said, 'I don't like this. Do you want it?'

Unused to dealing with children, Cedric was taken aback. 'Er, well,' he replied warily, eyeing the dripping cone, 'not really, though it's terribly nice of you.' And then feeling something more was required, added, 'But how very kind!'

The child smiled genially, and then casting the confection to the ground, stamped on it with evident pleasure. A splodge of cream fell on Cedric's trouser cuff and he beat a hasty retreat.

CHAPTER SIXTEEN

'Well, at least we've had a formal identification,' Nathan said, 'so that's one thing less to agitate the super; he's pernickety like that, wants everything to go according to the book.'

'And you don't, sir?' Jennings asked.

'Not if it's obvious and slows everything down, I don't.'

'Ah, the pragmatic initiative,' the detective sergeant murmured.

'What?'

'Oh, nothing, sir. Just thinking aloud,' the other said hastily. 'Er, so what was she like, the aunt or whoever?'

'Like I've said, she's the wife of that MP who has been spouting about the firearms trade, Tom Carshalton. Last year it was the excessive granting of shotgun licences, but he's gone up a notch since then and now it's illicit arms smuggling.

There was a big thing about it in the press last week.'

'So what's his angle?'

'Doesn't like it; ought to be stopped. Says the police should be doing more. In other words the usual thing – blame the poor bloody infantry!'

Jennings nodded, but asked again about Ida.

Nathan contemplated his pipe, and then said thoughtfully: 'Nice pins.'

'What!'

'Her legs were nice. She was quite attractive, I suppose, in a middle-aged way.'

Jennings explained patiently that he had been less concerned with the lady's legs than with her general demeanour and whether she had said anything useful to aid their enquiry.

Nathan shrugged. 'She had got it about right: a balance of sorrow and gallant stoicism. Just a few tears to show heart, but not too many as to cause embarrassment. What you might call "decorously poised". But then her being an MP's wife, that's to be expected . . . They do it all the time.'

'What, view corpses?'

'No, Clever Clogs, cultivate a stage presence. It comes with the job.'

'So you mean she was acting?'

Nathan shook his head. 'No, I do not mean she was acting, or at least not in the crude sense. It's a kind of social instinct – not something you would know much about.' He smiled benignly. 'Mind you, she wasn't alone. She had got that travel writer from Reydon with her, the one that's always on the wireless. A bit of a bumptious bloke, if you ask me.'

'Vincent Ramsgate? Oh yes, but he's rather good, isn't he? I've read one of his books,' Jennings said eagerly. 'It was the one all to do with Rhodesia and the—'

'Have you now?' Nathan interjected quickly, parrying a lengthy résumé. 'I am surprised Agatha Christie allows you the time.'

Jennings looked piqued but let it pass. 'So she didn't say anything helpful, anything that might give us a lead?'

'What, like: "Oh I say, Officer, I know just the person who's likely to have done it!"? No, I hate to disappoint you, old son, but she didn't. Quite the opposite, in fact. Kept saying what a charming person the girl had been, and how impossible it was to imagine anyone wanting to harm her. "Everyone loved Tippy," she insisted.'

'No they didn't,' Jennings said, 'or at least that's not the impression I had when we interviewed those film people. I don't mean that any of them said anything *against* her, but then nobody said anything *for* her either – not unless you count that Alicia woman, and she seemed pretty phoney. Laying it on with a trowel, she was.' He sniffed. 'A bit like "the lady doth protest too much, methinks", if you get my meaning.'

'What?'

'It's in *Hamlet*, the bit where—'

'Yes, yes. I'm sure it is . . . Now, let me tell you something: I've had some information which may have a bearing. It's from some old girl with a spaniel. She dropped in last night all of a twitter, and saying she had seen a figure like Tippy Tildred on Sunday morning on the lower promenade, wrapped in a towelling thing and wearing a straw boater or some such. Thinks she may have been carrying a small beach bag too. At the time it hadn't meant anything as a lot of visitors deck themselves out like that; but she had noticed her as there hadn't been anyone else about, it being a Sunday and most people in church or cooking the family joint.'

'Well, that's something. Did she say what direction she had been going in?'

'No. I asked her that, but she said she really couldn't say. Apparently, the dog was on the verge of doing its business – the first time for three days, so she had got better things to think about.'

'Hmm. Still, that's better than a poke in the eye. But like we've established, there was no sign of a hat or anything when Hackle and his cronies discovered the body – not even shoes. At least, according to them there wasn't.'

'Exactly. Which rather suggests that her things had been left nearer to that area than we first assumed. When the woman saw her she must have been either going somewhere to leave them or coming from somewhere where she had put them on. Either way, after she had been shot the body would still need to be transported to the dunes; but the distance is likely to have been shorter, i.e. not from the edge of town or an outlying district, but somewhere closer to hand.'

Jennings nodded but said nothing. An awful thought had struck him. It would be just his luck if he was instructed to make an inventory of all properties within a mile radius of the seafront, to launch a thorough search of the owners' cupboards, sheds and dustbins and get detailed accounts

140

of their activities between the relevant hours. Those not available for comment would have to be contacted, and those pleading absence on that Sunday would need their alibis strictly verifying . . . On the whole Jennings rather enjoyed ticking lists and making notes, but there were some procedures that were a bridge too far! Perhaps if he played his cards right he could offload the task on to some junior lackey who could report to him when complete. Yes, that would be the thing . . .

He opened his eyes, which had been momentarily closed, to see Nathan staring at him quizzically.

'Did you hear what I said?' his boss asked sternly. 'I asked if you were up for a pint at the Red Lion, but all you can do is stand there and wince with your eyes shut! One of your earache spasms, I suppose.' He sighed and added grudgingly, 'Oh well, I'll fork out this time, but you can get the crisps – ordinary Smith's, mind, none of those tarty new ones at twice the price!' He reached for his hat, and Jennings gave thanks to something or other.

On their way to the Red Lion they passed, but did not observe, Felix and Cedric descending the steps of the post office. The latter had been sending soothing postcards to friends saying they were having a marvellous time, and assuring the recipients that Southwold's growing reputation for gruesome skulduggery was grossly exaggerated. 'It has been nothing to do with us!' he wrote (and lied) gaily.

Just as Cedric was breathing a sigh of relief at the completion of the chore, Felix gripped his arm and hissed, 'Watch out, we don't want to bump into *them*!'

'Who?' Cedric asked, adjusting his spectacles.

'Them – the heavies, Nathan and the Jennings boy,' Felix whispered.

They hesitated on the steps, looking resolutely in the opposite direction as the two policemen strolled by and continued up the high street.

'You don't think, do you,' Cedric muttered, 'that we are being just a trifle paranoid? I mean, I know that we didn't exactly hit it off with them the last time we were here, but other than the coincidence of our being associated with another homicide case, I cannot see that there is much to fear.'

'There is always much to fear with the police,' Felix replied grimly. 'You may remember the problems we had in London with the Beasley affair.[4] Besides, if they learn that my hat was there, let alone me not reporting the fact, it could turn sticky. We don't want that, do we?'

Cedric agreed that stickiness would be distasteful, but added mildly that it was a moot point which was the more risky: the hat being revealed or concealed. 'Quite likely the latter,' he suggested. 'Tampering with evidence is generally frowned upon by the authorities; they don't like it.'

'I did not tamper, I took it,' Felix replied with some asperity. 'I had every right. It was *my* hat and it shouldn't have been there! I can't think why it was.' He thrust his hands into his pockets and pouted.

'Yes, I've been thinking about that. You know, it occurs to me that the girl herself may have taken it. After all, she did show a distinct fancy for it at the Sole Bay,

[4] See *A Little Murder*.

if you remember.' Felix did remember, and shuddered. 'And when you were at the studio last week doing your mournful wanderings among the paths of "the labyrinth", I noticed her fingering the brim. You had left the thing on the sideboard, and it seemed to have caught her attention again. She was obviously very drawn to it.' Cedric shot a sly glance at his friend: 'Perhaps she whipped it to go with the new bikini. I wouldn't have put it past her.'

Felix's face froze, and it was difficult to tell which possibility dismayed him most: the police uncovering his misdemeanour, or Tippy's dastardly theft. Neither was savoury. 'I think I need a coffee,' he announced, 'oh, and a large flapjack too. They do excellent ones in that cafe further up the street.'

With eyes primed for Nathan and Jennings, they slunk into the sanctuary of the tea shop's back room, where Cedric chastely ordered a pot of lapsang, and Felix commandeered a flapjack plus a cream bun.

CHAPTER SEVENTEEN

Busily absorbed in matters of consumption, they did not see Alicia's entry until she was seated at the table next to theirs. She gave them a vague wave and rather pointedly took out her newspaper.

Cedric leant towards his companion. 'We are evidently not in the communing mood today,' he whispered. Felix nodded, too busy with his bun to care.

To complement his second cup, Cedric withdrew his cigarette case, selected a filter tip and lit up. The smoke curled in the direction of the neighbouring table.

The newspaper was cast aside. 'Oh, I say,' Alicia exclaimed, 'that's splendid; you've got some gaspers. I've left mine behind. Could I be awfully rude and cadge one off you?'

'By all means.' Cedric held out the case and invited her to join them.

She brought her chair and coffee over; and gazing at Felix, now about to embark on the flapjack, observed that having an appetite was all right for some but for others it was deadly. 'I only have to look at a cake,' she grumbled, 'and it goes to my hips. Or here,' she laughed, gesturing to her bosom. 'But you're like Tippy, thin as a lath . . . though of course, *she* never ate anything except gin and lettuce leaves. Obviously that's not your diet!'

'Certainly not the lettuce leaves,' Cedric observed dryly.

'Actually, she didn't eat many of those either,' Alicia continued, 'in fact, it's amazing she didn't peg out long before this business. Silly little thing.' She smiled, but the voice held a note of scorn.

Felix ceased munching and looked up. 'Silly? Hmm, you're right about that,' he agreed darkly. He spoke with feeling but didn't enlarge.

'But, Alicia, I thought you rather approved of her – at least, that's what you implied when we were interviewed by the police officer.' Cedric remarked mildly.

'Well, of course I did! When in a corner lay on the charm, everyone knows that.' She took a final puff of her cigarette, studying its diminished length with evident regret.

However, deeming one good turn a day to be quite sufficient, Cedric refrained from offering her another and instead asked: 'So what corner would that be?'

She grimaced. 'Being interrogated by the fuzz, of course. They are so eager to find clues and make an arrest they'll grasp at anything if it suits their book. A friend of mine was once caught in a nightclub raid – the Cat's Pyjamas in Soho – and, oh my goodness, was there a fuss!

No, if I had told them that Tippy Tildred was a nasty little troublemaker and that any of us would have shot her given half a chance, they would have marched me down to the station in a trice!' She paused, and added, 'Well, that may be a bit of an exaggeration but you know what I mean. There would have been endless questions and probings and one would never hear the end of it. Too tiresome for words!'

Felix nodded in fervent agreement.

Alicia looked at her watch. 'O Lord, is that the time? I must fly. I'm supposed to be meeting Robert in five minutes. He's in an awful state – Tippy was simply beastly to him, you know. In fact, if it had been me I'd have done her in myself. There was good reason, all right!'

'Oh. Do you think he did?' Felix asked with interest.

She gave a mirthless laugh. 'Robert? Oh, I shouldn't think so. Not one to chance his arm is our Robert. Preserving number one is his priority! Always has been.' She dropped a shilling on the table, telling them to give the waitress the change, and with another laugh and a flurry of Chanel, set off to bring cheer to the apparently wounded Kestrel.

'Interesting, really,' Cedric mused after she had gone.

'What is?'

'The fact that she showed no curiosity about the girl's death: perfectly ready to admit her dislike, but not a word of actual interest as to how it happened or who might have been responsible. I wonder why.'

Felix shrugged. 'They are all the same these thespians,

totally self-engrossed . . . Oh, by the way, I've been shown the rushes for that scene where I am found loitering in the labyrinth. They're rather good, I think – Fred has got exactly the right angle and has caught that teasing little smile I give just before being enveloped in the swirling mist. You should take a look sometime.'

'Oh, I will,' Cedric assured him earnestly.

Out in the street and wandering back to *Cot O'Bedlam*, they came face-to-face with Vincent Ramsgate (party garb replaced by an inoffensive raincoat and plain trilby). With head down, he at first appeared not to have seen them and would have hurried past, had not Felix, negotiating a stray cat, blocked his path. He stopped and greeted them politely.

'Ah, nice to see you,' he exclaimed. 'Just the day for a stroll – if you can keep out of the wind, that is. You'll probably be glad to get back to the fug of London, I expect! Going soon, I daresay?'

'Er, well,' Cedric began. But then remembering Ramsgate's book lying unopened at the cottage, he felt he should make some reference to the gift. 'It was really most kind of you to leave that book the other day,' he said; and then, fearful he might be required to make some perceptive comment, added hastily, 'though what with all this unsettling business going on, I am afraid I haven't had a chance even to open it. I shall reserve that pleasure until once more sheltered by that London fug!'

For a few seconds Ramsgate seemed to hesitate, regarding him intently, and then said dismissively, 'Oh, don't give it another thought, old man, absolutely not. Put it on the back boiler, that's my advice! As you say, this frightful business looms over everything. I've got the grieving aunt staying with me this very moment. She came to identify the poor girl and collect her belongings – a beastly task.' He gave a rueful sigh, adding, 'In any case, we scholars have far more pressing things to attend to than to read one another's publications, wouldn't you say? Keep it for a long winter evening!' And briskly sidestepping them, he pressed on in the direction of Queen Street.

Felix thought Cedric looked peeved. He was right. 'I don't know what he means by that,' the professor remarked coldly.

'Means by what?'

'Bracketing us together as scholars. The term may well apply to me, but he is a mere populist. My Cappadocian book is a keenly researched study, not some pappy stream of personal anecdotes!'

'Oh no, of course not,' Felix agreed. He gazed after the man's retreating back, frowning slightly. 'Considering we were the life and soul of his wretched party, I think he gave us rather short shrift. Not exactly chummy, was he? A bit shifty, I thought.'

'Hmm. And presumptuous with it,' Cedric said, still bridling. 'And I have no desire to read his book, either now or in London. Put it on the back boiler? *In* the damn thing more likely!'

Felix, alert to the cloud hovering, said brightly: 'I have a superb lunch ready for us, a melange of Sole Bay prawns, lobster tails and sautéed local samphire. I have also managed to track down a bottle of that excellent Meursault you are so fond of. It's in the fridge now – we don't want it overchilled. Come on!'

Thus, like Ramsgate, the two friends also pressed on – though in their case to a goal possibly more indulgent.

However, the prospect of such goal did not stop Felix from stopping to peer at some colourful fabrics displayed in a draper's shop window. As they walked on he referred to one of the samples, but Cedric made no answer, his mind being elsewhere.

'Wake up, didn't you hear?' Felix prompted. 'I said that that piece of brocade might be suitable for the little side window in your drawing room, the one where the cat damaged the blind. It's about the right colour. You ought to go in and take a look.'

'What? Oh yes, yes I will, sometime,' Cedric replied vaguely.

'Well, don't get too excited, it was merely a thought!'

Cedric stopped and frowned. 'I have been thinking,' he said.

'Extraordinary. What about?'

'Kestrel. What do you think Alicia meant when she said he was in such a stew?'

Felix shrugged. 'Could have been anything.'

'Yes, but it was something to do with Tippy; Alicia implied she had behaved badly to him, had said or done something intolerable.'

'Nothing surprising there,' Felix said with feeling. 'What about my—'

Cedric sighed. 'I was thinking about something a little

150

more pertinent to her death: i.e. he may have had a hand in it.'

'Really? So what makes you say that?'

'That night we were coming back from Buss Creek ... why was he lurking behind those three? I very much doubt it was because he was fascinated by Charlie or Frank. No, the object of his attention, as we rather assumed at the time, was clearly Tippy.'

'Got it!' Felix cried. 'He fancied the girl, she spurned him, he killed her. And now he's in floods of tears and having to be comforted by Alicia.'

'That's putting it a little crudely but it could have been something like that. After all, it's not just in books or opera that one encounters the *crime passionnel*.'

Felix looked doubtful. 'Well, he might fancy himself as Al Capone or Errol Flynn, but I can't imagine him using a real gun.'

'Then you imagine wrong. I overheard him telling Rosy Gilchrist all about his prowess in the Surbiton Pistol Society and how he had won some prize: £15, I think it was.'

'Was she impressed?'

'Looked bored out of her mind.'

When they got back to the cottage and Felix busied himself with assembling the luncheon and rearranging the flowers, Cedric continued to look preoccupied.

'Are you still brooding about Kestrel?' Felix asked, tweaking a lily and discarding a rose.

'He has been rather playing on my mind,' the other replied, 'but I'm not sure if—'

'Oh, I shouldn't let him play too long,' Felix giggled, 'you might become obsessed.'

His friend closed his eyes: 'Oh, very droll.' Opening them, he said, 'You know, it might be worth having a word with Rosy Gilchrist. Occasionally, she can be quite discerning, and I saw her in close conversation with him recently. You never know, she might just have a view.'

'We will invite her to tea,' Felix said briskly, 'and she can be guinea pig for my new biscuit recipe. It was given to me by Rosemary Hume herself! Yes, why don't you telephone The Swan and tell her you have a vital matter to discuss and would value her opinion.'

Without waiting for a response Felix had whipped into the little kitchen, switched on the oven and donned an apron.

Two hours later Rosy was seated on the sofa in *Cot O'Bedlam* sipping tea and munching one of Felix's exquisite biscuits.

'The secret,' he explained, 'is not to use too much flour or to overbake, *or* to be heavy-handed with the mixing. A light touch is needed: the keynote is delicacy.'

Rosy nodded appreciatively. 'Oh yes,' she said, 'one can certainly taste the delicacy – in fact, I've never tasted such good delicacy in my life!' She grinned and requested another.

Cedric cleared his throat. 'Without wishing to sound overly curious, we should be interested to hear your views on Robert Kestrel. You see . . .' And he told her of their conversation with Alicia, the previous episode on North Green and their tentative suspicions.

Rosy had not expected this and was momentarily flummoxed. Would it be fair to reveal what the dead girl had confided – or hinted at – in the Walberswick pub? It seemed a bit rotten. And yet in view of what the girl had implied to her about Robert's 'problem', plus Alicia's comments as relayed by Cedric and Felix, it did rather look as if he had an involvement with Tippy that had been far from satisfactory. But would that really drive him to murder – to exact revenge for being scornfully rejected, as Cedric seemed to think? Probably not.

But blackmail might. What had Cedric quoted Alicia as saying? Something like: 'Not one to chance his arm is our Robert. Preserving number one is his priority' . . . Thus to risk all for thwarted passion might not be his priority – whereas safeguarding his own interests and reputation could be. According to Tippy, she had threatened not only to expose his sexual 'inadequacy' but also to tell his wife. Some men might not care, but Robert just might. *Preserving number one is his priority*, she mused.

'Come on, Rosy, what do you think?' Felix urged impatiently.

Rosy beamed. 'I think I would simply love another of your biscuits!' she said.

Eventually, and reluctantly, she did tell them what Tippy had so maliciously revealed, and indeed what the girl had hinted she might do about it.

'Poor sod,' Cedric remarked, 'not a happy circumstance.'

'Especially if he is guilty,' added Felix.

'But that's just it,' Rosy protested, 'we don't know that

he is. What we have is interpretation; there's not a shred of evidence. It's simply speculation and gossip, *our* gossip!'

Yet even as she said this, a doubt nagged insidiously at the back of her mind.

CHAPTER EIGHTEEN

As it happened, the process wasn't as grisly as she had feared. The first few moments while waiting for the sheet to be drawn back had been a trifle fraught, but after that things were all right. Mercifully, the girl's face was unscathed and the features sufficiently recognisable as not to need a prolonged perusal. A glance was enough. The whole procedure had been quick and remarkably painless with no ill effects; indeed, Ida had experienced no feelings at all. Vincent's presence had doubtlessly helped and she was grateful for his understated sympathy.

Afterwards he had taken her to a restaurant for a bolstering lunch, plus some post-Dutch courage, or as he had first rather smugly put it, 'post-Baviorum fortitudinem'. Latin being total Greek to her she had not caught the gist of this, but light dawned when the waiter brought a bottle of Möet to the table.

'If one can't drink champagne at times of grief and upset, when can one?' her host had said jovially.

The logic of this escaped her (though did not bother) and together they did full justice to both meal and wine.

Thus fortified, Ida could turn her mind to the last phase of her Suffolk duty: collecting the girl's clothes from her room at the temporary film studio. In fact, she had no intention of personally collecting the stuff (hauling an additional suitcase all the way to Liverpool Street and beyond was out of the question!), and had detailed British Rail's freight department to do the job. Nevertheless, it was only right and proper to put in an appearance at the place, supervise a little of the arrangements and to say some gracious words to the girl's companions. With luck, it shouldn't take too long.

Thus with lunch over they drove to Southwold, where Vincent dropped her at the gates of the drive while he rushed off late to keep some dental or chiropody appointment. Relaxed by the meal and with the worst over, Ida felt perfectly poised to attend to the matter alone. Thus, adjusting her hat, and composing her features into an expression of benevolent concern, she entered the porch of the big house and tugged the bell pull.

From within there came a loud clanging, but to her slight irritation nothing happened. She waited and tried again. Eventually, just as she was about to yank the rope for the third time, the door opened and she was confronted by a short scraggy woman wearing heels of monstrously stacked elevation and puffing a cigarette. On her jumper was displayed a large label, which said CONTINUITY. The woman frowned.

'If you're from the press again, you can forget it,' she said truculently, 'we've had enough of you journalists asking questions about the poor kid. *Some* of us have proper work to do, and I can't spend my time nattering to you lot.' She broke off, and eyed the visitor more intently, appraising her smart appearance. 'Although,' she continued, 'if you're from the BBC that might be a different matter. I'll have to ask His Nibs, but we're shooting just now and he won't want any—'

Hastily, Ida explained that she was neither a reporter nor from the BBC, merely a relative of the murdered girl come to deal with her belongings and express condolences.

'Oh, well,' the other conceded, 'that's different, I suppose. You had better come in.'

She deposited Ida on a wooden bench in the hall and told her to wait while she went to fetch 'young Hackle'. (Ah, so the name *was* Hackle, Ida thought. At least she hadn't got that wrong!) In the far distance she could hear shouts and occasional bursts of laughter, and rather strangely what sounded like a bugle being blown. But in the sparse and rather desolate hall all was sombre and quiet.

Almost quiet. For the silence was punctuated by the ticking of a grandfather clock. And then, in tandem with the clock, Ida could hear something else: a heavy rhythmic breathing from the alcove under the stairs . . . Oh God, was there somebody lying there drunk! She peered nervously at the recess but could see nothing. Then with a snort and guttural yawn something stirred, and out from the darkness a huge and even darker shape emerged. It lurched towards her, and she froze as it laid its gigantic head upon her lap. For one absurd moment she thought that the champagne had done its worst. *I must not drink at lunchtime*, she counselled herself hysterically.

The next moment she heard a voice. 'Ah, Mrs Carshalton,' Bartholomew Hackle cried, as he came buzzing down the passage. 'I am so sorry to have kept you waiting! I knew you were coming, of course, but I was horribly entangled with one of the military scenes and everything went rather haywire!' He stopped, and addressed the head in her lap: 'That's quite enough, Pixie,' he said sternly. 'I am sure our visitor hasn't brought any nice sweeties for you.' He looked at Ida and said, 'At least I don't suppose you have?'

Ida confirmed that she hadn't. The dog must have sensed this for it obligingly removed its head, and with a valedictory wag of its tail lumbered down the corridor.

She had thought that being in the dead girl's room might be mildly unsettling. As it was, after her encounter with Pixie the place felt almost like a sanctuary. She removed her hat, sat on the bed and took stock.

To her relief there didn't seem to be much there: the wardrobe door was open revealing a couple of dresses slung on hangers, a raincoat and a crimson jacket. Stockings, a pair of Capri pants and an assortment of blouses were draped over the back of the only chair; in one corner was a muddled heap of plimsolls and stilettos, and on top of a rickety table was a hairbrush plus a conglomeration of make-up items, mainly lipsticks and nail varnishes. Magazines of the 'glossy' type littered the floor.

Ida suspected the room might have held more things originally but that they had been taken by the police. She vaguely recalled one of the officers at the mortuary saying something to that effect and assuring her the articles could be reclaimed. (Goodness, why should she want to do that? Wasn't there enough to deal with already?)

She gazed at the two dresses in the wardrobe. How small they seemed. Rather pathetic, really . . . No, she thought grimly, not pathetic – far from it: for one so slight Tippy Tildred had produced great disquiet! And with that in mind she opened the bigger suitcase and started to fill it.

She had almost finished when there was a knock on the door and a young man came in bearing a cup of tea. He held it out to her. 'Bartho said you might like this. But he hopes you don't take sugar because there isn't any: Pixie has eaten it.'

Ida thanked him for the kind thought, inwardly wincing at the pallid milky fluid. Its one redeeming feature was surely the lack of sugar, but she had no desire to put it to the test. Instead she placed the cup and saucer on the windowsill, smiled at the hovering youth and enquired his name.

He said it was Frank, and she asked him if he was one of the cast.

'Oh no,' he grinned, 'you wouldn't catch me doing that acting stuff! I am the best boy,' he informed her proudly.

She must have looked startled for he went on to explain that it meant he was the principal grip.

'Oh *really*?' Ida replied in her best MP's wife's voice. 'And what is it you have to grip exactly, the props I suppose?' (Perhaps he would be handy in removing the suitcases to the hall.)

Frank sounded slightly put out. 'No, that's the job of the scene-shifters,' he said dismissively. 'I do all the lighting and electricals with Charlie. He's my assistant, but I'm number one: like I said, best boy to the gaffer – that's Fred.'

'How splendid,' Ida enthused, 'so you are an absolute vital cog!'

'Well, you could say that,' he agreed modestly, flushing with pleasure.

'I trust Tippy realised that,' she couldn't resist saying. 'The poor girl wasn't always discerning of others' talents. Still, she was a very lively person; you must all miss her.'

He agreed sombrely that she had been fun (though whether that meant she was missed, Ida wasn't sure). The young man added awkwardly: 'It must be sad – I mean, you being her aunt and all that.'

'Oh, very sad . . . although of course I wasn't her "full" aunt, a sort of partial one: she was the child of my stepsister.'

'Yes, but she liked you – thought you were very funny, you and Mr Carshalton.'

Ida was taken aback, but any latent pleasure was quickly dashed.

'Oh yes,' Frank went on, 'in fact she kept telling Charlie and me that she had a hilarious story about you both, which she might tell us one day if we were good.'

Ida regarded him intently, looking for signs of malice or

160

mirth. She couldn't detect any. 'And were you good?' she asked casually.

'Of course not! We're never good, Charlie and me!' He beamed cheerfully.

Ida gave a reciprocal smile, while inwardly thinking: *Hell, if that wasn't typical of the little beast!*

Thus death duties completed, courtesies exchanged with the moviemakers and her niece's belongings packed ready for removal, that evening Ida relaxed on her host's sofa and took a long sip of Scotch. My God, she had earned it! The whisky was a particularly good blend from Adnams; and despite (or perhaps because of) being served in the Sassenach way – strong yet with ice and soda – to Ida it was bliss.

She adjusted a cushion behind her head and smiled at Vincent Ramsgate. 'Ah,' she sighed, 'only the funeral now and then we can put our feet up.'

'And very pretty feet you have, if I remember correctly,' he said gallantly, and gave a large wink.

They spent a convivial evening laughing, gossiping, reminiscing about things over and done with . . . And at one point, inevitably, speculating about Tippy Tildred's murderer.

It was, they decided, the deed of some deranged tourist with an unhealthy dislike of girls with cropped blonde hair. 'Alternatively,' Ramsgate suggested, 'it might have been Hackle, the producer fellow. With a name like that he could be capable of anything!'

Further suggestions were made and jokes exchanged. During this time the host drank moderately, the guest excessively.

The following day in the train returning to London, and with a crashing headache, Ida wondered if she had been too careless in her remarks the previous evening. Perhaps her allusions to the activities of a mutual friend had been a trifle indiscreet . . . well, more than that, really. After all, Tommy had told her he had the information on good authority. So presumably it was 'kosher', and he would be furious if he thought she had breached that confidence. As a politician's wife, Ida knew that it was a deadly sin to repeat things of a delicate nature, and apparently this item had been strictly 'under wraps'. By divulging it to Vincent the wraps were less firmly tied.

She sighed, annoyed with herself. Normally, she was pretty good at keeping her mouth shut regarding inside information, but last night she had been thoughtless. She put it down to the strain she had been under having to cope with the tiresome aftermath of the child's demise! Fortunately, when she repeated to Vincent what Tommy had confided, he had laughed and seemed unimpressed. 'My dear,' he had said, 'how simply fascinating – but I suspect that as so often with these things, there is plenty of smoke and not a single spark of fire. You'll see, it will be just one of the Home Office's perennial panics: sound and fury signifying absolutely nothing.' He had filled her glass and they had moved on to other topics.

* * *

By the time the train neared Chelmsford and she espied the familiar Marconi building against the skyline, her head was eased and any qualms regarding her indiscretion fast fading. It would be good to alight onto the platform at Liverpool Street and re-embrace the capital's grime and clamour. Coastal Suffolk was all very well and beautiful, but it was in London where real life began!

Hailing a porter and securing a taxi, she drove to their flat in Westminster eager to hear from Tommy how the party conference had gone and what further chances he had seized to secure his rightful office. She smiled, took out her compact and powdered her nose.

CHAPTER NINETEEN

The girl's death – an enigma, that's what it was, Jennings told himself as he demolished the remains of his ham sandwich. Almost as big an enigma, he reflected, as that rum film they were making up on the East Cliff.

Having failed to get a coherent answer from the cameraman, he had asked that Alicia Gorringe person what it was all about. 'Oh, it's obvious, darling,' she had replied, 'the tyranny of existential angst and barren illusion. Just up your street, I daresay.' She had then roared with laughter – though whether at the film's theme or at himself, he couldn't be sure. Both, he rather suspected.

Well, he thought sternly, there was nothing barren and illusory about the corpse on the dunes; and as a puzzle it was much more intriguing than the stupid film!

* * *

Jennings was currently off duty and he had cycled back to Walberswick to catch the afternoon sun and to eat his lunch at a spot near the jetty watching the ferry and the gulls. He liked doing that as it straightened his mind and gave a pleasant respite from the acrid fumes of Nathan's pipe. He had once offered to buy his boss a sweeter brand of tobacco, but the suggestion had been met with a bemused grunt and a blank stare. Responses that he had taken to be a negative. Oh well, it had been worth a try . . .

It wasn't that he disliked his superior, but his phlegmatism could be an irritant (Jennings liked the word phlegmatism, almost as much as opaque); but then, he supposed, that was a trait of the elderly – or at least the nearly elderly – a sort of wry complacency, an assumption of worldly wisdom, which, in his view, didn't always cut the mustard.

No, it did not! This Tippy girl, for example: it was unlikely to have been a crime of passion as Nathan had seemed to assume. From what he had read (via Agatha Christie and his psychology manuals) such things were generally brutal: killings executed in a burst of sudden fury. And of course, given the personal nature, by a sole assailant.

Yet from what they had ascertained, the girl's body had most probably been deposited on those dunes post-mortem. In which case there must have been more than one person involved. Nobody, except some Neanderthal titan, could have lugged the body to that spot unaided. And given the gun and the neat shooting, it must have been something premeditated, surely, not done in a rash moment.

Jennings lobbed a macerated crust at a lurking gull. He

166

missed, but the bird leapt upon it with predatory greed. Watching the performance, it occurred to him that perhaps that had been the motive: avarice. The girl had a swish background and the aunt was married to that fashionable MP Tom Carshalton. Perhaps she had had money – or most likely had been in line for a legacy or inheritance, which, should she die prematurely, would have devolved elsewhere.

He frowned, dwelling upon the possibility. Certainly, the mercenary element featured strongly in the Christie novels (and *there* was a woman who knew a bit about human nature, all right!) so could that be the case here? Was there some crazed relative Tippy had supplanted as legatee in a family will and who had been desperately seeking reinstatement? It wouldn't be the first time. After all, money – its need and love of – was an age-old goad. Yes, well, that was something that could be checked easily enough. A quick enquiry of solicitors and family members should do the trick.

But if that were done and nothing found, what then? Jennings pondered, and picking up a piece of driftwood threw it aimlessly at nothing. It fell in the mud, the action stirring his inspiration not one jot.

Gradually, however, other ideas did begin to form: if not for money or thwarted love, then how about revenge? A wronged wife, perhaps. (By all accounts the girl had been pretty free with her favours, actual or hinted.) But that too would have entailed an accomplice; a woman on her own could hardly have engineered the shifting of the body. But then why should anyone share in such a dangerous risk simply to pander to another's vanity or hurt feelings?

No, it had to be something else: something potent, something that had *necessitated* her disposal. Jennings stared unseeingly at the fishing boats.

And then for some absurdly illogical reason the title of a favourite novel slipped into his mind (not an Agatha Christie but by another literary hero), and he saw its shabby red cover and worn spine jostling with other titles on the shelf above his bed. For a brief moment the random image of Eric Ambler's classic *Journey into Fear* filled his mind and eclipsed all else.

Fear! Yes, that could be it! Somebody, or some persons, had been fearful of Tippy Tildred, and the only way they could destroy that fear was by destroying its source. In killing the girl the threat (whatever it was) had been stilled, and the fearful made safe.

In mild triumph Jennings selected a small pebble, hurled it at another gull and instead hit a passing fisherman on the shin. Head down and face averted the assailant made off swiftly towards the bridge, with the anguished protest of 'Bloody hooligan!' ringing in his ears.

Early that evening and in buoyant mood, he returned to the station eager to mull over his conclusion with Nathan. After a few cheery exchanges with the duty officer he walked along the passage towards the chief inspector's room. The air, normally redolent of pipe smoke, seemed unusually mild, and for a wild moment Jennings wondered if Nathan had broken the damn thing or been persuaded to take the smokers' pledge.

He knocked on the door but had no reply, and on gingerly turning the handle found it locked. He was surprised and felt a pang of disappointment.

He returned to the reception desk. 'Where's the chief inspector?' he asked the clerk. 'Wednesday isn't his night off.'

'Oh yes it is – leastways, this Wednesday is. It's his birthday and he's taken his missus to the pictures in Lowestoft.'

'Huh,' Jennings snorted huffily, 'he would, wouldn't he! And just when I've got something important to tell him.'

'Ah well, I expect it'll keep till the morning. But meantime he's given me these for you to do. They are the files on the Blyford burglary case. He wants you to go through them again and make any adjustments.' The constable handed him a thick set of dossiers. 'He told me to say that they shouldn't take you too long but to be sure to have them ready first thing.' The constable gave a cheerful leer and Jennings scowled.

As directed, the following morning Jennings presented his boss with the dossiers neatly stacked and duly checked.

'It took me quite a time to shuffle them into the right order,' he remarked tartly, 'all over the place, they were; added at least fifteen minutes to the job. Whoever was at them last must have been in a right old hurry.'

'I was,' replied Nathan dourly.

Jennings sighed inwardly. As he had suspected. 'Er, I've been thinking,' he began.

'So I gather,' the other interrupted, 'it was the first

thing Webb apprised me of when I arrived. "Sir," he said, "DS Jennings has got something of the utmost significance to impart, and doubtless has been dwelling upon the matter the whole night through."' Nathan gave a lopsided grin and reached for his tobacco pouch. 'So what is it?'

'It's to do with the Tildred case,' Jennings replied stiffly.

'Oh yes? Solved it, have you?'

Ignoring that, Jennings explained his theory about the motive having been fear: that the girl constituted a threat to someone – probably because of something she knew and could thus reveal – and that it had been imperative to keep her quiet. 'She was a deadly danger and had to die!' he observed with sober relish.

Nathan regarded him expressionlessly. And then rather to Jennings' surprise, nodded and said, 'You could be right, old son. I've been thinking along those lines myself – but it's not exactly glaringly obvious, is it? I mean, on the face of it you'd think she was too flimsy to pose a threat.'

Jennings looked puzzled. 'Flimsy?'

'Yes – too young (only nineteen) and too lightweight. By most accounts she seems to have been a shallow, flighty little thing. An irritant, perhaps, but no more than that – what you might call a tiresome gnat or mosquito, not a blooming great tiger.'

'Ah, but mosquitoes bring malaria,' Jennings said darkly. 'And speaking personally, I'm always ready to swat a gnat, they can be damn persistent.'

'And was she being persistent? Putting the frighteners on somebody?'

'Either that or she had the potential to do so, and they weren't prepared to wait and see.'

'Hmm. Nothing of interest was found in her bedroom. The usual teenage junk, of course, but nothing *useful*, unless you count the postcard from that Hector Klein fellow in London.'

'The one that she had scratched a thick red line through?'

'Yes, that's the one.'

'So why had she done that?'

Nathan shrugged. 'Your guess is as good as mine. All he had written was "I trust the Southwold air is calming the injured spleen." Sounds a daft sort of thing to write, but evidently she didn't think much of it. It's funny, these kids, they get sort of shirty. Take my Hester for example—'

But Jennings wasn't interested in his Hester. 'But maybe the link lies in London,' he said eagerly. 'Perhaps there is somebody there who she had been bugging and who had felt it was time to put a stop to things – to swat the gnat. Yes, London could be the key!'

'Exactly, Jennings. So would you be so kind as to get on the blower to the Kensington lot and liaise with them. Get them to dig out information on her friends and contacts, and then make a list of all the possibles. Ask them if there was any chap she was seeing regularly. Indeed, once you've submitted your preliminary report you may find you need to pay a visit to the smoke yourself – a foretaste of Scotland Yard, as it were.'

His superior smiled benignly, while the subordinate was torn between cursing the mound of paperwork that lay before him and rejoicing in the prospect of an important trip up to London. Did the chief really think he was Yard material? He certainly rarely showed it! Still, you could never tell with Nathan – a bit of an enigma, really, just like the bloody case!

CHAPTER TWENTY

Owing Lady Fawcett and Rosy a lunch, Felix and Cedric had entertained the two ladies at The Crown for supper, during which Angela had quizzed them about the cottage. 'I do trust it is comfortable,' she said, 'you can never be sure with these holiday lets. One does hear the most frightful tales. You know the sort of thing I mean: damp in the bedrooms, mice in the larder and *very* peculiar things in the dustbin!'

They assured her that apart from its name, the cottage couldn't be better. 'I tell you what,' Felix suggested, 'instead of taking coffee here, why don't we take it there? Then you can see the cottage *and* sample some particularly fine chocolate truffles we've just found – home-made in that little shop in Pinkneys Lane. You should get some to take back to London. They beat Fortnum's any day! But come and try ours first.'

Thus it was arranged. And a little later with supper over, the four strolled back to *Cot O'Bedlam* where Felix bustled with the coffee and Cedric presented the vaunted truffles.

Angela sat and scanned the room. 'It's very cosy here,' she observed appreciatively, 'and such pretty wallpaper. But the essential thing is that it's all so comfortable: I can't stand this mania for hard wooden Swedish furniture – most unsettling.'

Her eye fell on the small sofa table where Cedric had left the unsolicited *The Limes of Paradise*. 'Ah, I see you've been given one too. Mine has the most lavish signature sprawled all across the flyleaf. In fact, you can barely see the paper for the ink. What about yours?' She picked up the book, and as she did so a folded sheet of notepaper fell out. 'Oops! Sorry, I've lost someone's place – yours, I daresay, Cedric; Felix only reads *House & Garden* or the *Tatler*.' She smiled at the latter, while Cedric looked blank and said that he hadn't had a chance to look at the thing.

'Well, somebody certainly has, there's this . . . oh, I *see*, it's a letter addressed to Ramsgate. He must have given you his own copy by mistake.'

'What does it say?' Felix asked.

'Say? Well, really, one is hardly in the habit of prying into . . .' But despite such protest, Lady Fawcett began to give the note her casual attention. It was when she whipped out her reading glasses that it was obvious she had found something of interest.

Eventually, and with eyebrows levitated, she silently passed the letter to Felix, who scanned it quickly and

174

then emitted a protracted splutter of mirth. 'Disgraceful!' he brayed.

Rosy grabbed it from him, and with Cedric at her shoulder, read the following:

Dear Mr Ramsgate,

You probably won't remember me, but we've met before – two years ago at a house in Knightsbridge that my uncle had borrowed from a friend. You were in bed with Ida, and Uncle Tommy was roaring with laughter and wearing his underpants on his head – or at least I suppose they were his, could have been Ida's perhaps. I had just happened to open the bedroom door and that was the scene – too funny for words! Of course, Ida was simply furious with me afterwards but I promised not to tell (and never have). Actually, they were terribly sweet and gave me a bicycle that I'd been craving – the sort with silver mudguards, drop handlebars and all the latest gadgets (to soothe the shock, I suppose!) And they funded the most superb holiday in Switzerland (at Le Beau Rivage, if you please!). I'll never forget it and would so love to go again. Fat chance of that!

You haven't changed a bit, and with just that same jaunty chuckle . . . Oh, and talking of remembering and not changing: one of your friends at the party rings a bit of a bell – quite a big one, actually. I am absolutely sure he was the man I saw in the hall when I came back down the stairs to let the dog out from the basement. He was coming out of Uncle Tommy's study – or at least the room he was using while they were staying there – and seemed in a fearful hurry. Neither of us spoke – and, besides, I was still giggling from what I had seen in the bedroom so wasn't really up to saying 'Good afternoon' or anything polite like that! Anyway he dashed out of the front door like a bat out of hell, and when I looked out I saw him getting into a car with another chap in the passenger seat (an odd little geezer with a round face and bright-blonde hair). If he hadn't been in such a hurry I might have asked him if he had been making whoopee with you and the others! I've got rather a good memory and it was definitely someone at your party. Funny old world, isn't it?

I'd love to see you again and – as Aunt Ida would say – have a little powwow about 'this & that'. Incidentally, I've still got your specs case, which I later found under the bed (must have been dropped during the fun & games!). I often did wonder whose initials they were, and now it's obvious! As you know, I'm doing this filming with Bartho Hackle and we're all staying at his cousin's house on the East Cliff. Any messages will find me there. Chow for now,

T. T.

'Crikey,' Rosy breathed, 'who'd have thought it!'

Cedric picked it up and read it again. 'I think,' he said slowly, 'that on the face of it, this is what one could call mild dynamite. You do realise the potential significance?'

'Most certainly,' Lady Fawcett answered cheerfully, 'she had got him over a barrel.'

'And now she is dead,' said Rosy. She hesitated, clearing her throat: 'Uhm, you don't suppose there could possibly be a—'

'A link?' said Cedric. 'Feasible but tenuous. It is a long jump between murder and this letter. We shouldn't fall into the trap of inferring the convenient and making a hypothesis a fact. It could be simply a coincidence. The fact that the girl clearly enjoyed a spot of blackmail does not necessarily mean she was killed because of it.' He gazed at them soberly over the rim of his spectacles.

Felix was unimpressed. 'I'll stick with the hypothesis,' he said, 'and better still with the details of the letter. No wonder Ramsgate didn't want to tarry with us in the high street the other day – too damned embarrassed! I thought he looked shifty.' He tittered, and digging his friend in the ribs, exclaimed, 'I mean to say, all in one bed – wouldn't that make things a trifle congested? I should have thought that—'

'Bound to have been one of those extra wide ones, which are becoming so fashionable: emperor-size or some absurd term,' Cedric replied in a lighter tone. 'Heal's furniture department is full of them, or so I gather. Besides,' he added, 'it may not have been simultaneous; perhaps they had one of those tripartite agreements which—'

'Oh, really,' Rosy protested, 'must you be so prurient? We hardly need to know the details. The point is they had a thing going and Tippy Tildred was blackmailing them for all she was worth, and so together they decided to do her in. It was a joint action. How's that for a theory?'

Cedric wagged his finger at her. 'No. As I said, we must not jump to conclusions; it is so easy to be precipitate. Nevertheless, as a mere theory, one must admit it is very intriguing. For example, if that *were* the case I wonder which of them would be the prime mover.'

Felix sniggered again. 'If you mean who called the bedside shots, I suggest that—'

'No, that is *not* what I meant. I mean who might have the most to lose if the arrangement was ever revealed, and thus who had the most zeal for the disposal?'

'Ah, that's an easy one,' Lady Fawcett said firmly, 'it would be Ida. She was always mean-spirited, and such a crashing social climber!' She spoke with a glint of satisfaction. 'Oh yes,' she declared, 'it's common knowledge: Ida Carshalton already sees herself as a prime minister's wife, and the last thing she would allow is to have either of them compromised by this sort of thing. Rumour has it that her dressmaker is working on an evening frock of tartan taffeta.'

There was a bemused silence as they absorbed this last item of information.

'Er, what's taffeta got to do with things?' Felix enquired.

'I suspect,' said Cedric dryly, 'that the significance lies not with the fabric but the tartan.'

'*Precisely*,' Angela beamed, 'she is obviously preparing to be received at Balmoral. Mark my words, she's convinced the premiership is in the bag.'

'That's a bit premature, isn't it? He isn't even party leader yet,' Rosy objected. 'What about the rival?'

'Oh, Figgins doesn't count, or at least not in Ida's estimation. He's bound to drop out anyway, and then the way will be clear for the Carshaltons . . . Unless,' she added darkly, 'the hanky-panky comes to light, in which case they are ditched. Ida wouldn't like that. She wouldn't like it at all.'

'Hence the suppression of Tippy – at her instigation?'

'Of course,' the other assured her.

'Hmm. Plausible, I suppose. But as a hypothesis – which Cedric is so insistent about – don't you think it begs a large question? I mean, if, as you suggest, Ida is so obsessed with status and public power – albeit via her husband – why on earth would she be so crass as to engage in the sexual thing? A mild discreet dalliance is one thing, but a full-blown three-in-a-bed caper, or whatever the arrangement is, is quite another. Indeed, that goes for him too. For a pair so intent on Downing Street, it strikes me as just a trifle unwise. Wouldn't you say?'

For a moment Lady Fawcett looked downcast; but she rallied and declared authoritatively that in her experience ('years in the diplomatic service with Gregory, you know') there was always the thrill of danger, and that naked ambition was frequently accompanied by naked imprudence.

There was an explosion of titters from Felix, who declared that his immediate ambition was for a naked gin clothed in as little vermouth as possible. The others concurred, and conversation turned to other things: the ineptitude of the second cameraman. 'He made a fearful hash of Felix's profile,' Rosy remarked cheerfully.

* * *

However, the subject was instantly revived. For Lady Fawcett, who had stood up to supervise the mixing of her drink, hesitated and then emitted a sudden gasp. With an uncharacteristic yelp of 'Oh my God!' she sank onto the sofa staring distractedly at Felix's meticulously arranged flowers.

At first he assumed the choice was not to her taste – though was a little surprised as her feelings were not normally so frankly expressed.

He was about to ask what was wrong, when, with one hand gesturing towards the letter and the other clasped to her brow, she cried: '*Borrowed from a friend?* But that was us, Gregory and me! It must have been *our* spare room – when we had the other house in Wilton Place! I've suddenly remembered. We had gone down to Cannes; and because the Carshaltons were in some accommodation fix – caught between buying and selling their house or something – Gregory said they could borrow ours for a few weeks while they sorted things out. It was somewhere around the July or August, yes, that was the time . . . Oh my goodness, to think that *that* sort of thing was going on. One had no idea!' She looked highly indignant.

'But at least it was in the guest room,' Cedric said comfortingly. 'You are sure of that?'

'Oh yes. Ours was locked. And besides, the bed would have been too narrow: Harrods were going to deliver a new one once we were home. I remember that it had a nice deep mattress. But Gregory said it was too soft and insisted on sending it back, such a bore . . .' Her voice trailed off, but revived firmly: 'Anyway, so there you are. *Our* bed is in no way implicated!'

* * *

There was a nonplussed silence as each was torn between shock and mirth.

Rosy was the first to speak. 'Well, I suppose that sort of puts the girl's tale in a tangible context, links it to a definite place and time. All very circumstantial, I know, but maybe we really ought to consider going to the—'

'The police? Oh no,' Lady Fawcett interjected quickly, 'most unwise, if you don't mind my saying. They are bound to jump to the wrong conclusions – I mean, they might think one was involved!'

'But aren't we? We have in our possession this explicit letter left here by Ramsgate himself, and which presumably nobody else has seen. If it were blackmail alone it wouldn't matter a fig, but it's a case of murder – and so presumably the police might think such evidence "germane" to their enquiries.'

'Perhaps. And doubtless they would also think the fact that these absurd antics were enacted in *my* house was equally "germane" to their enquiries. Why, I might be accused of being a madam! And who was this other man down in the hall – not to mention the creature in the car? Just think, there may have been a whole string of them traipsing in and out! No, Rosy, I really think that the less said the better.' It was one of the few times when Rosy had seen Angela Fawcett looking resolute.

Cedric cleared his throat. 'Angela is right: the less said the better. In fact, it could be very dangerous to expose ourselves in that way: we might be accused of slander.'

'But surely—'

'Look,' he said patiently, 'you have just used the term

"evidence"; but that letter is no such thing. While it could be construed as blackmail by those of a cynical mind, such as ourselves, it doesn't make any explicit threats or demands. It could simply be the foolish prattle of a garrulous teenager craving attention. If we go to the police brandishing that note and accusing Ramsgate and the Carshaltons of conspiracy to murder, at best we might be a laughing stock and at worst, as I have said, be accused of traducing the innocent. There is such a thing as calumny. Apart from our conjectures – whether founded or not – we have nothing definite to offer the police, so let us be silent.'

In a way Rosy was relieved by Cedric's response, and indeed its obvious approval from Angela and Felix. She had no desire to be embroiled in more complexity, least of all criminal. True, her head was abuzz with questions, but for the moment she was content to shelve the whole damn thing and to play the part of the average holiday visitor: detached from all matters sinister or murderous! Thus, when Felix offered some more chocolates and suggested a game of rummy, she responded eagerly.

An hour later and when Cedric was helping Angela on with her coat, the latter asked what he intended doing with the letter.

'Oh, the usual thing,' he answered coolly, 'swallow it of course, it's what all the best spies do.'

'Seriously, my dear, what will you do if he asks for it back?'

Cedric shrugged. 'I doubt if he will – not if he's got any sense. There are times, as my wise friend recently remarked, when silence is golden. If I were in his position I should clasp discretion like a lifeline and take a long holiday. He may not have committed murder, but who wants to be exposed to public gossip and ridicule, especially someone of his renown?'

'Hmm. Exactly,' his guest agreed vehemently. 'I'll kill that Ida Carshalton if I ever see her again!'

And with that threat affrighting the summer night, the two ladies began to stroll back up the little path and onwards to the welcoming lights of The Swan.

When she reached her bedroom door, Lady Fawcett turned and whispered to Rosy, 'Remind me to take two aspirin at breakfast: Amy is arriving at midday.'

CHAPTER TWENTY-ONE

For the second night Rosy lay awake for longer than she cared. Cedric's counsel to shelve the whole matter was all very well, but she was assailed by a number of niggling questions. The situation as described by Tippy certainly had its comic element – the makings of a good Whitehall farce, in fact. But unlike such farces, the script had been penned by a murder victim and was not (presumably) an imaginative invention. Despite what Cedric had rather pedantically insisted about the blackmail not being explicit, it was quite obvious that that had been the whole point of the letter.

How seriously had Ramsgate taken it? To have slipped the note casually between the pages of a book suggested not very – and still less to have then mistakenly given that book away. Still, people did have moments of aberration. (Dr Stanley, her brilliant boss, had them all the time!) She wondered if they had met for the requested 'powwow'. And if so, how had he handled it? Like the Carshaltons, with promises of indulgent holidays and presents? Or had he sent her packing with a flea in her ear – or perhaps even more robustly with a threat to report her to the police? Maybe he had ignored the whole thing, made no answer and sat tight hoping that, like a bad dream, it would just dissolve . . . Or had he, after all, as in the best gangster novels, sent a trusted hit man to 'take her out'?

Rosy grinned into the dark. No, despite her own facetious conclusion earlier, that hardly seemed likely. Far more likely (and prosaic) was that Ramsgate had been in the middle of deciding how to handle the girl, when the murderer struck. Thus the question of what response to make had suddenly become irrelevant, and he and the others left horrified and safe.

Rosy plumped the pillow and turned on her side ready for sleep. But just as she closed her eyes she also recalled the other bit of the letter, the bit about Ramsgate's companion emerging from the study next to the hall. According to Tippy he had been at the party. Well, there had been a lot of men at the party and they had all seemed fairly affable and well acquainted with Ramsgate. It could have been one of any number (the old boy who had mistaken her for Lana Turner, for example!). Tippy had coyly implied the man might have been one of the bedroom revellers. But that was pure surmise. And after all, he had been in the hall, not bounding up the stairs!

She closed her eyes and mind, and drifted into sleep. But it was not of the most soothing kind, being beset with images of crime and carnage, plus ludicrous scenes of Tom Carshalton (whom she had never met) crawling furtively on a landing, Lady Fawcett commanding a bordello and poor Robert Kestrel going quietly berserk with a sickle.

Luckily, when she awoke the perturbations of the night seemed far away. From outside her door came the cheerful sounds of the chambermaids' chatter and the buzzing of a hoover. The sun, thrusting its way through the shutters, was almost dazzling; and she was ravenous for breakfast! Somehow the linking of poor Tippy's death to someone in her immediate circle seemed absurd – a lurid fantasy of no account. The girl had been done to death by some stranger, a mindless nutcase visiting Southwold for its salubrious sea air. Yes, that was it.

Of rather more account, Rosy felt, was her promise to remind Angela to take the two aspirin in preparation for her daughter's arrival. She grinned. Amy Fawcett had the temperament and guileless nature not unlike that of a boisterous water spaniel. Lacking her mother's wafting elegance, she made up for it with an explosive zest, which, though often enlivening, could also overwhelm, (hence the aspirin).

Her train was to be met at Darsham by Bartho and Angela. Thus deeming it best to steer well clear of the Fawcett–Hackle reunion, Rosy decided to spend a peaceful time amid the curiosities of the Sailors' Reading Room, followed by a light snack in the cosy tea shop in the high street. Afterwards, she might perhaps have a wander in the precincts of St Edmund's church. The latter held a special resonance – partly because of the ancient beauty of the church itself, and partly because at their last visit to Southwold it had been where she had attended the funeral of Angela's old school friend Delia Dovedale, whose life had been so spectacularly destroyed. Funerals were not particularly Rosy's penchant but that one held a vivid memory, and she recalled that Delia's grave lay unobtrusively beneath one of the several spreading trees . . .

In fact, she had never known the woman; but having once been a guest in her house and privy to all the complexities of her death, it seemed fitting that she should re-pay her respects. There would never be another chance.

At breakfast, and having prompted her companion regarding the aspirin, Rosy asked where Amy would be staying: 'Up with the others on the East Cliff?'

Lady Fawcett frowned. 'I am not sure that the facilities there are entirely suitable: a trifle spartan, I believe. And besides, there is the problem of the dog.'

'Which one – Mr Bates or Pixie?'

'Both, really. They may not approve of each other.' She paused fractionally, and then added, 'And actually I am not sure – protocol being what it is – that it would be entirely fitting for Amy to be under the same roof as Bartholomew; I mean they *are* semi-engaged.'

'But surely that makes it simpler.'

'It may be simple but would it be *safe*? One has to be practical, Rosy. Dear Amy can be so impulsive.'

'Ah . . . so where will she be staying: here with us?'

When her companion shook her head, saying she had secured her a charming room at The Crown, Rosy thought she detected the merest flicker of relief. 'They are most welcoming of dogs,' Lady Fawcett explained, 'and in any case it will be nice for Amy to have a little distance. I am sure she doesn't want to be under her mother's eye all the time.'

Rosy smiled in agreement, but couldn't help wondering for whom the distance would be the greater benefit: daughter or mother.

Breakfast over, Rosy decided to reverse her morning's planned itinerary. Her first visit would be to St Edmund's and to seek out Delia Dovedale's grave. And then, with sober duty accomplished, she would relax in the quaint and cosy Reading Room before enjoying a snack lunch in the high street or perhaps in the back bar of The Crown. The alternative, of course, would be to join the film crew on the East Cliff. Doubtless, the spectacle would be entertaining – but busy and noisy. (The battle sound effects of Tobruk and Sole Bay were ear-splitting, not to mention Bartho's vigorous use of the megaphone!) And for the time being she preferred a restful solitude.

Being in no hurry and glad of the walk, she turned left out of The Swan and took a detour, approaching the church precincts circuitously via the lighthouse and St James Green. It was a beautiful morning, and despite the recent shock and tragedy, Rosy could not help but take pleasure in her surroundings. The bright air held the faintest tang of salt, and the little streets with their huddled sleepy cottages exuded not just charm but a reassuring stability, a sort of protective peace . . . which Rosy knew to be illusory, but savoured all the same.

She meandered down towards Church Green. And as she approached the gate to the churchyard, as with the lighthouse (and although familiar with its location) she felt a start of surprise to be faced with such loftiness towering up amid so modest a context.

She picked her way among the trees and shrubs, seeking Delia's grave. Her recollection was right, and she found it easily enough beneath one of the trees. Rosy stood contemplating the small patch with its clear but modest headstone; and the images of the funeral with all its disquieting consequences flittered before her. A sadness, a regret for one she had never known but of whom she had heard much, stirred within her. And she remembered the portrait over the stairs of the woman whose reputation had been of loudness, but whose eyes had looked quiet and benign . . . Poor Delia.

Rosy started, feeling slightly guilty. Poor Delia? But what of Tippy whom she *had* known: why no feelings for her – or at least only of the impersonal sort? The sort you naturally felt when someone was killed brutally and pointlessly: decent laudatory sympathy but not much else.

She shrugged inwardly. Ah well, the heart was an illogical thing; it couldn't be dictated to. And after a last lingering look at Delia's grave, she turned and walked briskly towards the church.

Rosy had not been inside St Edmund's since the day

of the funeral. And then, of course, it had been filled with people, spectacle and sound. She had been moved, but by the activity rather than the surroundings. Now, in silence and alone, she had a chance to properly look and absorb. She gazed around, awed by the nave's soaring height and its trumpeting angels, the sense of space and light and sheer gracious beauty. It was a world at once majestic and enfolding, a world that soothed yet stirred.

Slowly, she began to walk down the central aisle, her eyes magnetised by the huge intricately decorated rood screen, and beyond that the splendour of the high altar backed by its glowing stained-glass window. The harmony of light and colour drew her on towards the choir stalls where she stopped, delighted by the animal and human figures ingeniously carved on the arm rests.

She put out a hand to caress a monkey's polished head, when a voice behind her said: 'They are enchanting, aren't they? I always think that those medieval craftsmen must have had such fun devising them. Probably the best bit of their project.'

Rosy spun round, expecting to be faced by some clerical official – or, given the graciousness of the surroundings, even a bishop!

It was neither deacon nor bishop, but someone more familiar: one of the guests at the Ramsgate party, Mickey Standish.

'Hello,' he said smiling. 'You may not remember me but we recently met at Vincent's house and tried to exchange a few words against the din. You are Rosy Gilchrist, aren't you?'

She smiled back. 'Yes, I am, and I remember you perfectly well, Mr Standish.'

'Oh, Mickey, please. We may be in solemn surroundings but there's no need to stand on ceremony!'

She laughed and asked him what he was doing there: 'I thought that when you were in Suffolk you spent much of your time fishing.'

'Oh, I do. But I also have a peculiar penchant for ancient churches. My family were as poor as church mice – well, more or less – and so perhaps I have a sort of homing instinct. But this one is particularly lovely and one always finds something new and unexpected. Thus, when I stay with Vincent I generally try to come over here and have a little potter; it's a soothing pastime . . . By the way, I trust you have bid good morning to Southwold Jack?'

'Who's that,' Rosy asked, 'the gravedigger?'

'No,' he laughed, 'the bell-ringer; the little fellow with the red pants and sword and the axe. He's up on the wall there. I'll show you.' He took her to the west end and pointed out the clock-jack soldier, axe poised all ready to strike the bell.

Seeing Rosy's fascination he offered to show her other features, and she readily agreed.

Her guide proved both knowledgeable and witty, and Rosy found the time passed most agreeably. Then as they paused before the font to admire its vivid carvings, he looked at his watch and exclaimed, 'Ah, *tempus fugit*, I fear. I have to drive back to London this afternoon . . . But I tell you what, if you can bear it, would you like to share an early lunch at the King's Head? They do excellent sandwiches and serve very good beer. Any chance?'

Rosy grinned, saying she thought there might be a fair chance. And thus leaving the church they strolled back into the sunshine, crossed St Bartholomew's and made for the pub.

Ensconced in the cosy King's Head they ordered sandwiches, and Mickey persuaded Rosy to try a local beer rather than her usual gin and tonic. To her relief she found her companion as entertaining out of the church as he had been in it, and they quickly fell upon topics of mutual interest, principally baroque painting and the jazz trumpeter Miles Davis. Of the latter Rosy had only scant, albeit appreciative, knowledge; but Standish was obviously an aficionado and he talked enthusiastically about Davis's latest arrangements.

However, slightly to her dismay, he also returned to the subject of her aunt, Marcia Beasley, and the mysterious circumstances that had surrounded her death. This was not a topic Rosy had any desire to pursue, and she listened bleakly when he said cheerfully, 'Oh yes, as mentioned, I came across Marcia a few times in the war. In those days I was pretty young and wet behind the ears, and as an older woman Marcia always struck me as being the epitome of sophistication. She had a boyfriend, didn't she? – well, one of several, I suppose – and occasionally one would see them propping up the Ritz bar. She always looked a hundred dollars!' He regarded her intently, and said, 'Obviously you were much younger than her, but I expect you were close, weren't you?'

Rosy felt a flash of irritation. Why was the man being so damned inquisitive? Just idle curiosity – or was there something darker? Huh, perhaps he was an MI5 snout trying to pump her! But surely they hadn't opened up the whole thing again, had they . . . ? Of course not, she thought impatiently, she was just being hypersensitive about the wretched affair, and he, poor chap, merely showing a polite interest.

'Oh yes,' she replied, 'Aunt Marcia always looked pretty good. But actually, we were never close. I knew very little about her life and she certainly never took any interest in mine!' Rosy gave a light laugh, and bent down to pat a spaniel who had wandered over.

Mercifully, Standish turned to another topic – though also concerning the dead, namely Tippy Tildred. But at least this was something more expected and less personal.

'It's funny about that girl on the sand dunes,' he remarked. 'Not quite what one expects in Southwold! And, of course, ghastly for all of you having known her on the film project. Pretty bad luck on the director too: it must have cast a blight over everything. How is he coping? Or is that the end of it all?'

Rosy assured him that Bartholomew had no intention of cancelling things and was pushing on with his usual zeal. 'Of course he and the scriptwriter have had to make some adjustment to the structure and a couple of the scenes, but other than that he's going great guns.'

'Hmm. From what he was telling me at the party the script is so fluid and gnomic that I should imagine any change would be easily absorbed.' Standish smiled. But then his face clouded as he said, 'But it's such a dreadful business, isn't it? And absurd, really – she was such a kid, or so it struck us at the party: prattling and posing all over the place! Vincent took it rather badly – he had been amused by her, although I had the impression one or two of his female guests were less so. Not one to have endeared herself to the ladies, I imagine! But hell, who would have expected that to happen?'

Rosy nodded. 'Yes, it was an awful shock.' She hesitated and then added quietly, 'Especially as it was us who found her – Bartho, me and Cedric and Felix. We had gone for an evening stroll, and suddenly there she was – lying in front of us. It was terrible.'

Standish winced. 'God, it must have been! What bad luck, coming to Southwold for a bit of a jolly and then being faced with something grotesque like that. Appalling.' He frowned in kindly sympathy, and then after a pause said, 'As mentioned, I'm afraid I've got to get back to London pretty soon, but may I give you my card? Do look me up when you return and perhaps we might grace the portals of Ronnie Scott's jazz club in Gerrard Street. Do you know it? I believe there is rather a choice repertoire scheduled.'

Rosy took his card. 'I have heard of it but I've never been. It sounds fun.'

'Good. That's a date, then. Call me at your convenience, Miss Gilchrist.' He gave her a mocking salute, rose from the table, and negotiating the spaniel now fatly sprawled across the entrance, walked briskly from the pub.

Left alone, Rosy finished her drink and studied his card.

It was a good address: close to Chelsea Embankment. Very chic. The nameplate read *M. Z. Standish, Accountancy Consultant*. She wondered what the Z stood for. Zaccariah? Perhaps she would find out at Ronnie Scott's.

CHAPTER TWENTY-TWO

Amy's arrival on the platform at Darsham was accompanied by much noise, drama and confusion. When the train halted, a window was yanked down and its door violently rattled. The door did not yield. 'It's stuck!' an anguished voice yelled.

'Try the next one,' Bartho was about to yell back, but the next moment he was assailed by a suitcase being hurled from the window. This was followed by a handbag and a bulging holdall. Moments later, accompanied by banshee shrieks, Amy's agitated face appeared two doors further down. 'He's gone!' the girl bellowed.

'What?' Bartho shouted, as he ran towards the carriage.

'Mr Bates – he's disappeared down the other end of the corridor!' She gesticulated wildly in the direction of the engine. 'Tell them to keep the train!' she cried.

Bartho wrenched the door open and hauled the

protesting girl onto the platform. A whistle blew and the engine roused itself. 'They'll take him on to Lowestoft!' Amy wailed. 'He won't like it; he can't stand fish!'

The train, having gone a few yards, lurched to an abrupt halt. A guard's peaked cap poked out from a window near the driver's end. ''Ere,' an irate voice called, 'is this your blooming hound? Good riddance, nasty little beggar!' The next moment the whippet had been tossed unceremoniously onto the platform.

More noise. Yelps from the dog, squeals from the owner. As the two collided, yelps were replaced by staccato barks, and squeals by hooted endearments. Bartho rescued the jettisoned baggage and, as hastily as he could, hustled girl and whippet out of the station and into the car park.

Lady Fawcett had tactfully elected to remain in the car rather than to greet her daughter on the platform. Recalling her own youth, it had seemed diplomatic to allow the two young people to meet on their own. However, having heard a little of the commotion emanating from the station she felt that her decision had been not only kindly, but immensely sensible. She looked at her handbag and wondered if a third aspirin might be injudicious.

'Mummy!' Amy roared as she rushed towards the car, arms waving jubilantly, 'You'll never guess, Mr Bates has been so naughty . . .'

'Oh dear,' murmured her mother, and gave a brave smile.

Other than the traveller's joyful chatter, the journey back to Southwold was uneventful. Amy had, of course, been inquisitive about the murder, but both Bartho and Lady Fawcett had decided that at this early stage the barest details would suffice. The subject was unlikely to go away and there would be plenty of time for the girl to indulge her curiosity.

As they reached the outskirts of the town, Bartho thought it a good idea to make a brief detour before depositing her at The Crown. Thus at the police station they turned left down Pier Avenue and drove to the seafront. 'Ooh,' Amy exclaimed, 'you never told me Southwold had a pier. Has it got slot machines? I'd love to have a go sometime! I've got a lucky streak, you know.'

'No, you haven't,' her mother said, 'you cost me a fortune at the Conservatives' summer fete. They made so much I nearly cancelled my subscription.'

'We'll approach the centre via North Parade,' Bartho said, turning right, 'and then you can get a good view of the lighthouse. It's quite spectacular – it rears up at you from the very midst of the town!'

Amy was duly impressed. But she had also glimpsed the row of colourful beach huts below the promenade. 'How quaint,' she enthused. 'Can one go in?'

'No,' Bartho said quickly, 'they are all private.' He accelerated briskly and steered the car back into the high street and drew up in front of The Crown.

After Amy and her impedimenta had been safely decanted and guest and dog shown the bedroom, Lady Fawcett suggested it would be nice for them all to take a stroll on South Green. 'I expect you and Mr Bates will want to stretch your legs after that long train journey,' she said to

Amy, 'and I'll ask Rosy if she would care to join us.'

Amy thought that a fearfully good idea and that she could then tell them all about her Shropshire visit and the prowess of Mr Bates.

Thus a little later and joined by Rosy, they wandered on to South Green's gracious expanse, where, in time-honoured tradition, the visitor was introduced to the elegant mix of Edwardian and Regency villas skirting its edge, the six canons on Gun Hill, the octagonal casino, and the vast vista of sea, sky and whirling gulls.

The whippet was in its element, sniffing the air and scampering around in an ecstasy of adventure. His capers were interrupted at one point by his mistress, who insisted on placing him on one of the gun barrels for a photograph. Like Felix earlier, the whippet posed obligingly (albeit precariously) and gave a couple of jaunty yaps – though unlike the other film star, seemed reluctant to display his left profile to best effect.

For a few minutes they sat on one of the seats overlooking the sea while Bartho gave Amy a meticulous account of *The Languid Labyrinth*, its layers of meaning, contemporary resonances, subtle ambiguity, and the tantalising fusion of myth and reality. 'If you like Cocteau,' he said earnestly, 'you will love this!'

Amy did not know if she did like Cocteau, or indeed quite who he was. But she did know Alfred Hitchcock. 'I say,' she said, brightly, 'since you are the director, have you given yourself a titchy walk-on part – you know, just to show that you're the boss?' She giggled, and added, 'Perhaps you could even tote Mr Bates behind you on his lead!' She looked fondly at the dog, who, having made its gun-top debut (and perhaps lulled by Bartho's commentary), was now immobile and studying a blade of grass.

'Well,' Bartho replied doubtfully, 'that might be seen as a bit derivative . . . and in any case it's not the sort of film that—'

Fearing that he was about to take the spiel further, Rosy hastily asked about Amy's Shropshire trip.

Amy replied it had been splendid and the dog's contribution first-rate. 'He gave the girls such a nice time,' she enthused, 'and went like the clappers!' Addressing the whippet, she crooned, 'Didn't you, my pretty boy?' The pretty boy regarded her with round innocent eyes and then promptly fell asleep.

'Yes, well we don't need to hear the gruesome details,' her mother said quickly. 'Now, why don't we all have a nice ice cream? They do excellent ones in that shop in Queen Street.' She gestured towards the edge of the green and set off smartly. The dog, roused from its well-earned rest, followed dutifully.

CHAPTER TWENTY-THREE

Cedric had fallen asleep at midnight, but in his usual way had woken at three: the usual pattern of the elderly, he supposed. Elderly? No, of course not – he wouldn't be that for at least another decade! Nevertheless, it was something that those beyond a certain age seemed to share. Come five o'clock he would doze off again until seven perhaps, or with luck seven-thirty. But until then there was always the crossword. He stretched out his arm for the bedside light and picked up the discarded newspaper.

He had just polished his reading glasses and embarked on the third clue down, when he heard a faint noise: a sort of creaking, scrabbling sound coming from below. Very slight but distinctly there.

In his warm bed, Cedric froze. A rat? He had always had a fear of rats ever since a friend of his had related an anecdote of finding one sitting on the driving seat of his tank in the Ardennes. 'I kid you not,' his friend had declared, 'he was the size of Göring and with a face like Goebbels.' Apparently, the creature had scampered away, but such had been the drama of the narrative that it had always remained in Cedric's imagination. However, dismissing such nonsense, he concentrated his attention on the crossword. It really was a devil this week; the setter was clearly of a fiendish bent . . .

Oh hell, there it was again! A definite click. And what was that, a footfall? Ridiculous! It was doubtless Felix gone to spend a penny. But in which case surely he would have seen the passage light under the door; Felix was not one to blunder around in darkness. No fear, arc lamps at full blast!

Cedric lay and cogitated. If it wasn't a rat all would be fine – he could investigate with impunity . . . But of course it wasn't a bloody rat, he thought impatiently, merely one of those 'things that go bump in the night' – the bugbear of an insomniac. Still, perhaps he ought just to listen on the landing, but he certainly had no intention of traipsing all the way downstairs.

He got up and cautiously opened the bedroom door and cocked an ear. Apart from the slow ticking of the clock from the kitchen, there wasn't a sound. He closed the door, but before returning to bed opened the window and peered out . . . Nothing. Darkness and the hoot of an owl . . . Or had there been something else? He couldn't be sure. But as he was about to adjust the curtain he thought he saw a faint glow of light at the curve in the lane. A torch, a car headlamp? Perhaps the moon wafting from a cloud, its beam flickering in the branches of a tree . . . Well, it wasn't a rat, that was for sure, and it probably wasn't anything else of consequence. There was another cottage further up the lane. Perhaps its occupants had been out admiring the night sky or returning from some late-summer ritual, or whatever it was the denizens of Southwold did at three in the morning!

Cedric clambered back into bed, where, jettisoning the crossword and worn out by the unaccustomed activity, he fell fast asleep until breakfast time.

'Well, you were making a racket in the night,' grumbled Felix, helping himself liberally to marmalade and toast, 'enough to wake the dead! It's a wonder I didn't have a nightmare.'

Cedric shrugged. 'I thought I heard something, that's all.'

'Heard something? I should think you did, crashing about like that! I thought you were going to wrench the window out of its casing!'

'It was a trifle stiff. It's the wood in these old cottages, it gets warped,' Cedric replied indifferently.

'Like a lot of us,' Felix quipped, 'including that Kestrel fellow. He was most uncivil the other day. I had merely said that I thought his handling of the breakwater scene was a trifle exaggerated, and he scowled like hell and said what did I know about acting. I ask you! Simply no manners, some people.' He consulted his watch. 'Oh my goodness, never a dull moment! I must dash for the next shoot. Apparently I am to reappear at the height of the Somme as some dead Tommy.' He hesitated and frowned. 'Though why not an officer, I cannot imagine. See you later!'

Left alone, Cedric finished his breakfast at a placid pace and even completed five more clues from the previous night's failure. He then thought about Felix and gave a rueful smile. These celluloid capers were beginning to take him over, which was all very well provided the interest was confined to Southwold. To have it continued in London would be wearisome. Once back in town he must steer him firmly in the direction of *Bountiful Blooms* again and the floral requirements of the Queen Mother. It was time normality was resumed! There was a crash in the porch: the paperboy with the morning's delivery. Cedric retrieved it, eager to see the crossword solutions. Then, the main task done, he glanced at the editorial column . . . Hmm, the usual mix of gloom and facetiousness. He scanned the previous page and noticed an article on the Covent Garden flower market – its charm and historic role in supplying the nation's florists. How timely. He would cut it out for his friend's attention as a subtle reminder of the real world.

Having checked the obituary column (an essential daily perusal), he was about to clear the breakfast things when his eye fell on an item concerning the recent party political conference. *MP for North Finsborough on Sparkling Form* the headline ran. Cedric frowned slightly. North Finsborough? Why did he know that name? Oh, of course, it was the constituency of Tom Carshalton, relative of the Tildred girl. He read on.

What had the makings of a rather staid assembly in Eastbourne last week was certainly given a welcome fillip by Tom Carshalton. Long regarded for his genial style and safe judgement, he has now shown himself a remarkable mimic and comic raconteur – a talent that won him much applause (and surprise) from the delegates. We have to admit that in comparison with the PM's rather lacklustre performance Carshalton struck a very lively note, delighting party loyalists not just with his merry wit but by some hard-hitting thrusts at the opposition. It was an impressive contribution – and perhaps the prime minister should take note.

Cedric raised an eyebrow. On sparkling form, was he? Full of merry wit? How resilient of Carshalton to be the life and soul of the party conference while his young relative had just been brutally murdered and the funeral not yet held. Evidently a rising star and not one to be fazed by such an event . . . But then, he reflected, perhaps that was the mark of a true politician: to hold steadfast in the field of battle and not be deflected by such personal bombshells. Clearly a man of dedicated ambition. A bit like young Hackle, really.

Yes, indeed, as Angela had remarked, given the grim circumstances Bartholomew was being remarkably sanguine. After all, the girl had been a member of his cast. He had known her in London and must have thought she had some quality to offer – if only as a foil to the lavish Alicia. And yet, a bit like Carshalton, he seemed relatively detached from the event. It was the film that absorbed his emotional energies, that and preserving the reputation of his cousin's beach hut. Still, Cedric mused, you never quite knew with the young: a bit like Hartley's past, they were a foreign country and did things differently there. Or so it often seemed.

He wondered idly what the boy had done with the two things they had found on the floor of the hut, the lipstick top and the Monaco franc. Kept them safely? Shoved casually into a pocket? Or (and it wouldn't surprise him) thrown firmly into the sea? As far as he was aware, Hackle hadn't mentioned them again. Perhaps he should make a mild enquiry . . . Or would that seem officious?

His mind turned to something else: the weather. It had been drizzling earlier on, but over breakfast the gloom had lifted to be replaced by a surly sun, which now had suddenly burgeoned into blazing light. A lover of heat, Cedric's instinct was to retire into the conservatory and bask lizard-like, but stern duty directed him elsewhere. He would take the opportunity to go for a brisk walk across the Common . . . No, not a brisk walk, a relaxing ramble to savour the pleasure of summer sunshine and the unaccustomed freedom of rural space. He would take his camera and perhaps have a potter around the imposing water tower, which, like the lighthouse, had become a Southwold landmark and entirely dwarfed its modest neighbour, the Victorian original. So far he had only viewed it from a distance and this would be the time to look more closely. It was hardly an aesthetic edifice, but certainly striking and well worth closer investigation.

He set out full of purpose along Godyll Road skirting the Common – but was waylaid by a cricket ball flying from the direction of Eversley House, the boys' prep school. Luckily, it didn't hit him, but it was a near miss. Small boys rushed forward to utter shrill and grovelling apologies; and indignant though he had been, Cedric was sufficiently disarmed to linger some time at the edge of the turf and applaud their game.

As he watched he pondered his own youth. Had he really had that raucous energy and bounding zest? He supposed he must have, but couldn't be sure, and certainly not on the cricket pitch or rugger field (far too cold and windy!). Fencing had been his preferred pastime at school, that and a little table tennis. But the more rumbustious sports had eluded him – and he them. There had, of course, been chess, he mused, and also—

'Howzat!' A falsetto voice yelled, and Cedric's ruminations were broken.

He continued on his way towards the tower, stopping occasionally to gaze up at the sky and admire the swirling undulations of an orange kite. Its fluttering progress awoke childhood memories, and with a start he recalled the curious exhilaration of being in control of something so high and so remote.

But then for some reason (a twittering lark, a cheer from the schoolboys?) he glanced back, and saw walking some yards behind him a man with a dog. The dog was scruffy, the man familiar: the policeman Nathan.

Dog and handler looked much the same, both heavy-jowled and of bloodhound mien. And for one wild moment Cedric wondered if the hound was a trained sniffer and he was being trailed by the Southwold constabulary. Surely not. Really, he was becoming like Felix: paranoid! Clearly, Nathan was off duty and simply taking his own pet for a walk. Pet? The creature looked distinctly dodgy to Cedric.

But then so did its master. For as the chief inspector drew level (Cedric having paused to allow the straining creature room to thrust past), he coughed and hesitated as if about to say something; but then, slightly to Cedric's surprise, pressed on. Whether such volte-face was due to the strength of the dog or to Nathan having second thoughts, Cedric was unsure. But he was relieved, anyway. The chap had clearly recognised him, and the last thing Cedric wanted was to be further reminded of the murder at such a time as this. He was here to relax, dammit!

But it was too late. The sight of the police inspector had unsettled him, and the appeal of the water tower began to fade as once more his mind was beset with images of the beach hut and what they had found there. He wondered again whether he should ask Hackle if he had kept the two 'clues'. There were two options: to satisfy his curiosity by mentioning it to the young man (albeit perhaps risking a snub), or tactfully to say nothing and thus remain in ignorance. Hmm . . . tricky.

He recalled the way the chief inspector had just looked at him: not suspiciously, exactly, but with a distinctly quizzical glint. He had definitely been about to speak. Perhaps the police had found something or had a fresh theory and were thus planning another spate of questions. If that were the case, then the second option of not saying anything to Hackle would be by far the more sensible. After all, if one knew nothing how could one possibly comment? Yes, when in doubt a discreet silence was invariably the best course, as was keeping a discreet distance. After all, it was the Hackles' hut, and it was entirely up to Bartholomew what he did with those things. Why should he and Felix get dragged in?

He continued in the direction of the tower, stopping to take a couple of photographs. But somehow its interest had palled, as had the sunlit marshes. And instead of moving closer he decided to return to the cottage and follow his original instinct: to sit in the warmth of the conservatory or on its veranda and immerse himself in making notes for his new researches. A most agreeable prospect. And perhaps by that time the troubling picture of the beach hut and its possibly gruesome secret would have been erased . . . or at least blurred.

CHAPTER TWENTY-FOUR

'Oh, by the way,' Felix said later that day, 'I bumped into Rosy Gilchrist earlier on and she wants us to join her and Angela for a drink this evening. I gather Amy has arrived and Bartholomew is taking the girl out for a gargantuan feast somewhere – The Wentworth at Aldeburgh, I think. So apart from the pleasure of our scintillating company, they think it would be a chance to have another look at the letter that Ramsgate left here. Apparently, Angela is worried.'

'Huh, not the only one,' Cedric replied, glancing up from his reading. 'I happened to encounter that police inspector this morning, Nathan, and he gave me some very sideways looks! I can't think why, unless they are about to give us another grilling. It's all most annoying . . . Anyway, when does Angela want us?'

'About six-thirty on the dot. We must remember to

take the letter. I know you joked about swallowing it but I assume it's still in the book?'

'Yes. It's clipped to the end of the fourth chapter, the one called "Heavenly Riches" or some such absurdity.' Cedric returned to his Trollope. But not for long.

'I have a theory,' Felix announced suddenly.

'Really?' said Cedric, slightly surprised. 'What about?'

'The crime, of course. It's not about the price of fish, you know!'

'Er, no, of course not,' Cedric replied hastily, putting the book aside.

Felix leant forward in his chair. 'That Tippy Tildred, how many times had she applied blackmail?'

'Well, obviously to Ramsgate in that letter, but—'

'Yes, as you say, obviously. But what else had been implied there?'

Cedric pondered, not quite sure what to answer.

'If you can't remember, I will remind you,' his friend said helpfully. 'She had made reference to her aunt and uncle, the Carshaltons. She had talked about their having given her a bicycle and funding an expensive trip to Switzerland. This apparently was shortly after she had interrupted them romping in the Fawcetts' spare bedroom. There was absolutely no reason for her to mention it in the letter except to imply to Ramsgate that if he wanted the matter kept secret he too would be expected to produce similar largesse. In other words, she had been milking them, and now, having recognised Ramsgate as the third person on the bed, she was going to try him.'

'Yes, all right, so she had two potential sources, we already know that.'

'But she had a third as well.'

Cedric looked perplexed.

'Robert Kestrel, of course. You may recall what Rosy Gilchrist told us: that she had said he had made a play for her and then couldn't deliver the goods, and that she was so angry that she had threatened to tell his wife. She may not have applied blackmail as such, or at least not then, but she had obviously made it clear to him that she had information that she could divulge should she care to. It strikes me that here was a girl who was both spiteful and unscrupulous and also bold. She had no qualms about confronting or riling people. I mean, consider her attitude to you and me – no respect or courtesy, brazen in fact! And I bet that before long she would have tried it on us as well if she thought she could get away with it.' Warming to his theme, Felix looked indignant.

'Er, perhaps, but I am not quite clear—'

'What I am saying is, that judging by her track record and general manner, there may have been others whom she had approached and who, for one reason or another, she had made to feel vulnerable. Take that chap in London, for example – Hector Klein, the one who had dropped her. Admittedly, Hector drops everyone. But it had obviously rankled, as Alicia said she had been hopping mad and was vowing revenge. So who knows, she may have been threatening him just as she had Kestrel.'

Cedric was unconvinced. 'Hmm. Feasible, I suppose, but likely?'

'I bet you,' said Felix darkly, 'that she had a string of potential victims, and that any one of them might have decided she was a better bet dead than alive.'

Cedric laughed. 'Fair speculation, I suppose. But anyone in particular?'

Felix sniffed, nettled by Cedric's mirth. 'Not especially, but the name Hackle comes to mind.'

Cedric stopped laughing abruptly and stared at his friend. 'Bartholomew? But why?'

'One gathers they had known each other in London, though exactly how closely one doesn't know; but certainly before the advent of Amy. Who knows, like the sensible Klein, he may have discarded her in favour of Amy Fawcett, and out of vengeful pique she was putting the frighteners on him about some dark secret that he doesn't want his future mother-in-law to know. Angela can be very picky when she chooses.'

'I think your remarkable brain has overlooked something,' Cedric observed dryly, 'something that blows your theory to pieces. If Hackle had murdered her he would hardly have invited us all into that beach hut where the thing had been done – or apparently done.'

There was a long pause while Felix frowned and considered Cedric's objection. Eventually, he shrugged: 'Bravado,' he said carelessly. 'They can get like that, murderers, it's the thrill of the thing – that or vanity. It's a well-known trait: they like to chance their arm.' He gave a firm nod, thus clinching the theory.

Cedric regarded his friend thoughtfully. 'On the whole, dear chap,' he murmured, 'I think your skills of imaginative concoction vastly outdo your skills of deduction . . . Now, why don't you go and concoct us something *exquisite* for tomorrow's supper while I finish this chapter. And then, time allowing and as we have plenty of lemons, we might give ourselves a little treat with a couple of White Ladies: something to line the stomach in preparation for our charming companions.'

Felix beamed and took his fertile mind off to bustle inventively in the kitchen.

In fact, the proposed cocktails were unforthcoming, for something intervened to curtail matters.

Twenty minutes later and culinary issues evidently settled, Felix came back on to the veranda. 'I can't see it,' he said.

'What?'

'Ramsgate's letter; it's not there.'

'Oh, of course it is,' Cedric replied irritably, 'you haven't looked properly.'

Felix sniffed. 'If you say so. I'll leave it to you to find. Personally, I am going to have a bath: it's been the most gruelling day. This morning our revered director changed his mind yet again about one of the scenes and I had to repeat it endlessly; and then, in the afternoon, Fred expected me to walk that monstrous dog of his while he did something technical to his camera. I can't think what, but it took ages and my right arm is utterly worn out with throwing sticks for Pixie. And it's not as if she prances after them, but lumbers relentlessly; and then if you stop throwing the things she heads you in the butt. Exhausting!' He retired upstairs to the balm of the bath salts.

Meanwhile, Cedric continued reading to the end of his chapter, and then laying the book aside, went to find the other.

It was still on the sofa table where he had left it. He picked it up and flipped through the pages to the end of chapter four, 'Heavenly Riches'. There was nothing there. He leafed through the other pages, even shaking the damn thing in the vain hope the letter might have somehow got stuck and would fall out. But Felix was perfectly right: there wasn't a sign.

Cedric swore softly in frustration. Where the hell was it? He knew he had put it there, and now he came to think of it, had even used a paper clip. He stared in bafflement at the page where the letter should have been. For God's sake *why* wasn't it there? One's mind played tricks, he knew that well enough. But not in this instance, surely. He could remember the scene vividly: making the joke about swallowing it, folding it in half, taking a paper clip from the desk and fixing it securely, shutting the book and putting it back on the table . . . Of course, if he was really going mad doubtless such vivid images would be par for the course. But he was not going bloody mad, he was as sane as anyone else!

He paced about the room fretting and cursing, an exercise interrupted by Felix in the doorway, clad in what at first sight appeared to be a Roman toga, but which Cedric recognised as his friend's new dressing gown. Damp from the steam, the *en brosse* hairstyle stood up in fretwork spikes, and the air was filled with an odour not of sanctity, but a heady cologne of industrial pungency.

Despite his agitation, or perhaps because of it, Cedric couldn't resist a little mockery: 'Ah, enter Caligula,' he observed dryly, 'arrayed and scented and poised for slaughter. I take it the bath was to His Imperial liking?'

The diminutive emperor tossed his head and indicated the proposed cocktail would be welcome.

Cedric shook his head. 'Fix it yourself. I have more urgent matters to attend to.'

Felix was startled. 'More urgent? I can't think what.'

Cedric sighed helplessly. 'You were quite right, Ramsgate's letter is not in the book, yet I know I left it there.'

After making the usual hints and suggestions to jog his friend's memory, Felix fell silent, and instead helpfully poured Cedric a bracing whisky. 'Try this,' he urged jocularly, 'it's just the thing for confusion and amnesia.'

'I have *told* you, I am suffering from neither,' Cedric retorted testily. But he accepted the glass gratefully and took a sip. Excellent! He closed his eyes. And then a happy thought struck him: 'Ah, very likely it was the cleaning lady. She probably picked up the book while dusting, saw the letter, read it and kept it. Yes, that's it, the only explanation. I shall have to speak to her firmly!' He took a further, triumphal, sip of his whisky.

There was silence. And then Felix cleared his throat. 'Well,' he said slowly, 'that *would* make sense, except that we only found that letter after her last session. And she is not due again until tomorrow. The woman hasn't been here.'

His friend groaned and stared disconsolately at the carpet. But as he did so something tiny caught his eye: a piece of glinting silver metal. He got down onto his hands and knees and crawled to where it lay in front of the table . . . Yes, as he had hoped, it was the paper clip. Vindicated!

'Well, at least now we know you are not barking,' Felix remarked cheerfully. 'But it still doesn't tell us what happened to the letter.'

'What happened to the letter was that somebody took it. And not being the cleaning lady, it was somebody else,' Cedric replied grimly. 'Whoever it was found it in the book, pulled it out, and in so doing dislodged the paper clip.'

'Well, don't look at me,' Felix exclaimed. 'As Rosy Gilchrist so kindly observed yesterday evening, I only read the *Tatler* and *House & Garden*.'

Cedric shook his head. 'Oh, not you, dear boy. We've had an intruder, that's what.'

'An intruder – when?'

'Last night, of course, when I was "blundering about" and disturbing your sleep by opening windows. I thought I had heard some sounds downstairs, but dismissed the whole thing – it seemed so improbable.'

They stared at each other in puzzled dismay. And then Felix, hearing the kitchen clock strike six, cried, 'Oh lord, it's nearly time to go to The Swan. If we don't hurry we shall be late and find the ladies prone in a fume of gin. Quick, we must change. On with the motley!'

They hurried to get ready, but not before Cedric had said wryly, 'Well, this won't reduce Angela's worry, not one bit it won't!'

Their news produced shock and scepticism, plus, as Cedric had predicted, alarm from Lady Fawcett. 'But it's back in circulation now,' she protested, 'and anyone may get hold of it. And should it be revealed that it was *my* house where these things happened I shall never live it down! And supposing Amy gets to hear of it? She would be most embarrassed, especially when things are going so well with her and Bartholomew.' She looked reproachfully at Cedric. 'And I thought it was so safe with you. I really think you should have taken better care of it!' She sounded uncharacteristically annoyed and Cedric felt chastened.

'Look,' Rosy said, trying to defuse matters, 'I very much doubt if it exists at all by now. It will be torn in pieces or gone up a chimney in smoke. Obviously, the whole point of the break-in was to retrieve the thing and then destroy it.'

Lady Fawcett looked mildly mollified, and Cedric nodded in agreement. 'Exactly. And more to the point, who was responsible? Ramsgate, presumably – although somehow I can't envisage him sneaking in so silently. Unobtrusiveness is not exactly his style. Still, I remember his saying he had been a commando in the war – unlikely though it seems – so he must have some skills in stealth and daring, I imagine.'

'And was he also a lock-picker?' Rosy enquired.

'Didn't have to be,' said Felix. 'Needless to say, as the name implies, *Cot O'Bedlam* wisely kept its spare key under the mat. I tripped and noticed it there the other day. I meant to remove it but was in such a tearing hurry to get to the film studio I forgot all about it. The intruder may have come prepared to force a lock, but he certainly didn't have to. It was an open door, virtually.'

'But how did he know where to look?' Lady Fawcett asked. 'I mean, that letter could have been anywhere.'

'A lucky guess,' Cedric said, 'and one that paid off.

Ramsgate had realised he had left the thing in his book, and after bumping into Felix and me the other day may have assumed that that's where it had remained. At the time I was rather irritated with the chap and made it very clear that I really hadn't had a chance even to glance at the thing. He seemed relieved, and firmly advised me not to give it another thought until I was back in London. In fact, he made rather a point of it. So perhaps, based on that hope he took a long shot: came to the cottage, checked under the mat first, as all good burglars do, entered the drawing room, saw the book on the sofa table – it's quite a hefty volume with a vivid jacket – opened it up, found the letter, cried "Yippee!" and buggered off. His hunch had worked.'

Cedric took a long sip of his whisky and sat back, rather pleased with his account.

'I am sure you are right in all the ancillary details,' Felix murmured approvingly.

The other looked at him sharply. 'What do you mean "ancillary"? What's so ancillary about them?' Cedric sounded indignant.

'They are ancillary because the central character in your scenario wasn't here last night. He was in London giving a live broadcast about his precious *The Limes of Paradise*.'

'Oh? And how do you know that?'

'Because Sam Thwaite, our scriptwriter, had heard the broadcast and was telling us about it this morning. According to him it should have been cut by half and then some.'

'Well, that is hardly conclusive,' Cedric replied, nettled. 'He could have delivered the talk and then driven back here in time to break into our cottage.'

'Not really. The talk was one of those late-night ones on the Third Programme. Apparently, it didn't begin until eleven and then there were questions afterwards. The noises you heard were at about one-thirty. Even if Ramsgate had left Broadcasting House by half-midnight and driven like the clappers, he wouldn't have got here by that time.'

Cedric said nothing but spread his hands in a gesture of acceptance.

'Mind you,' Rosy said thoughtfully, 'although Tippy sent the letter to Ramsgate he wasn't the only one who might have been concerned about it. I mean, what about the Carshaltons? They have a lot to lose, should things come to light.' She glanced slyly at Lady Fawcett, and added, 'Even a bit more than you, Angela.'

Lady Fawcett said nothing, except to mutter that she wouldn't trust that Ida Carshalton an inch.

Cedric reflected on the newspaper article he had read that morning reporting the MP's strong performance at the party conference. Both from that, and from earlier press references, he suspected that beneath the amiable exterior there lay a tenacious will. The man knew what he was doing all right, and what he wanted. Would that include engineering the break-in – perhaps by sending some loyal minion to do his dirty work? Conceivably.

On the other hand, would he have known about the letter in the first place? They had been assuming that Ramsgate had relayed Tippy's mischief to his merry bedfellows; but there was no proof of that. Perhaps he had kept quiet on the subject . . . It was possible, but probable? Unlikely. After all, as he had told them himself, Ida had been staying with him only recently in his house at Reydon when she had come to view the body. They were old intimates, in every sense. He was bound to have confided the matter to her – and she in turn to her husband. One way or another Carshalton would have surely known.

These thoughts and others were shared and debated, and no firm conclusions reached . . . except that as the letter was no longer in their possession they had nothing concrete to offer the police – even had they wished to. 'Why,' Felix declared, draining his glass, 'they would think we were a bunch of fruitcakes and making it up as we went along!'

'I still think that Ida Carshalton had a hand in it somehow,' Lady Fawcett muttered darkly, 'you mark my words.' She turned to Cedric: 'Well, my dear, I trust you won't hear any more bumps in the night – all most unsettling. Still, I suppose that danger is passed now – although personally I would check the back door mat as well. Pull up every drawbridge, that's my advice. Clearly, Southwold is a hotspot for danger.' She gave a smile, but glancing at her watch, replaced it with an anxious sigh: 'Oh dear, I do hope Amy is having a nice time with Bartholomew and that the dog is behaving itself; the last thing one wants is any more upheaval!'

CHAPTER TWENTY-FIVE

Angela's disquiet regarding her daughter and the dog was mercifully unfounded, for Amy's report of her evening at Aldeburgh with Bartho had been rapt and fulsome.

'Oh yes,' she enthused, 'they really did us proud. A wonderful menu – better than in London, I can tell you! Masses of fish things and mussels, and some lovely creamy scallops. I simply didn't know where to begin!' She paused, and then added, 'Well, actually, we began with champagne and sort of went on from there.' There was an explosive laugh: 'And do you know, the waiter even asked if Mr Bates would like some in a saucer. Wasn't that sweet? But I said no fear, he had had too many treats already and I certainly didn't want a tipsy whippet on my hands!' More peals of laughter.

'And what about Bartholomew?' her mother asked. 'I

hope he enjoyed himself. It was really a very generous treat.'

'Oh *yes*, he was on crashing form – we both were, and had *so* much to talk about.'

Lady Fawcett smiled (privately trusting that the other diners had enjoyed as merry a time as the young couple). Her smile wavered slightly when Amy went on to say how fascinated Bartho had been by Mr Bates's Shropshire exploits.

'Er, is that what you were telling him about at dinner?' she enquired casually.

Amy nodded. 'Yes, some of the time – though, of course, I also insisted he should give me details of the murder . . . But do you know, Mummy, he said that obviously Mr Bates was a very gallant little fellow and clearly had a lot of stamina. And I said, "You bet – gallant *and* lucrative!" Bartho was very impressed.'

'Well, that's nice,' Lady Fawcett murmured, again wondering about the other diners. With luck, most might have been deaf.

Returning to The Swan she encountered Rosy, just returned from a perplexing session at the film studio (the film's tortuous narrative did not get any clearer). And after her own session with Amy, Lady Fawcett suggested that some tea might be welcome.

Thus they sat in the lounge and chatted, and Rosy raised the question of the murdered girl's funeral. 'It may be ages before it is announced. I mean, I suppose it all depends on when the police are happy to release the body, though maybe they've done that already. I wonder if it will be in private or a big public thing – and if the latter, do you think one should attend?'

Her companion cogitated. 'Since you were one of the unfortunate finders of the poor girl you might perhaps consider it appropriate – though certainly not a requirement. But speaking for myself, I shall feel no such obligation. A bouquet of flowers will be fitting. I normally send lilies – though dear Gregory couldn't stand them. For his funeral I had to substitute the most garish gladioli, his favourite flowers. It was really rather embarrassing, they looked so abrasively vulgar on the coffin – red and yellow, I recall. But then anything to give the poor boy pleasure . . .' Her voice trailed off and she looked wistful.

'So what will you choose for Tippy?' Rosy asked gently.

'What? Oh, Tippy . . . well, not lilies, too dignified. Something vivid and skittish: some colourful freesias, perhaps. She might have liked those . . . But,' and Lady Fawcett lowered her voice confidingly, 'I can tell you one thing, Rosy, I have no intention of attending the service itself. After all, people might think I was in some way associated with the Carshaltons!'

At that moment they were interrupted by a member of staff. 'Excuse me, Miss Gilchrist,' the girl said, 'but there's a telephone call for you. Will you take it in your room? I can put it through for you if you like.'

Rosy was startled. Apart from a couple of girlfriends, she didn't think anyone knew she had left London. 'Male or female?' she asked.

'It's a gentleman,' the girl answered.

'In that case best take it in your room,' Lady Fawcett whispered, 'always safest.'

Rosy laughed and stood up to do as suggested.

She mounted the stairs wondering who on earth it could be. Most of her male friends lived in London or thereabouts, and in any case why should any of them want to suddenly contact her here?

She was puzzled – and then a name struck her: Mickey Standish. He certainly knew she was staying at The Swan, and perhaps after their meeting the previous day and his slightly hasty departure, he wanted to continue the conversation. Or more likely, simply confirm the jazz club invitation. She went to the phone expecting to hear his voice, and when she didn't, felt oddly disappointed.

In fact, the voice she heard was familiar – too damn familiar. The caller was not Standish, but Stanley: Dr Stanley, her boss from the British Museum. Rosy cursed. Surely to goodness he didn't want her to get him some more Southwold rock! She closed her eyes and listened to the insistent tones.

Initially, he was all brisk bonhomie, but she knew it wouldn't last. He wanted something: to cut short her leave? To organise an exhibition he had forgotten to tell her about? Or simply to remind him where he had left a set of lecture notes? Oh well, she would find out soon enough.

'I heard that there had been a murder up there, and naturally assumed the victim was you,' he said jovially, 'so I thought I ought to telephone just in case.'

'In case of what?'

'In case I had lost an invaluable assistant, of course!' There was a rasping laugh, which stopped abruptly; and the voice took on the old conspiratorial urgency.

'You see, Rosy, being in Southwold I think you may be in a position to help me,' he began earnestly.

'Oh, I see, you want me to procure a stick of rock, do you?'

'Since you mention it, no. Though if you could procure me some Adnam's ale, I should be grateful. You have a car, I gather. So transport shouldn't be a problem.' (Huh, she thought, walked right into that, didn't I?)

'Ale apart,' he continued, 'I want you to help me with a little project I have in mind. I have persuaded the museum Gauleiters that our department should mount a display of nineteenth- and twentieth-century travel writing. We have an excellent collection and many of the works are accompanied by some fine sketches and photographs. But in addition to the material itself, I am proposing that we should invite three eminent travel writers to give a short series of lectures on the subject. By way of introduction, I myself will deliver a general overview of the genre and its development. And by dint of my consummate charm I have managed to persuade the splendid Freya Stark and James Morris to honour us with their presence. As you know, they are two of the most brilliant exponents of the genre. It will be a most prestigious affair.' A smug chuckle reached her ears. 'You must admit, it's amazing what a little judicious tact can achieve. The museum is lucky to have me! Wouldn't you agree?'

'Oh, absolutely. Without your saving presence there

would be mayhem and utter ruin. So who's your third contributor?'

'Ah . . . as yet unsecured. Which is where you come in, Rosy. Naturally, he is not in the same league as the other two (far too lush and florid) – but the chap is popular, colourful, a lively communicator and commands a very high radio rating. Does the name Vincent Ramsgate mean anything to you?'

'Oh yes,' she replied grimly, 'it does.'

'Good, good. Thought it might. You see what we need is *diversity*. Thus, in my capacity as senior curator I shall supply the scholarly wit and insight, Stark and Morris the literary brilliance and integrity – and Ramsgate will pull in the more impressionable and less discerning (of which there are many) plus their wallets.' He chortled happily, and Rosy could almost see him rubbing his hands together.

'So what do you want me to do?' she asked.

'Go and see him, of course. Present your credentials. Tell him you are an emissary from the British Museum, *specifically* from the notable Dr Stanley, and that your superior would be delighted if he would consent to join his little venture. Butter him up a bit and tell him you swoon every time you hear his voice on the wireless. He'll believe every word: he's notoriously vain, you know.'

Rosy gave a wry smile. 'Is that so?'

'Oh yes, very pleased with himself . . . but some people are like that. Funny, really. But perhaps you've met him already? He lives just outside Southwold, near a place called Reydon, I believe.'

Rosy admitted that she had met him and indeed had been to his house – an admission that was met with a roar of delight. 'There you are, then! You are as good as old friends. Approach him as soon as possible and tell him it will be in the first week of November, and then report back to me with sparkling news. I knew I could count on you, Rosy.'

'Well, I am not sure if—' she began doubtfully, but didn't stand a chance.

'Splendid! Splendid! We'll hear from you soon.' There was a click and the line went dead.

Rosy sighed, kicked off her shoes and lay down on the bed. She pondered the possibility of putting strychnine in his Adnam's ale.

That evening Rosy sustained a blow. She had decided to have an early night and was just getting undressed when there was a gentle knock on the door. She put on a wrap and went to open it. Lady Fawcett stood there.

'I am so sorry, Rosy dear, I know you had wanted to get on with the latest Graham Greene, but I have just heard something rather strange – unfortunate, in fact. It was on the news. I thought it might be of interest to you. May I come in?'

Somewhat surprised, Rosy ushered her in and gestured to the armchair, while she sat on the bed. 'So what's this, then,' she asked, 'has someone set fire to the British Museum?'

'No,' replied Lady Fawcett soberly. 'No, not that, but something as dramatic, I suppose, and certainly more personal. It's to do with somebody we know . . . well, not *know* exactly, but we've certainly met him.'

Rosy was startled, and all manner of names started to race through her head. But at the next moment she heard Lady Fawcett say, 'In fact, I think you said you had bumped into him only yesterday. It's that nice man we met at Vincent Ramsgate's party, Mickey Standish – he's dead. Attacked by a chance intruder in his flat and money stolen. The announcer said he was found at seven o'clock this morning by the postman. Apparently, the door to his flat was open, and as the postman had a parcel to deliver he went in – and then saw the poor man in a heap on the floor. Hit on the head, I gather.' She frowned. 'Oh dear, it seems so awfully unfair. He struck me as most agreeable; and so tall,' she added irrelevantly.

'Yes . . . yes, he was tall,' Rosy answered faintly, inwardly reeling. It was ridiculous! He had been her guide around St Edmund's, they had chatted and eaten sandwiches together in the King's Head, and he had nearly tripped over the spaniel by their table. He had been going to take her to Ronnie Scott's. And now – and now he was dead. Just like that.

For a moment she closed her eyes, and then opening them, she said conventionally, 'How simply dreadful. Poor chap, I hope it was quick.'

'Oh, bound to have been,' the other replied, 'they don't mess about, these types. A quick in an out, that's what they're after. A smart bash on the head, grab the money and off they go.' Lady Fawcett nodded firmly to make her point.

232

How Angela had obtained this information Rosy had no idea (the bobby on the Knightsbridge beat?) but she found such assurance comforting nevertheless.

Left alone, Rosy remained sitting on the bed staring listlessly at the wall. It was awful, unreal – incredible. For a few absurd seconds she wondered if Angela had got it wrong, misheard the name or confused him with someone else. But she knew that was nonsense: Angela could be vague but she wasn't addled. No, it was surely Standish. Presumably, there would be more on the news tomorrow, or some reference in the newspaper. Tangible proof that she couldn't question.

Rosy frowned, puzzled by her own reaction. She had barely known the man, so why so bleak? So *felled*? Had she been a little in love with him? Certainly not (or at least she didn't think so). But in his cool, urbane way he had been amusing and strangely attractive. She had enjoyed talking with him: he had been witty, casually assured, interesting – and, she suspected, very shrewd. Unnervingly so. Why had he probed her connection with Aunt Marcia? He had obviously sensed the case was more complex than reported. Casual interest, or had there been something deeper? Perhaps he had been one of her ex-lovers – there had been several. Or conceivably, as she had first fleetingly wondered, had he been engaged in some covert investigation by MI5, digging up unfinished business . . . Could that have been it? Oh, hardly!

She continued to stare disconsolately at the wall. Well, whatever the facts, he had been so real, so damned *alive*.

Far more truly alive than that poor foolish girl had ever seemed . . . And now, now he was no more. Extraordinary.

One thing was pretty certain: she would never go to Ronnie Scott's now. Any other jazz club, but not that one.

CHAPTER TWENTY-SIX

It was a beautiful day and Rosy would have liked to spend it visiting Minsmere or perhaps pottering about at Walberswick, or watching the boats down at Southwold's harbour. As it was, she was required to chat up Vincent Ramsgate and persuade him that his presence would be vital to the success of Stanley's project. It wasn't a particularly attractive prospect. Right from the start the man's unctuous manner had rather irritated her; and although she was no prude, after the revelation of Tippy's letter her initial distaste was increased. Still, all in the cause of culture, she supposed – that and Dr Stanley's good temper! She looked at her watch . . . Better get a move on; she was due there at two-thirty.

The drive to his house in Reydon was pleasant, albeit at times perplexing. The last time she had been there was for the party when she had been a passenger and indifferent to direction. This time she took a couple of wrong turns in the twisting lanes that crossed the marshes, but eventually (and she suspected, via a circuitous route) arrived at the entrance to his grounds.

Moving slowly up the treelined drive she noticed again the rather peculiar statues dotted about the front lawn. Seen in broad daylight they seemed even more crude and charmless than they had in semi-darkness. Who on earth, for example, would want to live with a headless ape? Or for that matter a brass Pegasus bearing a clearly inebriated Peter Pan on its back – especially as the horse seemed to have only three legs and one wing. Deeply symbolic? Or had the sculptor simply lost interest? Perhaps the owner considered them witty and whimsical, a sort of reflection of his own intriguing persona . . . She parked the car and walked up the steps.

The door was opened by a woman in a hat and coat, and who introduced herself as the housekeeper.

'It's my half-day,' she explained, 'and I'm just off to catch the bus. But if you would like a cup of tea, I've left things on the kitchen table. Mr Ramsgate likes a cuppa, so be sure to remind him. He boils the kettle beautifully!' She laughed. 'He is in the study at the moment practising one of them broadcasts on his Dictaphone thing. Very particular, he is; always likes to get it just right – every pause and syllable. Mind you, sometimes he'll try bits out on me. "What do you think of this, Dilly? Now, be honest, my girl."' She giggled. 'Girl, indeed! He isn't half an old flatterer – *when* it suits him!'

Rosy smiled. 'And what do you say?'

'Oh, I always says the same: "Couldn't be better, sir!" That's why he asks me. No point in saying anything else really, is there?' She gave a sly grin and took Rosy along to the study.

As she entered the room, Ramsgate turned off his gadget and rose to greet her with the same effusiveness he had shown at the party.

'*What* an unexpected pleasure, Miss Gilchrist,' he enthused, shaking her hand vigorously. 'I hadn't thought we should meet again – or certainly not so soon!' He offered her a chair and returned to his desk, from where he beamed and (so it seemed) appraised her dress and ankles.

'But,' he continued, wagging a mock finger, 'you never mentioned the other evening that you worked at the BM and were one of Dr Stanley's satellites. This is indeed an honour!'

Rosy was slightly stung, and had wanted to protest: 'I am not his blooming satellite!' But instead she merely raised an eyebrow, remarking that 'satellite' was a bit of an exaggeration, although she much enjoyed his stimulus – a statement that was not without truth.

'Oh, I am sure you do,' he chimed, 'a considerable scholar, by all accounts, and a most formidable custodian – though not without his quirks, one hears. A bit of a tricky cove, I imagine!' He winked.

Ramsgate was perfectly right on both counts: Stanley was both a good scholar and a tricky cove. But somehow Rosy was irritated by the man's attitude. He exuded a kind of smug patronage that grated. Dr Stanley's vanity seemed healthy in comparison, and his eccentricity often comic. They were features born of an innate, almost innocent, self-confidence. Whereas Ramsgate's seemed cultivated, striven for. He was the showman, Stanley the natural.

'Yes,' she agreed, 'he has his moments. But as I explained on the phone, he is mounting this travel exhibition and is terribly keen to have a contribution from you. I think it could work very well if you would be willing to participate. You would lend a certain . . .' she paused to flash a winning smile – 'a certain panache.' In her mind's ear she could hear Stanley's voice: *That's it, Rosy, soften the sod!*

He gave a modest smirk. 'Well, shall we say that I *rather* suspect that I could hold my own amid such illustrious names. It shouldn't be too onerous – rather amusing, really. My current book is doing remarkably well: its author could be quite a draw!'

Good, Rosy thought, it's in the bag and I can go home. 'So you will do it?' she said.

'Ah well, that's another matter,' he replied coyly. 'Never mistake interest for acquiescence. I shall have to consult my schedule – one is rather busy at the moment. And then of course, if you don't mind my mentioning it, there is also the small matter of the fee; though doubtless Dr Stanley is fair-minded in such matters.' He cocked an enquiring eyebrow.

'Oh yes,' Rosy lied airily, 'awfully fair.'

'Ah well, in that case I had better go and consult the diary. It's amazing how one's life is controlled by its diktats! Will you excuse me? I think I left it in the sitting room; shan't be a tick.'

He rose and went to the door, and Rosy couldn't help noticing that he was wearing the most lurid shade of purple socks; socks that clashed with a pair of well-worn scarlet bedroom slippers. She was intrigued. Goodness, she thought, had the man delusions of papal grandeur?

Left alone, she took stock of the room. It was fairly predictable: book-lined shelves, a filing cabinet, unremarkable prints on the wall, a large reading lamp and a pair of department store leather armchairs. More arresting was a richly patterned Turkey rug in front of the desk. A souvenir from Istanbul, perhaps? She vaguely recalled hearing one of his broadcasts from that city.

But the desk too was striking. Distracted by its incumbent, she hadn't really noticed it before. But now she saw that it was a splendid example of eighteenth-century craftsmanship of the Irish style: dark, richly polished yew, solid ball-and-claw feet and meticulous, but unelaborate, carving. She smiled, thinking how jealous Dr Stanley would be: he had been after one like that for ages. She stood up to take a closer look, and through the clutter of books and notes, saw how finely the wood had been honed.

But then she saw something else: an ornate metal paper tray. And among its mess of odds and ends there lay, incongruously, a pair of tortoiseshell sunglasses and a lipstick case. Or it would have been a case had the top not been missing.

Rosy gazed at the little object, recognising the familiar Revlon logo. She picked it up, and seeing the name of the shade, *Brazen Maiden*, caught her breath. Oh, surely not! Could it really be the dead girl's – the missing bit of the item they had found in the beach hut? As Rosy had overheard her telling Alicia, Tippy had loved both the name and the vibrant colour.

Then fearing what she would find, she examined the sunglasses . . . Yes, they were there: the fake diamond studs in the side pieces. Rosy had not seen Tippy wearing the glasses, but she had heard enough to know they were the same. Apparently, they had been especially purchased to complement the red bikini, and Tippy had delighted in regaling Rosy with details of their colour and style. For a few seconds she heard the high breathy tone: 'They look awfully Italian, you know – the frames sort of flick up like a cat's eyes and they have the teeniest little diamonds set into the sides. I can't wait to wear them, and I wish to hell it would stop raining!'

And then she heard a deeper voice. 'Ah, I've checked my dates, and I find that—' Ramsgate, who had re-entered quietly, stopped in mid sentence. He walked up to her and took both articles from her hands, giving a lopsided leer. 'Not my accoutrements, of course – a tad too girlie. They belonged to a young friend,' he murmured. Rosy stared at the smiling mouth and icy eyes.

In retrospect she felt she could have dissembled: concealed her shock, made some frivolous response, or simply said nothing and smiled vaguely like a fool. Had she done so, things might have been different. So different.

As it was, she was too stunned to muster her wits, and thus heard herself saying woodenly, 'Yes, I know who you mean: Tippy Tildred, the kid who was shot in the beach hut. I suppose you picked up these things before lugging the body to the dunes.'

For the first time since their meeting Ramsgate regarded her with genuine interest. 'What deductive powers you have, Miss Gilchrist,' he said suavely. And then in a trice the tone changed: 'Sit down,' he snapped.

Mechanically, she did as he ordered. What else could she do? Rant and rave, throw herself at the French window, spit in his face?

The first thing he did was to go to the desk and rummage in one of the drawers. She watched as he withdrew a large pair of pointed scissors, and felt a pang of horror. Oh my God, surely he wouldn't do that! Instinctively, she tensed, while looking desperately for something she could shield herself with.

But Ramsgate did not approach Rosy, for he had stretched over to the telephone on the windowsill, and with a deft movement severed its cord. He returned to his chair. 'That's better,' he said, 'no unseemly interruptions. And you, my dear, won't be tempted to do anything foolish like demanding police protection. It's quite easy, I believe: one just has to dial 999 and they come running like ants, blue lights ablaze and whistles screaming. So noisy!'

Rosy drew a deep breath, and in a voice considerably stronger than she felt, said defiantly, 'Well, in that case I shall just have to walk out to my car, won't I?' She made a movement to get up.

'Sit!' he commanded as if instructing a dog. With a start, she saw he had produced a small pistol. He didn't point it at her, but lay it on the blotting pad, fingering it casually.

Seeing her staring at it, he said, 'Oh, don't worry, I only use this in an emergency, and at the moment there isn't one . . . or at least, not as yet.' He frowned and emitted a heavy sigh. 'Quite honestly, my dear, you have rather messed up my afternoon; in fact, you have messed up a lot of things. It's all very vexing.'

Somehow, Rosy found the light conversational tone far more chilling than overt threats. She sensed that his manner could change in an instant and that it only needed one false move and he would gun her down as he had Tippy. Yet despite her terror, she was sure there must be a way of foiling the bastard – some way of escaping and messing up his afternoon even more! But what? She gazed at the complacent features, seeking inspiration.

Vanity! That was it: the man loved to talk, and principally about himself. He was a born raconteur. She would ply him with questions – anything to delay his coming to a decision as to what to do with her. And in the meantime, God willing, the housekeeper might return early.

Rosy swallowed, and adopting the same casual tone as his own, said, 'I know Tippy was blackmailing you and the Carshaltons about the bed business, which must have been quite a blow, but was it really worth killing her for that? And in any case, how were you able to persuade her to come to the beach hut? Pretty difficult, I should have thought.'

To her relief he seemed ready to talk. 'Oh, the sex business wasn't too much of a problem,' he said airily, 'one can generally nobble the press – or some of them, at any rate. And after all, the indignation of the prurient public is matched only by its indulgence – a few good tub-thumping speeches and Carshalton would have been back in favour again, albeit a few rungs down; and yours truly could doubtless have written a rather juicy memoir on the theme, probably a bestseller . . . No, tiresome though that was, the real problem was to do with Mickey Standish, nothing to do with the Carshaltons. And being Mickey's problem it was also mine: we had a joint venture, you see, and that fool of a girl might just have blown it sky-high. So she had to be stopped.'

At the mention of Standish Rosy suddenly went numb. So he had been part of it too! She felt sickened and oddly betrayed, and for a moment had difficulty in fighting back irrational tears. 'Hold steady,' she told herself angrily, 'show nothing.'

'But as to the hut,' Ramsgate continued, unaware of the effect of his words, 'that was simple. I telephoned her to say that Mickey was looking for a good PA and would she be interested. The little miss had been sucking up to him at the party and I guessed that she would jump at the chance. As of course she did. I still had a key to Walter Hackle's hut, which he had lent me ages ago, and I told her that Mickey often used it in the afternoons to catch up on his reading, and that if she cared to go along at a certain time he would be delighted to interview her.'

'And that's what she did,' Rosy said dully.

He nodded. 'That's what she did. And we were waiting for her and she was shot.'

The stark words made Rosy's stomach lurch, but she said nothing.

'I fear that was Mickey's doing, albeit at my suggestion.' Ramsgate gave a sardonic laugh: 'For a man of his particular talents he was awfully cack-handed with a pistol, and my intention had been to do it myself. But she arrived before expected and he happened to be holding the gun. By a sheer fluke he made quite a good job of it.'

Despite her disgust and fear, Rosy was intrigued. 'What talents?' she asked. 'And if it's not a rude question, what venture?'

The man laughed. 'Inquisitive, aren't you! Still, since you won't be going anywhere I may as well tell you.' At these words Rosy gripped her bag to stop her hands from shaking. But she kept silent and waited for him to continue.

CHAPTER TWENTY-SEVEN

'Despite appearances to the contrary, Mickey Standish was a liar, a cheat, an arch-swindler and a consummate racketeer. He was also utterly ruthless when it suited him.' Ramsgate must have seen Rosy's eyes widening, for he chuckled and added, 'Oh yes, I forgot, rather a nifty locksmith too. It was something he had learnt at school from the caretaker and he used to practise his skill by getting into the masters' studies and raiding their wallets. It was he who intruded into your friends' cottage to retrieve my letter. Said it would be the sort of challenge he hadn't had for a long time!

'But I digress. You asked about our venture: illicit arms dealing, my dear. We had been at it for years. Mickey was a first-class broker and had connections all over the world. It has all been most profitable. It started on a small scale after the war, but since then we have taken on rather bigger fish – Cuban insurrectionists, for example, and the African Mau Mau. We have also dabbled with certain factions of the IRA who have reason to be grateful. Currently, they are quiescent, but I can tell you there are weapon caches lying in Ireland based entirely on our expertise and contacts. Mickey was the brains of the outfit – one of our country's top accountants and headhunted all over the place. He had his own consultancy, a financial wizard really, and did a slick bit of corporate embezzlement on the side. Afraid I can't add up for toffee.' Ramsgate grinned and shifted the gun to his other hand. 'But we both took care of the arms aspect; that was rather exciting really. Made a nice change from sitting on my arse writing travel stuff or being charming on the Home Service!'

'How nice,' Rosy said dryly. And then a thought struck her: if Standish had been so damn sharp and the 'brains of the outfit' how come he had bothered to collaborate with Ramsgate? Wouldn't it have been simpler, easier, to stay independent?

She cleared her throat, eyeing the plump finger idly caressing the trigger. 'So, uhm, how did this lucrative liaison come about? If Standish had such talent and financial expertise couldn't he have just gone it alone? I mean, presumably you had both been splitting the proceeds. Why should he have bothered to do that?'

'Ah! A good question, my dear – though in my own modest defence I like to think that I was of *some* practical use in the operation! One is not entirely without ability. Oiling wheels and smoothing paths, that's my forte – handy in our line of business.' He gave an ingratiating smile and

Felix's judgement came back to Rosy: *smarmy smoocher*. Yes, she could just hear the patter! 'Nevertheless,' he continued, 'to give you the crucial reason: I had a hold over him – just as that silly little idiot thought she had over us, though in my case the hold was considerably tighter.'

'So what was this hold to do with?' Rosy asked indifferently, suddenly sickened by the man's complacent vanity.

'A schoolboy prank.'

'*What?*'

'Yes, sounds silly, doesn't it? But it has proved most fruitful to me. It happened one afternoon when we were about fifteen, and when most of the school was watching a rugger match; but Mickey and I were in detention stuck in an upstairs classroom. When we finished our task, lines or whatever, Mickey suddenly produced a bottle of whisky he had filched from somewhere. "We'll celebrate," he said, "and give thanks we've been spared the bugger rugger." So that's what we did – and in the process got blind drunk. Or at least Mickey did, I wasn't so bad.

'Anyway, the upshot was we were caught by one of the prefects, who threatened to report us to the housemaster. This was a facer as it meant instant expulsion. Despite being October, it was a blazing hot day, and the window overlooking the quad two floors down was wide open . . .' Ramsgate had paused, gazing at the wall behind Rosy, as if reliving the scene. 'And then you see, one moment the prefect was there, and the next moment he wasn't. My friend had pushed him out of the window.'

Even as he spoke, Rosy noticed a flicker of surprise

cross the man's face; yet the gun was held as tightly. 'What happened?' she murmured.

He shrugged. 'The corpse was found an hour later, and as you can imagine there was one hell of a fuss. I won't bore you with the details, but suffice it to say that during that hour I disposed of the whisky bottle and hauled Mickey off for a walk to sober him up. The authorities never discovered the truth and assumed it was an accident: *death by misadventure*, as the phrase goes. From that day onwards neither of us ever referred to the incident again – not a single word. It has been a sort of tacit collusion, a mutual agreement to say nothing. But as you can imagine, his obligation to me has remained – hence our partnership.' Ramsgate gave a wry smile. And then he added thoughtfully, 'Whether it was intended as a joke, or the product of drunken fury, I am not sure. It could have been either. For a man of his intellect he had a surprisingly puerile humour; but then neither did he like being crossed – used to say it unsettled his nerves, if you please. But one thing is certain: not a drop of drink ever passed his lips again. Never.'

'Fascinating,' Rosy said grimly, the sarcasm hiding her terror. The danger would lie in his silence: once the man stopped talking, anything might happen!

But fortunately Ramsgate seemed ready to continue. A pensive look had come into his eyes. And with what sounded like a sigh of genuine regret, he said: 'Yes, he's a loss to me, is Mickey. And I don't just mean in the practical sense. In an odd way I had always liked the fellow. God knows why – I suppose precisely because he was such a puzzle: an extraordinary mixture of charm and bastard ruthlessness. Women adored him, you know: it was the ascetic quality, they found it tantalising. The more detached he was the more they wanted him. Like moths around a freezing candle! But he was indifferent, quite unmoved.' Ramsgate paused, looking thoughtful. 'But he was like that generally,' he added, 'not just with women. It was as if he didn't need anybody, not in the emotional sense. A bit like Kipling's cat that walked by itself: completely self-contained. Funny, really.' He stared at the revolver.

As did Rosy. 'But surely,' she said quickly, 'if what Tippy had witnessed in the bedroom had nothing to do with him why were you both so set on killing her? Yes, she saw him in the hall – but what would that amount to? Hardly grounds for murder!'

Ramsgate sighed and looked almost sorry. 'Yes, Fate up to his ill-timed tricks, I fear. As they say in the films, she was in the wrong place at the wrong time. The man she saw him with was Aldo Pollini the Mayfair nightclub owner who, as you may recall, was then urgently being sought by the police in connection with a prostitution racket and other illicit activities – including arms trafficking. In fact, he was one of our best contacts.

'Things were getting very hot for little Aldo – very – and he was all set to get out of the country. It so happened that his exit had been planned for that day. Sounds absurd, but Aldo couldn't drive – always had a chauffeur. Anyway, for some reason the driver never turned up – sick or drunk, I suppose. Aldo was left stranded and desperate to make that dash to London Airport. What did he do? Phoned Mickey in a muck sweat and begged for his help. Mickey agreed, but said he would have to stop off at the Wilton

Place house as he had left his briefcase there when doing some tax business with Carshalton earlier that day, and he needed it urgently.

'So that's what happened, you see. Mickey picked up Aldo at a prearranged spot, drove to Wilton Place, dashed in for his briefcase, encountered Tippy, dashed out again and drove like hell to the airport. Aldo caught his plane in the nick of time and all was well. Afterwards, Mickey drove up to Scotland and fished on the Tweed for a few days. He told me he had made a frightfully good catch.'

Ramsgate sat back in his chair, beaming brightly as if he had just finished telling a tale to an attentive child.

Rosy was no child but she was attentive all right! How could she prompt him to go on talking while she wracked her brain for some means of escape, some diversion to get her out of this nightmare?

She leant forward with an expression of thoughtful interest. 'But things weren't entirely all right, were they? I remember that business: the papers were full of it. And one of the intriguing aspects was the identity of the accomplice who had dropped him at the airport. That kept the press going for days until they eventually tired of it and switched to some other scandal.'

Ramsgate nodded. 'Yes, it rather died a death, didn't it? But unfortunately the whole affair was recently dug up by a couple of smart reporters from the *Manchester Guardian* hoping to steal the *Telegraph's* thunder. They had been doing some rather tiresome snooping and we were getting a bit windy. It would only take one person to report having seen Mickey with Aldo that day, and – if you will excuse the expression, my dear – we would very likely have been in the shit. Naturally such a "sighting" would not be proof of anything and Mickey would have produced a plausible tale or alibi. But the press can be persistent hounds, and once the seeds are there, who knows . . . ?' Ramsgate shrugged and said blandly, 'The girl had a pretty little mouth but it made a big noise. We couldn't afford the risk.'

Rosy's own mouth was dry as dust, and she swallowed hard trying to keep her voice normal. 'But was it really necessary to kill the girl?' she asked. 'I mean, it wasn't as if she knew about any of this, was it?'

'No. The silly little cow thought we were just up to sexual romps – well, so we were, or at least I was, and very nice too, if I may say. But when she started to twitch her foolish little nose and began bleating about seeing Mickey with Aldo (not that she knew who he was) we realised that one thing might conceivably lead to the other. If those two journalists were intent on making a retrospective feature of the affair with pictures of Aldo, it could easily have jogged her memory and given her ideas. She had to be nipped in the bud.'

'Or shot in the back.'

He gave a non-committal but affirmative shrug.

'And am I a silly little cow?' Rosy asked quietly.

He flashed a disarming smile: 'Oh *far* more tolerable! And if I may say so, far from silly. But,' and a frown replaced the smile, 'just as dangerous and probably more so. I am afraid you will have to go, my dear.' He regarded her thoughtfully.

The eyes watching her were hard. And gripped by a

sudden vice of fear, Rosy heard herself gasp absurdly: 'But you'd be mad to shoot me here, there would be such a mess!'

The words elicited not a gunshot, but a shout of laughter. 'Hah! Such solicitude for my carpet and the domestics, and what a shame I shan't be able to pass on your kind concern to them. But you are right, it would indeed be foolish – which is why you and I are going to take a little stroll in the grounds. As you may have observed, my house is beautifully secluded.' He stood up.

Rosy gulped and felt the sweat trickling down her neck. She *must* check him! 'What about Felix's hat?' she blurted inconsequentially.

He looked perplexed. 'Smythe's hat? What about it?'

'Yes, the panama – it was near the body.'

A slow smile spread over Ramsgate's features and he wagged his finger at her. 'Tut-tut! You are playing for time, Rosy Gilchrist: trying to divert the old boy from his regrettable task. It won't do, I fear.'

Seeing his mocking eyes, hearing those silky sardonic tones, Rosy felt her terror replaced by something else: hatred. Contempt suddenly welled up in her and she was gripped by a furious defiance. 'Just tell me about the effing hat,' she shouted. 'I want to bloody know!'

Ramsgate started. 'Good lord, Miss Gilchrist,' he exclaimed, visibly shocked, 'where did you learn that language? Surely not from your job at the British Museum!'

'You'd be surprised,' she snapped, thinking of Dr Stanley's tantrums. 'I just want to get it straight, that's all.'

'Ah! A lady of clear mind, I see. Well, since you are so insistent I suppose I had better indulge you . . . She was wearing it when she came to the hut – got it on at a rakish angle. Thought it would impress Mickey, I suppose. After the shooting it was too risky to move the body in daylight, so the plan was to leave her in the hut for a few hours until nightfall. We had taken her shoes and beach bag but stupidly forgot the damned hat. And then—'

'Wasn't it a bit risky leaving the body there?' Rosy asked, genuinely curious.

'Not really. Naturally, we had locked the hut; and in any case it wasn't used that often. It was worth taking the risk for that short time.' He smiled wryly, adding, 'Though I must admit that I was relieved not to see a bevy of helmeted bobbies standing guard when we went back! But getting her to the dunes was the difficulty. We had my shooting brake, of course, and at that hour of the evening there was barely a soul about. Nevertheless, carting a corpse from hut to car was still a risky business. We might have been exposed to comment.' Ramsgate laughed. Rosy did not.

'Anyway, the problem was easily solved by the deckchairs. That was Mickey's idea.'

'What deckchairs?' she asked. 'The hut doesn't have any.'

'No, because we had taken them. We laid them flat and put her between them – what one might describe as a stretchered sandwich – and then taking an end each, carried our freight to the car. Two chaps heaving a pile of deckchairs was less likely to arouse suspicion than if seen manhandling a corpse. Wouldn't you agree?'

Rosy felt rather sick and said nothing, her flare of anger gone and desperate fear returned.

'Anyway,' he continued conversationally, 'what we had

overlooked was that wretched hat. We had forgotten to put it into her beach bag earlier and the damn thing was still there. So we shoved it under the body between the chairs. Then once we had reached Ferry Road, we did the whole thing in reverse: decanted the thing from the shooting brake and on to the dunes. Fortunately, it was really dark by then and the whole area deserted – or so it seemed. The hat fell out, and it was then that Mickey said he was going to put it on her head – said it would gild the lily. Christ! But at that instant there was a faint whistle from somewhere further down on the shore: someone calling for their dog. So he dropped the hat, and with a deckchair each we hoofed it back to the car. I'm getting a bit old for that sort of thing, and as we were scrambling up the bank I tripped and nearly lost my shoe. Still, we made it to the car all right and got away.'

Ramsgate breathed a sigh of relief as if he was reliving the whole episode. He didn't quite mop his brow but he had that look in his eye. 'You know, I wouldn't want to go through that again,' he said.

'No,' Rosy said faintly, 'no, I don't suppose you would.'

Her response brought him back to the present and he gazed at her with hardened eyes, all amusement gone. 'That's quite enough now,' he said abruptly, 'no more of this stalling. Time flies and I'm a busy man. We must be off.'

CHAPTER TWENTY-EIGHT

Where will it happen? How will he do it? Under the trees? With the gun – or with a rope?

Such were the thoughts thundering through Rosy's mind.

Pathetically, she grasped a final straw: 'It must have been quite a shock when Standish was killed like that, I mean, you being such old colleagues. An awful blow, wasn't it?'

He had already gestured her towards the door and she hadn't really expected an answer. Thus when he paused she was surprised – and even more so when he replied casually: 'Hardly a shock, my dear, since it was I who snuffed him.'

Rosy's heart lurched. '*You* killed him?' she cried. 'But you can't have! He was coshed by some intruder in his London flat, his wallet was empty and spare change all over the floor. The newspapers said it was the work of some late-night chancer!'

Ramsgate gave a bitter laugh. '"Chancer" is about the right term,' he said. 'I took my chance and it paid off. But it was hardly spur of the moment: it was planned, all right. I knew his habits, you see, or some of them. Every Wednesday he would nip along to the Clermont to do a spot of blackjack and at 2 a.m. on the dot would leave to return home. It was always the same, whether he had won or lost. Very disciplined was Mickey. So with that in mind, I drove down to London that evening, parked in a side street – Farnham Place to be precise – used my spare key to get into the flat, concealed myself behind the proverbial curtain and waited. He arrived bang on time, came into the sitting room, lit a cigarette and sat at his desk with his back to the window and my convenient curtain.'

The man paused, before adding quietly, 'And then came the easy part. I stepped forward, gave him a smart rabbit punch behind his ear and then coshed him for good measure. Poor sod didn't stand a chance . . . Naturally, I roughed things up a bit, threw his wallet on the floor, and then scarpered leaving the door ajar. The worst bit was driving back here to Reydon, a ghastly journey. I was exhausted and with a hell of a headache: nervous reaction, I suppose – which is why, Miss Gilchrist, I could have done without your visit this afternoon. However, "tired and emotional" though I may have felt, as you have perhaps observed, I was able to rally.' He gave a mirthless laugh.

In the nightmare, Rosy heard herself saying icily, 'Wonderful melodrama, but why did you do it?'

'*Force majeure*: I had had a tip-off that the Home Office had got their sights on him about the arms business and that

Scotland Yard was due to descend at any minute. Standish was a cool customer, so cool that I guessed that if he was caught and charged he wouldn't hesitate to implicate me. As explained, over the years we had been close allies, but I had always felt that deep down he resented the hold I had on him re that incident with the prefect. Without that he would probably have gone his own sweet way beholden to no one. I think he saw me as an irritant, a liability, especially after the Tildred stuff. He was furious too about my leaving that letter in the book I gave Dillworthy. Not that one can blame him, really; it was damn stupid of me. But oh yes, if he had gone down he would have pulled me with him all right! Never share secrets: that's my philosophy. Which is why I must now—'

He never finished his sentence. For at that moment Rosy saw the dog's face . . . Mr Bates's inquisitive nose was thrusting itself against the glass of the French window behind Ramsgate's back. The next instant she saw two other forms – the human figures of Bartho and Amy. They were peering through the panes, the latter shading her eyes to get a better view.

Instinct drove; and without thought or care, Rosy threw up both arms and beckoned them frantically to come in.

'What the Christ are you doing?' Ramsgate cried, confused by her sudden antics. As he spun round to where she was signalling, the French window burst open and the three intruders were suddenly in the room.

The shock was mutual, but the man with the gun had the upper hand. 'Get over to that corner,' he snarled, gesturing with the pistol. 'You too,' he snapped to Rosy.

Obediently, she moved and stood next to Amy. Perversely, the dog wandered to the opposite corner and started to scratch.

There was a silence as Ramsgate seemed to be contemplating his next move. Bad enough having to kill one bastard, but three together was a bit excessive. He was unprepared!

Bartho was the first to speak. 'You don't know what to do with us, do you?' he said conversationally. 'When you gunned down Tippy Tildred in my cousin's beach hut it must have been easy: a skimpy kid all on her own, it must have been child's play; but now you've got a real problem on your hands.'

Ramsgate glowered, but with a nonchalant shrug said, 'Oh, it wasn't me, that was Standish. And as it happens, as your friend here knows, I've done for him. So watch your mouth, sonny boy.'

Bartho looked nonplussed. But before he could make a retort, the whippet, disgruntled in its corner, had started to whine and fidget.

'Oh, do sit down, Batesy,' squeaked Amy, 'you're being such a pain!' She looked angrily at Ramsgate. 'See, you've upset him. He's not keen on guns, and neither am I!' Her gaze returned to the dog: 'Come to Mummy, sweetie.' Dutifully, the creature trotted over and sat at her feet. 'Good boy,' she crooned, and stroked his ears.

But the dog was indifferent to such endearments, being fixated on Ramsgate's left ankle – its slightly protuberant eyes gazing with interest at the man's trouser cuff.

Ignoring the interruption, Ramsgate turned back to

Bartho. He levelled the gun menacingly. 'I admit your intrusion has rather disturbed my plans, but I can assure you that—'

But his assurance was never heard. For at that moment, Mr Bates, alerted by the sudden movement and rampant with desire, had sprung forward, and with thin forelegs clamped firmly around Ramsgate's calf, began to hump away for all he was worth.

It was a mild diversion but it did the trick. Kicking out in furious disgust, Ramsgate momentarily lost his balance and dropped the gun. He bent to pick it up – but not before the three of them had rushed to the door and out into the corridor.

To their left was another door. 'In here,' gasped Bartho, 'it's the lavatory.' He pulled them inside and drew the bolt.

'Where's Mr Bates?' Amy exclaimed.

'Resting, probably,' muttered Bartho.

'Oh, don't be absurd,' she wailed, 'the beast may shoot him!'

'Blow the dog, what about us! Look, we can crawl out of that window, but you'll have to breathe in. Come on, I'll give you a hand up.'

'No,' the girl replied doggedly, 'I am not having Mr Bates shot in the line of duty. I'm going back for him.' She made a move towards the door.

'Sh!' Rosy commanded, and grabbed her. 'He's coming.' They froze and heard brisk but unhurried footsteps. These passed the lavatory door and continued on down the passage.

'Why isn't he running?' Rosy whispered.

'Doesn't need to,' said Bartho, 'it's a dead end. It only leads to the cellar. I mistook it for the loo at the party. He thinks we'll be there.'

'Well, he'll soon find otherwise. Quickly!' She moved towards the window. But Amy had also moved – to the locked door, and before they could stop her had unlatched and opened it a few inches. Such caution was as well: for right on the threshold sat the whippet – looking, Rosy felt, distinctly reproachful. Baulked in flagrante and then summarily abandoned, it perhaps had good cause.

Mr Bates was the first to scramble through the small opening, followed by the puffing Amy. There was a hiatus as she squirmed about on the ledge.

'Jump!' Bartho ordered.

'I can't,' she protested in a bellowed stage whisper, 'I've got my knee stuck.'

'Well, get it unstuck, for Christ's sake!' Bartho exclaimed. 'We haven't got all night!'

She managed to do as he urged, but lacking the dog's agility fell in an ungainly heap. She was followed by the other two, whose landing on the flower bed was less dramatic. They hesitated, breathless, unsure which way to run. The dog, glad to be in the open again, had gone haring across the lawn. Amy was about to follow, but she was gripped by Bartho. 'For God's sake, not that way, we'll be in full sight of the front windows!'

'It's not those windows, it's *this* one, where we've just come from,' Rosy cried. 'He's bound to guess where we went. He'll take a potshot from there at any moment. Quick!' She hustled them round the side of the house, and keeping flat against the wall, they edged their way in the direction of a small shrubbery.

They might have reached it, had not a rabbit sprung into sight, hotly pursued by the whippet. There was a loud crack and the rabbit fell dead. The dog skidded to a halt, looking vaguely bemused.

'Oh my God,' Bartho breathed, 'it's him. Look, on the veranda steps – and he's got a shotgun.'

'Batesy!' Amy screamed. She started to race towards the dog, in full view of the house and in the clear sights of the twelve-bore.

Another shot rang out. The girl fell to her knees. Instantly, Bartho started to tear towards her, while the figure on the steps reloaded.

Mesmerised, Rosy gazed aghast at the image before her: the trio at the centre of the beautiful lawn – stooping young man, crouching girl, cavorting whippet; and outlined on the steps, reloading his shotgun, Vincent Ramsgate . . . wearing his fez.

The scene held a cinematic quality, a surrealism akin to one of the more bizarre sections of *The Languid Labyrinth*, and despite her helpless anguish – or perhaps as diversion from it – Rosy found herself puzzling over the man's headgear: he certainly hadn't been wearing it in the study. Maybe it formed part of his shooting attire: some men wore ratting caps, perhaps Ramsgate favoured a fez . . .

Dread replaced reverie as she waited in agony for what must surely happen. The man was mad, and the next victim would be neither rabbit nor dog. Drawing breath, she closed her eyes and tensed for the shot.

There was no shot. Instead, what she heard was the throbbing engine and crunching tyres of an approaching vehicle.

She opened her eyes and saw a large black Wolseley trundling its way up the drive towards the house. Rounding the bend, the driver must have seen and grasped the situation – the man on the steps lifting and aiming his gun, its targets huddled helpless on the broad sward – for with a crash of gears and flaying of gravel, the car leapt forward, and, with blazing headlights and clanging klaxon, drove full tilt to where Ramsgate stood.

He swivelled the gun wildly, loosed off one barrel, which shattered the car's wing mirror, and with another hit its radiator. And then slinging the weapon aside, he leapt down the steps and made off across the grass.

Had he not been wearing carpet slippers he might have made better progress. As it was, he stumbled, lost his balance and fell to one knee. He pulled himself up, hesitated, and then turned to face his pursuers. From his pocket he took the small pistol he had been brandishing in the study, and with arm outstretched pointed it towards them. For a few seconds, almost theatrically, he held it poised while they faltered ready to duck.

Then slowly, and still with an air of theatre, he bent his elbow and twisted his wrist so that the muzzle was levelled at his own face. The barrel went into his mouth and there was an explosion.

CHAPTER TWENTY-NINE

'And we only came to check his gun licence,' the young constable said to Jennings in a tight voice, 'he had a Purdey, you know.'

'Not any more he hasn't,' Jennings replied, 'unless Purdeys make harps as well.'

They were sitting on the front steps waiting for the arrival of the ambulance and Nathan with reinforcements from the station. The other participants, recovered from their ordeal, had gone inside to get water for the dog and find brandy for themselves.

'How's the girl?' the constable asked.

'Very lucky. The pellets whipped straight through her sleeve, all she needs is a plaster. The medics won't care for that much.'

'Hmm. If you ask me, Mr Nathan won't care for

that either.' He nodded in the direction of the Wolseley's shattered wing mirror, dripping radiator and its buckled front bumper where Jennings had been tardy in applying the brakes. 'If you don't mind me saying, you took a bit of a risk, didn't you, driving at him like that? He could have shot the pair of us!'

Jennings cleared his throat and straightened his tie. 'Ah, but it was a *calculated* risk, you see, and there's a subtle difference between that kind of risk and mere rash impulse. It's something you will learn as you go along,' he added paternally.

The young constable nodded but was not entirely convinced.

Inside the house, in the large drawing room where Ramsgate's party had been held, the three escapees were comparing notes.

'I am hardly complaining,' Rosy said, 'but what exactly were you doing here? I had the shock of my life when I saw you peering through that window!'

'Huh,' Bartho replied cheerfully, 'not half such a shock as you might have got ten minutes later if he had pursued his plan.'

There was a splutter of laughter from Amy. 'Or the shock *he* had from naughty Mr Bates! It just goes to show how right it is about dogs being man's best friend.'

'I doubt if poor old Ramsgate would have agreed with you,' said Bartho. He paused for a second, frowning, and then said quietly, 'My God, we've been lucky.'

'Exactly,' Rosy said, 'so what stroke of luck brought you to my rescue?'

'That was me, really,' Amy explained. 'I'm trying to lose a bit of weight, and Mummy thought that a brisk bike ride might be a "Good Thing". Bartho had been telling me about Ramsgate's party and some of the weird statues in his grounds, so we borrowed another bike with a front basket for Mr Bates, and pedalled over here for me to take a dekko. When we saw your car parked in the drive we thought it would be all right to join you – drop in on him like proper visitors and perhaps cadge a cup of tea. We rang the bell but nothing happened, so that's why we started to do a recce round the back. And, as they say, the rest is history.' She glanced down at her arm. 'Actually, the ride was very pretty, but I jolly well didn't expect to get a bloody sleeve at the end of it!' There was another yelp of mirth.

'I think you've been fearfully brave,' said Bartho admiringly.

Rosy also thought the girl brave, but was not sure whether this was an innate virtue or something she inherited from her mother and other members of the Fawcett tribe: the ability to sail through life brightly impervious to all but the most exceptionally tiresome (a cancelled dinner date?). Perhaps it was a bit of both.

The young constable had been right about Nathan's reaction to the damaged police vehicle.

'Huh,' he grumbled, as they watched Ramsgate's body being shrouded and stowed, 'it looks as if we may have to send you back on another driving course, old son. And the super will take a dim view too. Still,' he added grudgingly, 'there's one mitigating factor, I suppose: you probably saved their lives. That could work in your favour.' He gave a lugubrious wink.

'All in the line of duty,' Jennings replied modestly. And then in a casual tone, he asked: 'Do you believe in déjà vu, sir?'

'In what?'

'Déjà vu,' Jennings explained patiently, 'it's when something happens to you, and then you feel that it's happening all over again, and you can't really distinguish the first time from the second.'

'Sounds a bit complicated, if you ask me. And besides, what's that got to do with all of this?' Nathan gestured to Ramsgate's house and its surrounding terrain.

'This, sir!' Jennings thrust his hand into his pocket and drew out a long crescent-shaped object. 'I found it on the lawn just near where he topped himself.'

Nathan stared at it pondering. 'Oh Christ,' he said at last, 'it's another of your bloody orthotics. What's it doing here?'

'A very good question,' Jennings said briskly.

Clever me, thought Nathan wryly, and looked enquiringly at the younger officer.

'It is the twin to the one we found near the murdered girl: same colour, same size, same make – *and* it is made for the left foot, not the right.' Jennings fixed Nathan with a triumphant gaze.

'So what? There's probably a lot of 'em around. I suppose it fell out of his slipper when he tripped in the middle of the lawn. I take it the other one is still intact?'

'But that's just it!' Jennings cried. 'There *isn't* another

266

one: the one for the right foot is missing. It's what I've got in my desk drawer, the one I picked up from the beach. Like I said, they match exactly. He's probably been walking at a list for some time!'

Nathan regarded the other soberly. 'Tell me, Jennings, should you ever decide not to continue as one of Her Majesty's police officers, might you ever consider chiropody as a career?'

Impassively, Jennings replied that his current career suited him down to the ground. 'Anything else would be far too *pedestrian*,' he explained, carefully retrieving the insole from his superior's grasp. 'It's the challenges, you see: you never know where they will come from next. What you might call the constant adversity from high and low, inside and out – sort of keeps you on your toes, doesn't it, sir?' Without waiting for an answer he walked over to the damaged police car, leant on its bonnet and began to scribble busily in his notebook.

Nathan sighed.

He sighed again when an hour later he was giving a verbal report to the superintendent about the goings-on at the Ramsgate residence.

'Just because one foot support matches another does not make a man a murderer,' the superintendent said sternly. 'Neither, for that matter, does running berserk with a shotgun before topping yourself in full view of pursuing officers. Perhaps he was in despair at having his front steps rammed by DS Jennings.' The superintendent gave a superior smile. 'I agree that his behaviour was very odd –

most unfortunate, given the result. But he was obviously experiencing some sort of breakdown. An aunt of mine went like that once – quite barmy and quite out of the blue, though fortunately she didn't have a shotgun. Of course, I was only a nipper but I remember the fuss and—' He stopped abruptly, and with a discreet cough returned his mind to the present. 'Anyway, there is nothing to suggest that Ramsgate had any reason to want the Tildred girl dead; he had only met her that one time at his party. And despite DS Jennings' "evidence", may I remind you, Nathan, that two orthotics do not make a summer. I think we can do better than that, don't you?' With a curt nod of dismissal, he picked up his pen and resumed writing to the chief constable, modestly requesting the latter's support for his membership of the golf club.

Once outside the office Nathan both sighed and cursed. The problem was that the man was right. Jennings' 'evidence' might be a supporting factor if other elements could be established, but without those elements the foot things proved nothing – except that the world was full of coincidence or that the dead man should have patronised a better chiropodist.

He thought gloomily of his interview with Hackle and the two women. From what he could make out they had been paying a casual social call – the Gilchrist woman taking him some message from her boss at the British Museum, and the other pair dropping in from their bicycle ride in the hope of being offered a cup of tea. They said they were 'taken aback' when he suddenly turned nasty and started to bawl his head off and threatened them with the pistol. The girl with the dog said she was convinced he was going to shoot it . . . Well, yes, Nathan reflected, he could understand that all right; he wasn't too keen on dogs himself and that one had looked distinctly shady. Still, there was no need for Ramsgate to threaten its human companions. Unless, of course, he was mad – as his superior had assured him.

But did people often go suddenly mad like that? Not in his experience they didn't (though perhaps the aunts of police superintendents had such a tendency). From what he knew of Ramsgate the man had been sane enough, or at least nobody had complained before. Broken under pressure, perhaps? What pressure? An acclaimed writer and broadcaster, plenty of money to travel to foreign parts, and living comfortably in a large country house in Suffolk away from the public gaze – what pressure had he been under, for God's sake? Difficult to imagine, unless it was from the deadline for a new travel book!

Nathan scowled and began to light his pipe (also a failure and he had to start again). On the whole, he mused, those three hadn't been the most reliable witnesses: perfectly polite and willing, of course, but he couldn't help feeling that there had been a collective vagueness, an air of reticence that he couldn't quite put his finger on. The girl with the dog was the daughter of that Lady Fawcett staying at The Swan. She had been in the area before, when the Dovedale woman had been murdered; as had the younger one, Rosy Gilchrist. Funny that those two should be in the vicinity again with the Tildred case in full swing, and now the Ramsgate drama. Still, as he had tried to instil into young Jennings, coincidences were more frequent than assumed.

He relit the expiring pipe as he reflected upon this fact . . . For example, what about that florist fellow, Felix Smythe, and his sidekick Dillworthy? They had been around last time as well – and damned difficult they had been too! Not obstructive, exactly, but bordering. This time they had been more amenable, which wasn't saying a lot.

He heaved another sigh. Yes, strange that they should encounter that quartet again. Perhaps they were sort of camp followers – always turning up at a crime scene to discomfit and bemuse. Doubtless, Jennings would have a theory . . .

CHAPTER THIRTY

All things considered, Tommy Carshalton reflected, matters had turned out remarkably well. Just occasionally fate dealt a winning hand, and in this case it had been in the form of a trilogy of happy accidents for which one was profoundly grateful.

Despite its shocking manner, Tippy's demise had been especially fortunate – the girl had become such a millstone, and not just because of the whingeing blackmail but her absurd public display. It had started to attract comment from the press. And inevitably whenever she featured in the gossip columns it was always stressed that the MP for North Finsborough was some kind of relation. Oh yes, they couldn't wait to drag in the Carshalton name! What a stroke of luck he had been at the conference when the wretched thing happened, otherwise he might have been a suspect! After all, wasn't one always reading of relatives or family members murdering their young and frail elderly? And in his position there was bound to have been malicious rumours – started by Figgins, no doubt, oily little toerag. Yes, he had had a lucky escape all right.

But it was strange Mickey Standish being attacked like that, and possibly there was more to it than met the eye. Quite a bit, probably, given what his Home Office pal had recently let drop. He had always thought the man was a bit of an enigma, too damn cool for his liking. In fact, instinct had suggested he had been as shady as hell. And according to this recent whisper his instinct may have been spot on: gunrunning, that had been the chap's little sideline, apparently, or so his source had hinted. And if so, what an infernal coincidence when that was his own moral hobbyhorse!

Tommy brooded grimly on the irony, recalling the time when he had casually raised the subject at a dinner they had both been attending. 'Appalling,' Standish had earnestly agreed, and had congratulated him on making such an issue of it in parliament. 'It's time someone took a lead,' he had said. Hell, if what his source had hinted was correct, then the sod must have been mocking him all the time! Tommy scowled.

But still, that was neither here nor there: the main thing was that he was out of Ida's orbit now. She had lately become nuts about the chap, stupid girl, and he had feared an elopement. No, Tommy corrected himself, it wouldn't have been an elopement, Standish had been far too cool: but a dalliance, quite possibly – with Standish detached and Ida fixated. Either way it would have led to gossip and ridicule. Not the most helpful thing in the current circumstances.

He smiled. So that possibility had hit the dust – and a good thing too. Ida could revert to her normal role: playing the devoted political wife, loyal, supportive and unerringly diplomatic. Yes, good old Ida – he really must take her to Paris and anaesthetise regret about Standish with pearls and a new fur coat.

And what about Vincent Ramsgate, for God's sake? Extraordinary behaviour for a man of his success. It just went to show that other than Figgins (whose aspirational motives were painfully obvious), you could never know about anyone really. In the old days the chap had been a frightful old goat, and fun in a rollicking way. But those days were over – Anno Domini for Ramsgate and growing political status for himself.

But it wasn't just Ramsgate's physical decline, he mused. There had been something else. When Ida returned from her recent visit to Southwold, she had declared that in her opinion he was going dotty, or peculiar at least. And it hadn't just been the usual habit of wearing that absurd fez thing and other sartorial affectations. Apparently, his whole manner had altered.

Ida had reported that beneath the usual suave bravado he had apparently seemed edgy and abstracted, as if there was something nagging in his mind that wouldn't go away. At first she had assumed it was connected with the details of that damned letter Tippy had sent him regarding the nonsense in the Fawcetts' house, and naturally they had discussed it. But she had felt the edginess went deeper than that. He had been a perfectly attentive host, and had dined her lavishly. Yet she couldn't help feeling that beneath the amiable facade there had been something distinctly off key. There had been uncharacteristic silences, little bursts of illogical agitation; and on two occasions she had heard him talking to himself – admittedly, a common enough habit, but not generally indulged in the presence of guests.

Well, if Vincent Ramsgate had been losing his grip, then his suicide could be seen as a merciful deliverance. After all, with a mind verging on the unhinged who knew what the chap might have let slip – or deliberately divulged? And not just about that particular business either, but some of the other little charades they had all once enjoyed. Naturally, a stiff denial would have been issued, but the public loved nothing better than to be titillated and things could have become a bit bumpy. The past had been fun but he had a shiny political future now and it wouldn't do to have it tarnished, however faintly. Yes, all things considered, Ramsgate's death was probably just as well.

Tommy took a ruminative bite of his biscuit and was suddenly struck by a fresh thought and didn't know whether to be shocked or amused. Perhaps it was old Vincent who had done for Tippy! Maybe beneath that airy nonchalance he had been so obsessed about his precious name being linked with sexual high jinks that in a moment of wild despair – or vicious premeditation – he had decided to stop her little mouth for good. After all, stranger things had happened!

For a few moments Tommy fantasised upon the possibility. And then with a sheepish shrug pulled himself together. Really, the idea was as absurd as it was unsavoury. Anyone would think he was one of those crude crime writers Ida so enjoyed . . . And in any case, there were matters of far greater immediacy: devising the next stage in his anti-arms-dealing crusade. A sound ethical cause was always useful, and that last speech on the topic had been well received by colleagues and constituents alike. He must capitalise on that and make another thrust upwards (while Figgins went down).

Thus, imbued with fresh energy and dismissing thoughts of the three deceased, he grasped his pen and wrote: *It is a crying scandal that the iniquitous trading in illicit arms should be so carelessly ignored. The public has a right to know that . . .*

Elsewhere (reclining on the sofa in their flat and toying with an overly strong gin) Ida too was ruminating.

What extraordinary twists life held, she mused. Take Vincent, for example. Admittedly, as she had told Tommy, he had seemed a bit odd the last time she had seen him, but hardly odd enough to have committed suicide, or at least certainly not in that spectacular manner. They hadn't seen him for quite a while, so perhaps something had been going on in his life of which they knew nothing, and which had eventually tipped him over the edge. Could it really have been that stupid letter Tippy had sent him? Surely he was far too robust to have reacted in such an extreme way. Vincent was not one to be felled by prurient rumour – or at least he certainly wouldn't have been in the old days: hide like a rhinoceros and hands like an octopus! No, it must have been something else, something more serious. But presumably they would never know; and after all, other than satisfying natural curiosity, did it really matter? The reality was that he had gone, out of the world and out of their lives; had become another colourful piece of the past to be occasionally revisited or quoted.

Ida closed her eyes and thought of something more personally painful: the bludgeoning of Mickey Standish. A dreadful shock. Its manner had been beastly, of course, but far worse was the blow to herself. She had been robbed of her target: that maddening enigma whom she had known she would never have, but whom she had wanted so absurdly. Would she ever feel quite so tantalised again, so deliciously and sickeningly provoked?

Ida took a large slurp of gin knowing the answer, and for a moment felt the pricking of tears. It had been one of those insane yens, something self-induced; for after all, she had received nothing from him – no goad other than a sly wink, a steady look, a knowing smile. Bastard! But oh God it had been good, and she would miss the tension, the ancient thrill of the chase . . . And now? What now, for heaven's sake? She sighed, confronting the sudden lacuna and staring bleakly at the ceiling.

Ah well, she supposed, there would always be Tommy and the old political game. She was good at that. And after all, he was doing awfully well these days. If they both played their cards right, who knew what mightn't be achieved. Anything really, especially now the child was off their hands . . . Yes, once she had stage-managed the girl's funeral she would put the maddening Mickey out of her mind and concentrate fully on securing something more attainable: Tommy's premiership, of course, and then the knighthood – or with luck a peerage.

Taking another sip, Ida wafted a languid hand in the air. Yes, au revoir to sex and hello to salubrious honours! She smiled faintly. But along with the smile came a look of steely determination.

Tommy had promised that after the funeral business he would take her to Paris for a new fur coat plus some pearls. Pearls? Like hell! He could damn well buy her some diamonds. And good ones too, not like those meagre things worn by Figgins' smug little wife!

And with that happy thought, Ida rose (a trifle unsteadily), picked up the telephone and contacted her husband. 'Tommy, darling,' she wheedled, 'I think it's time I booked our Paris hotel, don't you? After all, once we have said our goodbyes to dearest Tippy I think we shall need to get off quickly; it will all have been such a fearful strain, don't you think? So what shall it be, the George Cinque or the Crillon?'

CHAPTER THIRTY-ONE

Three days after the Reydon drama Bartholomew announced the successful completion of *The Languid Labyrinth*. And after expressing his undying gratitude to his 'stellar' companions, he declared that its eventual release would mark a memorable stage in the history of British film-making.

Crew and cast were mildly surprised by this, but were dutifully jubilant – the only dissonant voice being that of the 'gofer', who was heard to mutter that he had thought the film was supposed to have been a good whodunnit and not some screwy Walt Disney. However, being merely the gofer, such observations were firmly ignored.

When Lady Fawcett enquired of the young director what his next project might be, she was told in no uncertain terms: 'Why, to marry your daughter, of course. We got engaged last night. Didn't she tell you?'

Angela had beamed. 'That's wonderful news,' she had exclaimed, 'you will suit each other down to the ground! But I wonder how Amy will take to the glamour of the film world – it will be quite a change for her.'

'Oh *no*,' Bartho had replied, 'filming is just a sideline. My real aim is to breed first-class whippets like Mr Bates. Once this is all over, Amy and I plan to set up a joint concern in Northumberland. She will see to the stud side of things and I shall handle the breeding. And you, Lady Fawcett, can have the pick of our first litter! I tell you, it will be the best whippet complex north of the Watford Gap!'

Lady Fawcett had paled and closed her eyes . . . Well, at least it won't be Kensington, she had thought gratefully.

'But there's always money in it,' Rosy said encouragingly, as they sat in the bar that night toasting the happy couple. 'It could be quite a lucrative venture, especially as whippets have become so popular all of a sudden.'

Her companion brightened. 'Yes. Yes, you could well be right – and certainly more useful than that outlandish film!' She took a thoughtful sip of her sherry. And then leaning forward, and with a softened wheedling tone, said: 'Now, Rosy dear, you don't think you could possibly help Amy choose her wedding dress, do you? The silly girl never listens to a word her mother says, and for her to do it unaccompanied would be disastrous.'

Warily, Rosy indicated that she would be only too happy.

'Oh, good,' the other said briskly, 'at least that's one

thing settled. Now, I suggest you go to Marshall and Snelgrove the moment we get back – one should never take too long over these matters.'

But then Lady Fawcett's face clouded somewhat. 'There's only one thing that is worrying me . . .' She hesitated, before saying, 'I gather one can change a name by deed poll, isn't that so?'

'Yes,' Rosy replied startled, 'but Amy won't have to do that, the marriage does it automatically.'

'I wasn't thinking of Amy's name. Bartholomew's actually . . . after all, Rosy, do I really want my daughter to be known as Amelia *Hackle*; it's not very melodious, is it?'

Rosy agreed that it wasn't. 'Not terribly. But then neither is Schoenberg.'

But the Fawcett request for help and advice was not the only one Rosy received.

Together with Cedric and Felix she had gone up to the studio to say goodbye to the departing film crew, and amidst all the noise and bustle of packing up, Bartho had sidled up looking distinctly twitchy. 'I say,' he said, 'I've just had a telephone call from Cousin Walter. He wants to give us a wedding present.'

'Well, what's your problem?' asked Felix. 'Never look a gift horse in the mouth, that's what I say.'

'If it were a horse it wouldn't be so bad,' Bartho replied bleakly, 'but it's something else.'

'What?'

'The beach hut. He says it's become a white elephant, and rather than sell the thing he would be delighted for

281

Amy and I to have it . . . Frankly, I don't fancy the idea. I mean, it wouldn't be quite nice, would it?'

Felix shuddered. 'I should think not!' he exclaimed.

'Why don't you tell him that Amy suffers from claustrophobia and couldn't possibly cope with being in a confined space? You could also add that she isn't too keen on ozone, either,' Rosy said helpfully.

Bartho brightened. 'Yes, that's an idea,' he began.

'In which case your cousin would sell the hut and thus the bullet hole would be found,' Cedric pointed out. 'He would have some explaining to do – as would you, I imagine. No, you will either have to accept his thoughtful gift or—'

'Set it on fire!' cried Felix.

Cedric closed his eyes. 'What I was *going* to suggest was that you get some putty to shove into the hole and cracks and then paint over the whole thing. All four walls. Alternatively, you could rip out the boards and replace them with others.'

'But that would make an awful commotion, and probably take ages,' Rosy objected.

'It would. Thus I think putty and paint would be his best bet.'

'Brilliant!' yelped Bartho. 'I'll get some straight away from that nice ironmonger in the high street, and then you can all help me to do it. It'll be finished in a trice!'

Cedric recoiled. 'Er, I hardly think—'

'And I don't happen to have packed a paint smock,' protested Felix.

Rosy fixed them with a stern gaze. 'Listen, we are all in this. We have already failed to report what we suspected to be vital evidence, so to complete the job we may as well conspire to conceal it entirely. Come on, the sooner it's done the better. And then at crack of dawn tomorrow we can all get the hell out of here and back to London. It can't be soon enough for Angela as she's dying to fix the wedding caterers. There's no point in hanging about!'

Felix and Cedric stared in wonder. 'If you say so,' Felix said meekly.

A week after the visitors' flight from Southwold, Nathan and Jennings were still brooding upon the murder and the Ramsgate suicide.

'The Kensington people haven't come up with anything useful about the girl and her contacts,' Jennings said glumly. 'I mean nothing of any significance that would indicate a London link. It's pretty disappointing; I really thought the key might be there.'

Nathan shrugged. 'Probably is, old son, but that doesn't mean that it can be uncovered. We're not all Hercule Poirot. In fact, if you ask me, that chap has done the police a great disservice. It's always assumed that we can pull rabbits out of hats, like he does in those stories you are so keen on. And when we don't, because of lack of evidence, the public gets shirty. It's one of the joys of being a policeman.'

Jennings sighed disconsolately. 'So what's the super saying? Grumbling about lack of progress, I suppose.'

'Ah, but that's where you're wrong. He *has* mentioned it, of course, but currently he is crowing about our success with the Blyford burglary. The jewellery is safe, three villains nailed, big headlines in the newspaper and a letter from the victim congratulating the chief constable on the efficiency of his police force – that's you and me. So cheer up, it could be worse. We may not solve this one, but we haven't got a bad track record. And besides, when you are lording it over everyone up at the Yard you can always reopen it.' Nathan grinned and stuffed fresh tobacco into his pipe.

Phlegmatic, that's what, Jennings thought. But also grinned.

'But the Tildred kid apart,' his boss continued, 'the one that really puzzles me is that Vincent Ramsgate. All that rampaging about and then topping himself like that. Very rum, if you ask me. Still, people do funny things.'

'Ah,' said Jennings darkly, 'but we mustn't discount the homosexual element.'

Nathan was startled. 'I didn't know there was one.'

'Oh yes,' the young man said, 'bound to be.' He nodded sagely.

'Really? What makes you think that?'

Jennings frowned. 'Well,' he explained, 'what gives the game away is the sartorial accoutrements. You can generally tell.'

'You mean clothes.'

'Exactly. I mean, would you go around wearing purple socks and a cap with a tassel, sir?'

Nathan reflected, and then said, 'Well, only at Christmas.'

'Hmm. But it wasn't Christmas, was it?' Jennings replied soberly.

'No, but—'

'Oh yes,' the young man said firmly, 'it's often the way: a spat here, jealousy there, a rival caught with his pants down – and then, all of a sudden, whoosh – suicides galore and a whopping great bloodbath! Oh yes, it happens all the time.'

Nathan lit his pipe. 'I see,' he said; and couldn't help wondering if, slaked of Agatha Christie, Jennings had switched his literary allegiance to racier reading.

ACKNOWLEDGEMENTS

I should like to thank crime writer Michael Jecks (The Knights Templar series et al.) for guidance regarding the topic of bullets and guns. His knowledge of this subject is immeasurably better than mine! Similarly I must thank Tanya Hayward of Kent and Essex Serious Crime Directorate, who, sparing time from the real world for the fictional, was so patient in answering my queries. Both sources helped enormously in clarifying my thoughts on the matter.